CORVIS EPIC

BLACK BIRD

from BLUE

PLANET

R. CODY CARVER

PTP

Pacific Time Publishing
Seattle | 2023

Pacific Time Publishing, 415 W Republican St #400, Seattle, WA 98119

Cover Art and Design by Perry Kirkpatrick
Ship diagram by Hamid Ullah

Facebook page: Corvis Santos

ISBN 9781649999115
Printed in the United States of America

For Kris, Tim, Steve, Zoe, Gray, Finn, Corbin, Colin, and Sloan

Contents

Dome I

Hiking Caverns

Yak Field

Factory Complex

Govt Machine Shop

Jupiter Residence

Residence Under Construction

Saturn Elem School

Sa

Enceladus Secondary School

Mimas Residence & Bubble

Library & Museum

Shop Mall

Newton Residence u. Dormitory

Tethys Residence

Ocean Residence

Community Garden

Mimas Elem

Ring Residence

Encela DC

Dome J

Enceladus University

Stardust Depot

Sweeper Station

Hydrocarbon Pipeline

Terminal

Dome E

Enceladus Zoo

Water Filtration Facilities

Saturn Stadium

Enceladus Sports Complex

Food Processing

Food District

Uranus Residence

Convention Center

Golf Club

So Elem

Residence Under Construction

Stripes Residence

Cultural Clubs

Titan Residence

Shop Mall

Worship Place

the's Park

dus Town
OME D

Cavern Residence

Newtons Elem

Venus Residence

Algae Vats Processing

Europa Residence

City Hall

Police

Dome C

Cemetery

DIAGRAM OF NURSERY

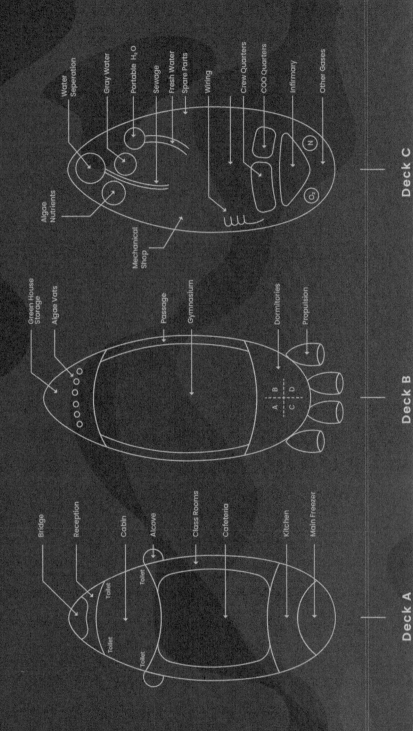

Deck A

- Bridge
- Reception
- Toilet
- Cabin
- Toilet
- Toilet
- Alcove
- Class Rooms
- Cafeteria
- Kitchen
- Main Freezer

Deck B

- Green House Storage
- Algae Vats
- Passage
- Gymnasium
- Dormitories
- Propulsion
- A B C D

Deck C

- Water Seperation
- Gray Water
- Portable H_2O
- Sewage
- Fresh Water
- Spare Parts
- Wiring
- Crew Quarters
- COO Quarters
- Infirmary
- Other Gases
- Algae Nutrients
- Mechanical Shop
- N
- O_2

1
Bleeding

YOUNG, BRILLIANT, HANDSOME, ONE of the best ICU nurses in New York City. All work, little play. He had never experienced love, so Corvis's heart had never been broken.

At 1830 hours, more than a half hour early for his shift, as usual, he peered into the lens of the retina reader. The door to his ICU opened and a little white robot with a red cross on its forehead scurried out. "Nurse Santos! You're needed in Room D, urgently," it said.

What else is new? I'm always needed... urgently.

He headed in that direction, the machine hot on his heels. "Now!" the bossy little thing squawked. He picked up his pace.

Three caregivers were hunched over the bed. Corvis couldn't see the patient. Caregivers didn't look up when the robot announced, "Santos is here."

Corvis took in his surroundings: another nurse wearing orange scrubs like his; IV running, normal saline; woman in chair, appears to be in late teens; monitor reads temp: 40° C, fever; basic metabolic panel, all within normal range. Edging his way between doctor and nurse, he saw in the adult bed, a tiny patient whose face was covered by a pediatric non-rebreather mask, empty medicine vials, syringe wrappers, crash cart at bedside.

Blood on pillow. Monitors beeping. IV pumps demanding attention. Commands shouted. Air humid and close.

Whose heart doesn't break for a suffering little child? I have all the signs of elevated adrenaline: fast heart, shallow breathing, jittery nerves. Good. I'll be at my best on this one.

"Can someone give me report?" he asked quietly but firmly.

"Eighteen-month-old female, complained of headache yesterday, high fever, vomiting. Mom thought it was a normal childhood illness. Two hours ago, child started bleeding from mouth. Mom brought child to ED. Child now bleeding from ears, eyes..." his colleague Wilma, an RN, said.

"What are we doing?" he asked.

"Replacing fluids..." Wilma replied.

With normal saline? Will they ever stop using normal saline? Old traditions, especially irrational ones, die hard.

"... Vitamin K given IM, four liters of oxygen," Wilma continued.

"Child's name?"

"Nereda Sanchez," Wilma said.

"Has the child traveled outside the country recently?"

"We don't know," the nurse replied.

"Hola, Señorita," he said to the weeping woman in the chair. "Yo soy Corvis, uno de los enfermeros. ¿Sabes si esta niña ha viajado fuera de los Estados durante las dos semanas pasadas? [Has this child has traveled outside the United States within the past two weeks?]"

"Yes, Corvis," she said in accented English, "I'm Nereda's mother. We just returned from Panama yesterday. The mosquitos are terrible this year. She got sick last night."

"Wilma, what are Nereda's crits?" I asked.

"Her hemoglobin was high in the ER, but it's dropping rapidly," Wilma replied. "Her pulse was fast, and her blood pressure was low. Her platelets were critically low."

"O-two sats?" Corvis asked.

"High seventies."

Dengue!

"Dr. Liu," he called out.

She instantly looked at him.

"Do you think it could be dengue hemorrhagic fever?" Corvis asked.

"Could be," she said, looking sad. "Two units of blood are coming, but the prognosis isn't good."

"I've heard that artificial blood is good for hemorrhagic fever," he said. "It carries more oxygen than human blood, and it expands. There's no need for typing and cross-matching. It can curtail capillary bleeding."

"Makes sense, Santos," Dr. Liu said. "Keep the real blood in the refrigerator when it arrives, and get two units of artificial blood... stat."

"Yes, ma'am," he replied. "By the way, studies suggest, that normal saline isn't a good fluid replacement for hemorrhagic fever. It can lead to fluid overload."

"Stop the normal saline," Dr. Liu ordered immediately, "but keep the line open. Get some lactated ringers."

Feels so good to be a valued member of a professional team.

Corvis called the lab. "Dr. Liu has ordered two units of artificial blood for Nereda Lopez in ICU Room D, stat. The child could die in minutes without it."

Rumor has it that the lab fills orders from the ICU faster than from any other unit. Another reason to work in the ICU.

By now, Nereda's sheets were saturated with blood. She was unconscious. Five agonizing minutes later, the artificial blood arrived.

Corvis spiked the first bag, flushed the line with saline, and started the thick, black blood replacement flowing into her tiny vein. Twenty minutes later he checked Nereda's crits again. Her hemoglobin was 6.9. Dangerously low, but it hadn't decreased from an hour earlier.

Charge Nurse Lewis entered Room D as Corvis was now on the clock. "You'll just have C and D tonight," she told him. "We were given another nurse for the shift."

Corvis changed Nereda's bed before checking on his other patient.

Smith, the man in Room C had been in a deep coma for days, his pulse and respirations declining. Corvis did everything for the man that he could possibly do, but at 0630 hours, Smith died.

Corvis sees people die all the time in the ICU. On those days that none of his patients die, he says to himself, *Thank God I didn't kill anyone today. Why does my heart beat fast every time one of my patients dies? I'm not afraid of getting fired. It's more personal. I'm not afraid of death. I can't be. Everybody dies.*

During his 12-hour shift, he ate a proton bar and dashed to the restroom twice to pee. Through the night, he offered Nereda's mother as much hope as he reasonably could. Just before his relief arrived, he talked to her once more.

"As you can see, your daughter's bed shows no sign of new bleeding," he said. "That's a good sign. But she's still a very sick little girl. If she survives, it will take weeks for her to recover."

She hugged Corvis. "I didn't expect her to live through the night," she cried.

He hugged her back.

High adrenalin sharpens the mind but drains the body, he thought. *I'm tired.*

2
Demand for a Second Dragomark

JiAnn • Enceladus, Saturn system

Everyone has a boss, but I hate being summoned, JiAnn thought. *The need to create a second Dragomark is the topic of this meeting.* This always grated. Convener Cly, Head of State of Enceladus Colony had a very small office, as did all officials on the tiny moon. She knocked and entered without waiting for his acknowledgment, much less an invitation to enter, knowing full well that this was a serious breach of protocol and an insulting cultural taboo. She was furious, and she hoped it showed.

He talked on his nearly invisible perso so she stood, as erect as possible given the severe, painful scoliosis of her spine, half outside, half in, his office. Her fist on hip, in the doorway, she glared at the Convener. From early childhood, she was accustomed to having others wait for her and wait on her. Waiting for Cly to finish his conversation exacerbated her irritation.

A screen on the wall above the convener's head changed from a Navajo geometric design in cream and coffee to another in yellow, blue, and orange. JiAnn loved fine art. Finally, the call ended. Loaded for bear, she didn't care how insulting it was to the Convener that she'd barged in.

Abruptly, she launched into the cause for which Cly had "invited" her to meet with him. Forcing herself not to shout she began in clipped tones, "Mr. Convener, if you want my resignation, I'll give it to you, but it won't change the fact that the satendrites will communicate with *only one* human!"

The Convener stood and put the ball of wool that he'd been rolling in one hand onto his narrow desk. "The feel of raw wool reminds me of the sheep I once herded on Earth," he said quietly. "And the lanolin softens my skin."

JiAnn didn't respond aloud. *What has that got to do with anything?* she thought.

Though they stood as far apart as possible, scarcely six feet separated them. His desk and chairs were made of bamboo grown on Enceladus, as were the two shelves on which a few books and a basket were artfully arranged. The gentle scent of pine, artificially embedded in the bamboo furniture, made the office seem larger than it was.

"I do understand," Convener Cly continued, looking at the floor in front of her feet, "and I've told the Council members, again and again, that there can be only one Dragomark, but do try to understand their concern. Even though Enceladus Colony doesn't officially exist, we're receiving daily requests for visas." His eyes scanned the spines of three hardcopy books, a rarity on Enceladus, quaint relics of places far away in space and time. "Earth is about to be incinerated in a nuclear war, and people are desperate. Council wants someone in the Bubble 24/7 to detect impending invasions. You alone, or even you and Mr. Ling, together, can't possibly provide that kind of coverage." Although he had two small chairs, Cly didn't invite JiAnn to sit. This wasn't going to be a long, casual chat. "Clearly, more than a half-dozen individuals on Earth now know about our colony, and many are willing to risk the long trip in order to escape the coming war."

She put both hands under her chin, fingers interlaced, pondering his observation. "How have you answered requests for visas?" she asked.

"We haven't even acknowledged receipt of their communiqués. We don't exist," he said with a sly smile. "But it's only a matter of time before ships arrive... uninvited."

JiAnn, 49 years old, dressed in a gray pinstripe suit over sheer black stockings, nervously ran her fingers through her long, healthy, salt-and-pepper hair. JiAnn wore no make-up, never did. "I'm as concerned about the risk of invasion as anyone. Believe me, Mr. Convener, I am," she said, "but I offer daily briefings, as it is, and I'll note, Council seems to ignore most of them, repeatedly asking questions I've already answered." JiAnn couldn't take her eyes off a beautiful Diné pot on the screen. "I can increase the briefings to two or even four a day if that would help."

"Truly I respect you, Madam Dragomark," Cly said, now focusing his soulful eyes on the wall behind JiAnn's left shoulder, "but could you humor Council and ask the satendrites, one more time, if they might consider a second Dragomark?"

We both know what Council members want. Dilute the power of the Dragomark, then divide and conquer. Ain't gonna happen. Not on my watch! JiAnn pressed the palms of her hands hard against her eyes, and slowly stretched the skin back toward her ears. Finally, she said, "I will. And you and I both know what they'll say." Intentionally speaking one word at a time: "It's simply... physically... impossible... for them to interface with more than one human. Each person has hundreds of *billions* of neuronal connections that the satendrites must test each, one by one. It's far more difficult for them to learn a new human being than it is for us to learn a new language. It's more like learning to communicate with a whole new species each time a new person arrives before them." She wanted to scream but took a deep calming breath instead. "I'll ask, but trust me, they won't speak, even to me, for a couple of days afterward." *Or ever truth be known.*

"That's a risk we'll have to take, Madam Dragomark."

"Do you want your door left open or closed, Mr. Convener?" JiAnn asked in a steely voice as she turned on her heel.

I have no intention of asking the satendrites, but my two-day vacation begins now. Truth is, I wish I could take a vacation, but right now I can't. There's too much at stake.

Futile Commencements

Enceladus Colonial Council didn't force her to decide. The satendrites, a colony of billions of single-celled organisms that floated above the entire south polar region of Enceladus, did. They showed JiAnn a caravan of 25 transports led by a single fighter, another fighter bringing up the rear. They were past Earth's Moon already and clearly not planning to land on Mars. The slow-moving cavalcade, obviously using outdated engines, was starting a year-long journey to Enceladus. She presumed they had not been granted visas. They likely hadn't even asked. *I've got to report this to the Convener. This is first clear evidence of attempted invasion. Unfortunately, it's more ammunition for those calling for multiple Dragomarks.*

Back in her small apartment, after Malcolm relieved her in the Bubble, she sipped her own blend of spiced tea and mulled the implications while gazing at the delicate plants in hanging baskets, trailing tendrils in the oval floor-to-ceiling window of her parlor. *I'll need to spend more time in the Bubble viewing the inner solar system through the "eyes" of the satendrites, more time conferring with Cly, then with the generals, and again with Council.* She felt exhausted just thinking about it. *Malcolm's younger. He can spend more time in the Bubble. Maybe I can carve out a small role for myself as Dragomark Emeritus. I'm certainly not old enough to retire. I could speak for the satendrites even while Malcolm interfaces with them. Something to consider.*

But her immediate task was to compose an announcement about the would-be invaders. *What would the satendrites say about the 25 ships, if they could speak?*

3
ICU

CORVIS • NY, NY

CORVIS FELT HAPPY GOING to work, slightly more rested, and a bit guilty after his first two-day break in six weeks. He had extended it an extra day by calling out sick. Medical staff found themselves in the midst of the second pandemic of the year, and he felt guilty knowing that he had increased the workload of his co-workers. This infection, no one knew yet how to fight. Some patients only get diarrhea. Most, however, get headaches and back pain at the same time. Multiple organs seem to be targeted in the very first phase. Staff were running in fluids, watching patients' intracranial pressures, and giving nothing by mouth while the patients asked if they were going to die; and "Can you please, kill the pain." Each ICU nurse had three or four critically ill patients to care for each shift. *I really was bone tired*, Corvis thought. Robot assistants helped with rolling patients side-to-side, giving bed baths, and taking vital signs, but certain things required a human; nurse's intuition to know what was needed and what will come next.

Corvis looked into the little camera. The retina scanner which lets only authorized people enter the ICU, failed to open the door. *Obviously, a malfunction. I'll ask maintenance to fix it*. He pressed the buzzer.

Waiting for a reply, he sniffed. Different parts of the hospital have their distinct smells. Oncology smells of necrotic flesh; med-surg smells of vomit and diarrhea. ICU always smells clean, with an occasional whiff of urine or feces. None of his patients could get up to use the bathroom. He was proud of his team. *We're like a well-oiled machine,* he thought. *We all understand that if a patient lies in body fluids our work gets even more complicated,*

After a full minute, he buzzed again.

"How may I help you?" Winnie asked over the intercom.

"The scanner didn't recognize me," Corvis said, "Will you buzz me in?"

"Sure," Winnie said, "Lorna wants to see you."

Corvis went directly to Head Nurse Lorna's office, and knocked.

"Come in," Lorna said, and while his hand was still on the doorknob, "You're fired. Report to HR. Give them your badge." Then she looked back to her vid.

His body moved backward as if he had received a physical gut punch.

"That's it?" he asked.

"That's it! No staff member fakes illness during a pandemic. Don't let the door hit your behind on your way out."

Stunned. Zombie-like, Corvis walked to HR. *That last phrase was gratuitously hurtful,* he sulked. His analytical mind stopped him from defending himself. *I deserved to be fired.*

I'm good at what I do. No. I'm one of the best. That's why I got this coveted job. But now I'm on my way to turn in my badge. I've been fired. For cause. Unprofessional conduct, he thought.

The receptionist in HR seemed overly cheerful. *She's gloating! No. She doesn't even know you. She's paid to appear cheerful.* He felt beyond awful, more like a catastrophic failure. He was sad to the point of tears. *It's so final. It's over.* There's so much identity tied up in a badge. It literally opens doors that ordinary people can't pass through. *I've worked hard for the privileges that go with being a nurse! But the pandemic required "all hands on deck." By indulging in a little personal luxury, I've revealed my unprofessionalism.*

"I can start off-boarding you now," the irritatingly helpful receptionist said.

"I'll come back later," he lied.

"That's fine," she said, still smiling. "Just remember that your final paycheck will be held until after your exit interview."

He just wanted to get out of there and left without responding.

He looked at his orange scrubs and felt a tiny surge of pride mixed with another wave of sadness. He no longer had a badge, but orange scrubs meant ICU, just like pale blue ones meant surgery. Employees knew the code and showed him respect.

I'll get another job. I'm good and I'm needed. And I'm tired. I need, I really need a few days off. I'm almost glad I got fired... No, I'm not at all glad.

4
Ripples

JiAnn felt cold. It's always cold on Enceladus. Outside the domes, a person could live scarcely five minutes without a spacesuit. Inside the domes, the temperature changes little. It's always around one degree above freezing outdoors. Inside most buildings the temperature is comfortable but at a high energy cost. Ice is the construction material. Micro fans keep frigid air circulating on the walls, while macroscopic ventilation keeps ambient temperature warm. JiAnn felt especially chilly as she entered the formal conference room. She consoled herself with the anticipation of wrapping her hands around a hot cup of coffee that predictably would be served. She and General Dioikis waited for the Convener to arrive.

"I don't know how or when," Convener Cly began, "but ripples will reach us." News from Earth took nearly an hour to reach Enceladus, but that was nothing in comparison to the historic events unfolding. Convener Cly had called an executive meeting of General Dioikis, JiAnn, and himself. "Transports from Earth, bringing new colonists along with limited supplies, are infrequent. Only one in the last year. Likely the last one. Ever. We don't need the supplies, but we always appreciate the additions to our gene pool that new colonists bring. General Dioikis, what do you observe?"

"Unfortunately, I have to report that all local wars on Earth are becoming more desperate and savage. It can't be long until nuclear war breaks out," the general noted.

JiAnn said, "The satendrites report that ships bound for both the Moon and Mars Bases are making constant round trips with quick turnarounds."

"Do either of you have any recommendations for the Council?" Cly asked.

"Not at this time," they both responded. The meeting appeared to have ended.

JiAnn stood to leave but sat again when the Convener spoke.

"Each new batch of pioneers arrives with continued interest in current events on Earth," Cly said, "The Council Members aren't the only ones worried about the threat of nuclear war on Earth. Our citizens may demand that we accept more refugees. Among other problems, such as over-stretched resources, there is the risk that immigrants bring with them blood-lust animosities, and we end up with war here in our colony."

Apprentice

Enceladus

JiAnn sat straight in her chair in the cramped Office of the Dragomark. Disciplining her face to show no emotion, though her heart was breaking, she told Malcolm Ling, the Apprentice "I'll be resigning as soon as we have a Candidate to replace you."

Malcolm, whose face seldom showed emotion, registered shock. They cleared calendars to reserve time for interviews, JiAnn surreptitiously wiping away hot tears.

Alone in her apartment the following day, she made calls. Each appointment she made with an excited candidate jabbed another dagger into her heart. Arrangements moved along too quickly, it seemed. *This will be easy for everyone*, she thought, *but me*.

Interviews

The Dragomark's parlor was small even by Enceladus standards. In the center of the room was an eighteen-inch round table and three small chairs. In the oval window hung a cascade of a dozen small baskets, growing an assortment of exotic plants whose leaves she used in her teas. Beautiful tapestries covered the walls. JiAnn's dress covered her from the middle of her neck to her ankles in nearly transparent, form-fitting fabric with a woven floral design that barely obscured her nipples and panties. At forty-nine, her body was still lithe, and she delighted in scandalizing her guests. She dabbed a drop of her most expensive perfume behind each ear, hoping the fragrance would unnerve the candidates.

Malcolm and JiAnn sat in two of the chairs, and the candidates, one by one, sat in the third. Malcolm reviewed the dossier of each candidate and introduced them with a summary of their qualities.

"All three candidates have arrived early," Malcolm said. "Your butl-bot is entertaining them while they wait in the hall.

First is Susan McAfee. She graduated *cum laude* a month ago from the University of Enceladus with a degree in Marketing and is already managing a team of twelve salespeople."

"Bring her in," JiAnn replied.

Susan stood only a little taller than JiAnn. Her black hair and tan complexion gave no hint of her ethnicity.

"Have a seat and tell us about yourself," JiAnn invited.

"I've been offered another promotion next month," Susan replied, "but I'm ready for a different kind of challenge."

"Why do you want to be Dragomark?" Ling asked.

She squared her shoulders and looked him in the eye. "Because the Dragomark has power and authority. And, because I'm the best candidate for the job."

After Susan left, JiAnn and Malcolm agreed that she wouldn't make a good Dragomark. Too power-hungry.

"Next is James Willey. James majored in Biology at the university. He married late in his senior year, and he and his wife Brenda are expecting their first child in less than a month," Malcolm said.

James' dark complexion suggested African roots. He gave the impression of an intellectual, slim of frame, yet fit.

"Have a seat," JiAnn offered. "How are you this afternoon?"

"I'm well and excited to have a crack at the position of Apprentice Dragomark," James said, pushing his ill-fitting glasses up on his nose.

"What makes you the best candidate for this job?" Ling asked.

"I don't know the credentials of the other candidates," James said, "so I don't know that I *am* the best candidate, but as for me, I gather data rapidly, carefully analyze it and draw conclusions. My analyses often surprise my peers. I form hypotheses, but I don't state them as fact."

JiAnn asked. "Why do you *want* to be Dragomark?"

James pursed his lips and adjusted his glasses. "I would like to know more about the cellular structure of satendrites," he said, picking at his fingernails. "That is if you don't think that would be too invasive."

"Thank you, James," Malcolm said standing.

"A Dragomark, even a female one, must have balls. I can tell you from personal experience." JiAnn spoke after James had left the room. "James is out."

Malcolm laughed. "Billy Birchfield is the final candidate..."

"What happens if he's not a good fit?" JiAnn asked.

"We have a huge pool," Malcolm said. "it just means more time sifting through them."

"But it would be worth it," JiAnn said. "Tell me about Birchfield."

"He graduated two years ago with a double major in Political Science and Physical Education. In addition to earning nearly straight A's, he was elected president of the student body. Since graduation, he has been a fighter pilot with the Enceladus Defense Department."

"Sounds like a soldier type. Let's talk to him," JiAnn said.

The room lights seemed to brighten two notches as he walked in. JiAnn felt warm all over. *He's stunningly handsome, which has nothing to do with being Dragomark. Or could it?*

He fit her image of a fighter pilot, too: big and athletic. But JiAnn wasn't sure he would find the role of Dragomark active enough.

"Mmm," Billy said, "someone's perfume is delightful."

JiAnn felt beads of perspiration form on her forehead. *I've been unnerved by my own trick!*

Malcolm presented data he got from Billy's teachers. "His form-one teacher told us that he answered the question 'What do you want to be when you grow up?' with the words 'Dragon barf.'"

Billy smiled sheepishly.

In form two, when children made suggestions for field trips, some wanted to go to the farm, others wanted to see the police station, and Billy wanted to visit the Bubble."

"Why do you want to be Dragomark?" JiAnn asked him, directly.

Billy shifted his tall frame uncomfortably on the little chair. "Because the Dragomark gives information... to the people of Enceladus... that they couldn't get from any other source," he said.

JiAnn glanced at Malcolm. They both nodded.

"All the controversy about whether or not they exist can be answered by that simple fact," JiAnn agreed. "They reveal what we could not possibly otherwise know, and these facts are verifiable. Have *you* ever seen satendrites?"

"Honestly, Ma'am, I'm not sure," Billy admitted. "As a little boy, I thought I saw a faint blue light. But little boys have active imaginations."

"Ultimately, it doesn't matter whether we can see them or not. What matters is that *they* see *us*, and they share with us what else they see." She stood and paced. "Our entire colony owes its continued existence to them." She sat down. "I'm only the second Dragomark..."

Billy smiled and twitched. "I hate to interrupt," he blurted, "but you're talking like I got the job. Did I?"

"It's not up to us..." JiAnn said, including Malcolm with a hand gesture.

Billy finished her sentence, "The Council has to approve?"

"No, I have to resign first. But the Council has nothing to do with the selection of a Dragomark." Her eyes pleaded with Ling. He touched her knee under the table. "It's up to the satendrites."

She took a deep breath, trying to keep her lips from quivering. She hoped her voice wouldn't crack. Remembering her own first encounter with the satendrites, she informed Billy, "Your test will begin at dusk. That's about three hours from now. If the satendrites accept you, Malcolm will *inform* the Council. Neither they, nor Convener Cly, have any say in the matter. I'll meet you at the Bubble," JiAnn said. "If the satendrites contact you, Malcolm will be the new Dragomark, and you will be Apprentice Dragomark."

She rose unsteadily. Malcolm and Billy also stood. JiAnn had forgotten how tall and muscular Billy was. His incredibly good looks combined with her realization that her time as Dragomark was ending made her feel faint. The edges of her vision grew dark. She looked at the men through an increasingly narrow tunnel, focusing on her next breath.

Malcolm will be the new Dragomark, she thought, as tears streamed down her face.

Billy noticed. "Are you OK?"

"Tears of joy, Billy" she lied. "We have a Candidate," she barely managed to whisper.

5
Billy's First Time in the Bubble

THEY MET OUTSIDE THE Bubble, a tower on top of the tallest building on Enceladus. Its entrance on the top floor looked more like a utility closet, with an eye-level label to the left of the door reading simply "Bubble." Everyone on Enceladus knew about the Bubble. Critical information issued from it.

Billy arrived early. JiAnn was already waiting beside the door. "I told Convener Cly that you're the Candidate," she said.

"I wondered," Billy said, "I invited my friends in the squadron to a little celebration at Mickie's Pub, and the first thing my friend Tyler said was, 'You've been holding out on us, Billy Boy!'" Billy smiled broadly. "I'm as excited as the first time I went down into the caves with Dad to go fishing."

JiAnn looked Billy up and down. He was wearing the same clothes he'd worn to the interview: a form-fitting long-sleeve light blue shirt, long slacks, white crew socks, and tennis shoes. "There's no heat up there," she observed, "so it's 0° C. Do you want to go home and change into something warmer? I'll be happy to wait."

"Naw. I just finished a workout. I'll be warm for some time," Billy said.

"I'll stay here so we can debrief immediately after. You shouldn't stay more than 10 or 15 minutes the first time. It's easy to get mesmerized."

Billy shifted his weight from one foot to the other. "Yes, ma'am. Anything else?"

"Clip this to your collar. It's an intercom," she said while punching in the code to open the door.

"Thanks!" he said as he disappeared, climbing up into the tower, two steps at a time.

JiAnn waited as ten minutes passed, then twenty. At thirty minutes she pressed the alarm on the intercom. Then she pressed it again. Billy finally responded to the third warning. "Wha, Wha... What is s... s... it?"

"You're cold, Billy. Do you need help coming down?" JiAnn asked, trying not to sound worried.

"N... Naw" he stammered, "I'm g... good."

She moved from the hall into the stairwell, worried that he might not be able to make it down on his own. JiAnn saw Billy, sliding his weight against the wall, taking one step at a time. "You're safe," she said, "just take it slow." In the hall, JiAnn said, "Let's go to a study carrel where we can talk privately. There's one just down here."

It took them a few minutes to reach it as Billy hadn't warmed up yet. "The first rule," she said, closing the door on the closet-like room, "is that we talk to each other about what we experience. But we think before we talk to the public. And the 'public' is anyone who is not a Dragomark."

Billy shivered. They sat knee-to-knee in a room that was barely large enough for two chairs and a very small desk between them. Billy slumped, his face downcast, and silently handed JiAnn the little intercom.

"Tell me."

"They rejected me!" Billy said with finality.

JiAnn smiled. "So, the satendrites said, 'Sorry, Bud, you're out!'?"

Instead of being amused, Billy looked at the floor, his shoulders rounded. "Worse. They didn't say anything at all. They tested me and I failed."

"How did they test you?"

"I introduced myself and said 'Hi. How're you doing?' I waited and then said, 'I want to make contact.'

"I didn't hear anything, but I smelled different smells," he said, holding his nose, "some nasty odors, some wonderful scents. I asked, 'Are you doing that?'" Cupping his hands behind his ears and hitting his elbows against the walls in the process, he said, "I heard quiet sounds. I listened closely, hoping they would answer, but I just heard random sounds. Some pleasant, some jarring."

"They didn't speak," JiAnn stated.

"No, they didn't." Billy scowled. "Then I entered different places and different times. They weren't just memories; I was really there! Playing catch with Dad, for example." Billy smiled. Then he held his head in his hands. "I relived my most awful secret... torturing a kitten. I said, 'I'm sorry. I'm really sorry.' But they didn't respond." Rubbing his head vigorously, he said, "I was also present at horrible, unspeakable atrocities that I, myself, had never participated in or even observed. I felt bad, guilty, and dirty. I know it was the satendrites messing with my brain." He held his palms up in front of him, "Then nothing." He looked miserable and shrugged.

"What do you mean 'nothing'?"

"Darkness. Silence. I thought it was over. But then the lights came," he said, squinting, "Tiny white lights, barely visible, then they grew blindingly bright," he said, his eyes widening, "so bright they made my eyes water. Then I saw different colors, different patterns, intricate Arabic filigree that kept multiplying and multiplying... endlessly." He spread his hands wide, hitting the walls, again. "They were beautiful beyond anything I could imagine." Billy's eyes moved as if still studying the patterns.

JiAnn waited a minute, then asked, "Was that the end?"

Chin in hand, he replied, "No. Then I saw Earth, not like pictures. I actually *saw* Earth come closer and closer. I saw oceans and lakes and rivers, cities and towns. And I saw people. I saw what they were wearing, what they were doing." Billy stood. He was silent.

Eyebrows knit as if holding back tears, he continued, "Five minutes into the test I began to hear that buzzing sound. No more earth. Desperate, I begged them 'Will you give me a second chance? Please?' They never answered. The buzzing got louder. I realized that I was cold. Then you were telling me to come down." He looked down at JiAnn, pleading. "Do you think they'll give me another chance?"

She looked at him solemnly. "First, if you had seen nothing, absolutely nothing, you would have failed to make contact. You *didn't* fail."

Relieved, Billy sat down again, but was now more erect. Completely attentive.

"What I'm about to tell you goes no further than this room," she began.

Billy nodded in agreement.

"We've learned that satendrites don't have cognition, at least not in a form remotely similar to human cognition. They don't have emotion. They don't have audition, touch, or smell. That's why they didn't answer any of your questions. But they have vision! Oh, do they have vision!" she said, spreading her fingers in front of her eyes.

Billy leaned in close.

"They have lenses, billions of powerful, microscopic, organic lenses that work in concert to see objects at incredible distances in minute detail. They can follow your interest when you are viewing objects, and alternatively, they can direct your attention to items that have changed since you last viewed them. What's more, they forget nothing they have ever seen. It's all stored in their DNA."

Billy crossed his hands under his nose looking into JiAnn's eyes. He appeared completely oblivious to the effect his sapphire eyes piercing into her soul, had on her, making it even more difficult for JiAnn to concentrate.

"So, when you saw Earth, they followed your interest, showing greater and greater magnification as you, unconsciously, directed them to do. Does that make sense?"

Not only Billy's head but also his shoulders nodded. JiAnn tried to move away from Billy, but she bumped against the wall. She tilted her head looking up. The one thing that made the room less claustrophobic was its high ceiling.

"They 'communicate' through vision. Vision is very complex. Rods and cones in our eyes sense light, darkness, and color. But nothing visual makes sense until electrical impulses converge in the visual cortex. The human brain is the most complex object in the known universe."

Billy sat straighter; he squared his shoulders, and his face showed animation. JiAnn's and Billy's knees touched. JiAnn reacted viscerally, but she didn't want to move; didn't want to break the contact.

"What you experienced, David, Malcolm, and I each experienced the first time: the feeling of being both in touch and yet rejected," her face soft and sympathetic. "That was the real reason I stayed nearby. I wanted to ease you back into *our* reality. Do you get what I'm saying?"

Billy nodded and smiled. "That's a relief."

"The first time they encounter a human, they find all those areas of the brain that have nothing to do with sight *irrelevant*; so, they avoid them in the future." JiAnn looked deeply into Billy's eyes. "You'll never experience the test again."

Billy's smile radiated happiness.

"Satendrites never interpret the vision they're sharing. Remember, they aren't capable of cognition. So where does that leave the Dragomark?" she asked.

Billy rubbed his chin, contemplating the question. "We're lying to the public," he said, a bit angrily.

JiAnn took it like a slap in the face. *Too much disillusionment for one session.* "Yes, we call it a ruse, but you're right. Instead of reporting the bald visualizations, we contextualize, we... embroider."

Billy interrupted, "You report your own opinions as messages from the satendrites!"

JiAnn stood and ran her fingers through her hair. She wanted to pace, but there was no space. She saw Billy's tight jaws and thin lips, his face like flint. She wondered if he might be angry enough to spill the beans. So, she tried to mollify him. "Yes, but we have to be very, very careful how we turn vision into suggestions. One thing must never happen: the satendrites must never 'say' something that later proves false. It must never come out as opinion, only fact, and perhaps implication." She sat back down.

Billy's brows were knit, lips working but not speaking. Finally, he asked, "So, why can there only be one Dragomark?"

JiAnn's heart sank. This was the most difficult question, but she had to try to explain. "That's an invention. Every person will contextualize the visions differently, but among Dragomarks there has to be one consistent message, so only one person *officially* sees what the satendrites see. Malcolm enters the Bubble frequently, but he never reports his visions to anyone but me. That is until he becomes *the* Dragomark."

Billy bit his lip. His face softened. A minute later he responded. "I get it. I don't like it, but I get it. You're charlatans... no, we're charlatans. But for a good cause, I guess."

JiAnn paused before responding. "I see... I *saw* my role... I used my office, with the benefit of visual information that I knew was accurate, to insert wisdom into the decision-making process. One condition of assuming the office of Apprentice is that you agree that the Dragomark is the *only* voice of the satendrites. Do you agree?"

"I agree."

"You're now the Apprentice, and you'll be Apprentice for a few years."

Billy's lips pursed, and his brows knit. "A few *years*!?" he asked, incredulous.

JiAnn worried.

6
Perfect Job

I'M RUNNING DOWN THE pitch, dribbling the ball. I'm almost to the goal. I kick! A bird is chirping. I look up, but I can't see the bird. I try to see whether I made a goal. Bird chirps again. I can't find the bird...

Persistent pinging. His perso was pinging. Sweating, he threw off his covers. It was always too hot or too cold in his efficiency. He opened my letr-page. A red-headed male face appeared in three dimensions in front of his eyes.

A voice said, "Corvis?"

"Yes" he said, rubbing his eyes. His watch read 2:31 AM. He turned on the light.

"I have the perfect job for you," the familiar voice said.

"I *have* the perfect job."

"Had, past tense. You got *fired* from a good job."

He clicked off the letr-page but knew he wouldn't get right back to sleep. Corvis looked around his unexceptional efficiency apartment: toilet separated from the rest of the room by a curtain that did nothing to subdue bad odors, tiny window with a great view of someone else's window, three feet away, curtains always drawn.

His whole life was efficient. *They say the life of an ICU nurse is never boring. Most of our patients are old, over 120, but we get the occasional crash injury or industrial accident. There's never been a cure for stupid. We struggle to help them live. Even with late 21st-century medical magic, too many times we end up comforting the bereaved. A robot wheels one body out to make room for another critically ill patient.*

His letr-page pinged. He wasn't surprised.

Please let me start over. Hi, Corvis. This is Jake.

I know. And you're writing me at 2:30 AM to remind me that I was fired. Don't need reminding.

OMG, Corvis, I'm sorry. I didn't think about the time zone difference! I'll call tomorrow.

It's already tomorrow, and I'm wide awake now. So…

My clients need a nurse and a space pilot…

My license is restricted to small private planes.

The computer will do the actual flying. Jake wrote, *You'll work at least 16 hours, seven days a week, and get paid nothing.*

You really know how to bait the hook, Corvis wrote. *Do tell me more.*

Not over the page. How soon can you get here?

Just so this scintillating conversation doesn't end precipitously, where, perchance, is 'here'?

I do love Congo and I like Jake. He's always amazingly persuasive. Jake and I worked together on projects for World Corps. Our one-year commitment ended. I returned to the USA. Jake stayed on. I envy him.

Have been thinking about taking a little vacation between jobs. My lease is almost up. A week in Congo wouldn't be so bad.

When is your lease up?

2 weeks

Could you be here in two hours?

I'm Twenty-three, and I confess, I'm an adrenaline junkie. Drop everything. Flying off to Congo. Exciting. Why not?

Can't possibly get there in less than 12 hours.

Great! I'll pick you up. Kinshasa International Airport, at 1300 hours. That's the last flight in from New York tomorrow, Jake wrote.

You even checked the flight schedule.

I do my homework. Your ticket will be waiting for you at Ethiopian Airlines. Bye! Jake clicked off.

You've got to be out of your mind! Corvis laid down and tried to get back to sleep, but that was futile, so he got up and packed a bag.

Realizing it would be at least an hour before he could get a snack at the airport, he dropped two slices of bread in the toaster. The smell of the toast got his stomach juices going. He made a peanut butter and jam sandwich and took a big bite. Then he poured himself a glass of OJ. While he ate, he wrote the landlady a note:

Dear Mildred,

Would you be good enough to pack up my stuff and
    rent a storage unit and store the stuff for
    me? I'll be back in a week or ten days.
You're a dear!
Corvis

He pulled three large bills out of his wallet, re-read the note, and realized the request was unrealistic. He put the money back in his wallet, wadded up the note and tossed it in the waste bin.

He scanned the room looking for anything he absolutely couldn't live without. Soccer ball and cleats he could replace. His eyes fell on a photo of himself smiling with his latest squeeze. He laid it, face down, on the dresser. *Sorry, Carter, you're more drama than I can manage*. He left the house key on the kitchen table and locked the door from the inside. *I'm not leaving that much behind*, he thought.

Knowing he could not get back in once he closed the door, he scanned his place one last time. *I want my cleats. They're almost new yet nicely broken in*. He opened his bag and threw them in.

Key on the table; dramatic. He closed the door.

Downstairs, he stood on the curb. A few dry snowflakes fell. Not a single floating vehicle was moving up or down the street. Even in New York City, there aren't many taxi-floats at 3:30 AM on a Wednesday. *Good thing I wore my overcoat. Hope I don't freeze to death out here. In a couple of weeks, I'll be back. Finish my offboarding, get my check, and find another job. New York: a great place for a young person. Full of excitement, this city-that-never-sleeps, except when you're looking for a float on a Wednesday morning, early. But it's also a place that can feel so cold, so very lonely, even in a crowded elevator.* He shivered and stomped his feet, craning his neck for a taxi.

Immortality

Between NY and Kinshasa, Earth

At 7:19 AM, nearly 2000 other passengers and Corvis started boarding the huge old air freighter. He walked past First class. The aisle narrowed through Second class. The aisle got narrower, still. He found his tiny seat, in coach, between, two morbidly obese, odiferous men.

Breathing was a challenge, air beyond stagnant. He wrangled his left arm out from under that of Obese Number One to open the air vent. Turning it all the way in either direction, it made no difference. Air was not going to move until takeoff.

Once airborne, he un-wedged himself, climbed over the human mountain, and walked around. He thought about his needs. *I want to live forever, but that's impossible.* In the late twenty-first century, a lot of other people in their early twenties felt beat. Nuclear world war was looming, and they believed they wouldn't live to see thirty. *When I'm not in the ICU I work out like a mad man. I want my body to live, really live, for as long as possible. I can't live forever, but I'm not afraid of death. Am I? I want something of myself to survive. Can't live without sex, but so far, I haven't met anyone I could imagine living my whole life with. I won't give up looking. Children? Yes, I want to have children. I want to nurture them and instill in them good values and hope.*

He sipped his black coffee. Third cup. *I want more. I want to be remembered. I don't want it all to just go black and instantly everyone forget that I ever lived.* Many people whom he'd helped, as an ICU nurse, told him they would never forget him. But did they even remember his name the next day?

Maybe immortality is calling me to Kinshasa.

7
Kinshasa, Congo

CORVIS BRACED HIMSELF FOR the bedlam that always awaits in the immigration-customs-taxi process of getting out of Ndjili International Airport. This time was considerably worse than he remembered. Panic possessed everyone. He watched, on the verge of tears, as an 80-plus-year-old, 4' 11" (150 cm) woman loped beside a flimsy box weighing more than she did, bound with twine, on the conveyor belt, tugging furiously, yet futilely, trying to pull it off. Emotionless people watched. He dropped his duffel to help her snare the box. The twine cut into his fingers. It was heavy even for Corvis. What she did with it after that, he had no Idea.

News of impending war headlined all the feeds. Desperate people sought loved ones, and hoarded necessities. Too much energy, and no place to hide from the coming holocaust.

It took almost 2 hours to clear customs. Just outside security, amid the gaggle, Jake was easy to spot with his red hair. He grabbed Corvis's bag and set off running. He tried to keep up, but soon his stamina gave out. He hadn't really slept in thirty-six hours and had a splitting headache. The mix of odors of jet fuel, diesel, and sulfur-rich gasoline lightened his head and turned his stomach. He walked half-dazed. Nearly 90° Fahrenheit outside and raining. He was sweating within, soaking without. Hot rain, poverty, panic, and fatigue all conspired to oppress and overwhelm him.

Jake's old 2079 Xamba float was parked less than a quarter of a mile away in the short-term parking area. Corvis couldn't make out what color it had originally been, so battered and patched it was. Jake threw my bag on top of a pile of detritus that once had been a back seat and jumped into the driver's seat. By the time Corvis got in, Jake was talking fast on his perso. Someone in a coverall uniform appeared on the screen on the dashboard. "Yes," Jake answered, "the pilot is here. Say 'hello,' Corvis."

He barely managed half a smile "Hello."

"The remodel of Valhalla II is nearing completion, right? Facilities for just over three hundred people. Algae tanks, functional?" Jake continued. "Water purification?" While he was talking, Jake floated the car nearly straight up. Even so, he had to fight to make fast progress.

Can I really still smell jet fuel even up here? Or is it just my imagination?

"... world-class infirmary. Twelve beds. More than they'll ever use..."

"Whoever has the least to lose goes first," he said, as we darted sideways between two on-coming, shiny new limo-floats that had more power and less nerve.

"Who's paying for all of this?" Coveralls asked.

"Congo government has funds dedicated to the mission," Jake replied.

As they cleared the city, Jake descended to just above the turnpike. It was clogged with all types of conveyances: trucks, goat-drawn carts, bicycles, tractors, and pedestrians, all moving, at a slow walk, when moving, at all.

Jake hadn't finished one conversation when another call came in. "I understand fuel is at a premium right now. How much can you get me?" More negotiations, plans, and haggling.

After half an hour, Corvis tried to break in. "Uh, Jake…" "Jake." "Jake!" Corvis hadn't even tried to use any of the restrooms he passed in the airport because of the long lines.

Jake looked at him but continued talking. *He's not hearing me. He won't stop, and I'll wet my pants.*

"I saw a sign for a Rest Stop!" Corvis shouted, "I need to freshen up."

"No need," Jake said, "the kids'll accept you just as you are."

He doesn't intend to stop.

"I have to *pee*!" he screamed.

The woman on Jake's perso, with her long black hair, stopped mid-word, shock on her face.

Jake still showed no evidence of having heard, but he landed the float close to the restroom.

Camp Lakoko, Gabon

Corvis listened to Jake switch from English to French, haggling with contractors, to German while sweet-talking potential donors. Always talking fast. At the same time, Corvis watched the lush green canopy of the forest pass beneath them, some trees blooming bright yellow. A large red macaw flew just below. The jungle appeared so beautiful from this perspective. Fast-talking in his auditory channel and breath-taking, peaceful splendor in his visual channel gave him serious cognitive discord.

As they approached the border between Congo and Gabon, they dipped down cutting into line, provoking a riot of honking horns and shouted expletives.

Jake had official papers issued by both countries. Corvis had only his US passport. The border patrol was not happy about the furor they had caused. While one officer scolded Jake, another, younger officer in an unwrinkled khaki uniform, eyed Corvis coldly. "This is no time for tourism," the stern officer said, resting his hand tensely on his large service pistol.

Dripping perspiration, Corvis stammered. "I'm, I'm not a tour... tourist."

Jake interrupted. "He represents an American charity that is resettling refugees from Camp Lakoko. We're headed there now."

A bored officer dismissed them with a wave.

Just a few miles past the border, Jake veered away from the highway, following a paved road that soon became a dirt track through the lush jungle. Corvis's head and nose cleared. Jake hadn't resumed his conversations once we crossed into Gabon. He became hypervigilant. Impossibly, the scenery became even more beautiful... until, suddenly, everything went brown.

"What happened?" Corvis asked.

"We're in the refugee camp," Jake explained, "Camp Lakoko."

A woman dumped a large basin of dark water over a fence. A sea of brown cardboard shacks was lightly peppered with tarps of different colors. The refugee camp went on for mile after miserable mile. "How many people live in this camp?" Corvis asked.

"No one knows for sure. Thousands arrive every day. Certainly, over a million are living here now. Some residents work as far away as Kinshasa, in the finest hotels."

By now, the sun was low in the sky as the track ended in a roundish clearing. "We walk from here," Jake said as he dropped his float down deftly to park it.

While they walked, Corvis tried not to step in amorphous piles of brown stuff. The putrefaction was oppressive. People looked at them with hopeless, empty eyes. Skin-and-bone children with swollen bellies, due to kwashiorkor, seemed too weak to cry. A million people here were relegated to live far from the view of city dwellers, with no running water, sewers, or garbage collection, and very little food or potable water, all because warlords had taken over their villages.

Half an hour later, they arrived at another clearing. In the gathering night, a fire glowed at its center, and what seemed like a thousand children encircled the fire. The smell of smoke felt cleansing after the long stench.

Jake said, "We're here," nudging his way through the crowd. Corvis, still overawed, followed in his wake.

One of the few adults, a tall man with a healthy dark complexion greeted Jake warmly. They made small talk in French. What little Corvis understood didn't concern him. He introduced Corvis to this man whose name Corvis could not pronounce.

When Unpronounceable began to speak, the children grew still. He spoke in Fang, a language Corvis once knew a few essential phrases of. He pointed at Corvis, and the children erupted in cheers.

"Why did they applaud?" Corvis whispered to Jake.

"Because he told them that you're the one who will take them to a better place."

Several children with scars and even missing limbs took turns giving Corvis high-fives. He patted one wooly head after another. Shook hands with many more. How could anyone hurt such sweet children? Corvis sat on a rock while Jake tried to address them in Fang. Laughter drowned out his words, so he spoke in French while Unpronounceable interpreted. Corvis admired Jake. He could charm the stripes off a tiger.

The scene told him about the children's physical wounds: a broken bone that had healed crooked, a missing arm or a leg, and one girl with awful facial scars and eyes clouded white. Many of the wounded were mere toddlers. His heart ached. *What about the scars I can't see? What's the damage to the psyche from this kind of torture?* But tonight, this circle of faces, lit only by firelight, reflected kindness, trust, and hope. They were all sisters- and brothers-in-suffering, and all had lost much. When Jake finished speaking, he sat on a rock beside Corvis.

A three-year-old, missing her left foot, crawled into Corvis's lap and snuggled in. He had only a fuzzy notion of what Jake had committed him to, but Corvis's nod sealed their contract.

8
Dangerous Animals

AFTER AN HOUR, HE had met the children, and the children had met Corvis. Their business was finished in the jungle. Now they just needed to walk back to the parking lot.

In the dark, Camp Lakoko looked nothing like it had at dusk. In fact, Corvis couldn't see three feet in front of his face. *How can a camp of one million people be so utterly devoid of light?* As soon as they left the clearing two large men offered to protect them from "dangerous animals."

Suspicious, "I don't think..." Corvis started.

But Jake interrupted, "Thank you. That would be terrific." As an aside to Corvis, he said, "Homo sapiens is the most dangerous animal here... or anywhere."

"Thanks," Corvis said, "I'm glad they're with us. They know the way back to the parking lot."

Moist night air intensified the putrid odors. They had walked about five minutes when a voice not three feet from Corvis's left ear said "Stop!"

Terrified, he wanted to sprint away; but he knew the owner of the voice would quickly overtake and kill him. But he couldn't stop, either. Corvis tried to think, but only the reptilian part of his brain was working. He kept walking. His breathing stopped, expecting something horrible.

"You dare to disrespect me!" the angry voice shouted. Corvis sensed two other strangers with the first. Knowing his end was near, but with no alternative, he stopped. Silence and darkness closed in. Time stood still.

"I didn't mean... to disrespect... you," came out in a breathless, barely audible whisper. "I didn't hear."

"Shut up!" the captor shouted.

Their escorts, the ones that in his panic he had forgotten, intervened, speaking to the men in Fang. Soon there was laughter, and then they were walking again. Corvis's nearest escort whispered in his ear. "I paid them twenty new francs. They won't bother you anymore. Can you reimburse me?"

"Gladly!" Corvis replied, his heart pounding out of his chest, his throat so dry he couldn't swallow.

Danger apparently passed, his adrenalin slow to return to normal, in what seemed like another hour, they arrived at the float, Corvis pulled out a hundred-franc bill.

"Sorry, man, no one can break such a large bill here." Corvis had only two 20s, which he gave his savior. Jake gave the other man some bills, as well. They all shook hands. Their guides slapped them on the back and wished them well.

Jake started his float. The dashboard gave off a small, dim light within. It was still pitch-black outside as they headed toward Kinshasa.

"Aren't you going to turn on your headlights?" Corvis asked.

"Did you learn nothing from our little stroll? Out here, it's best not to draw attention to oneself after dark."

Flying blind, obviously with only memory to guide him, Jake didn't make conversation. In the dark silence, Corvis's mind's eye flashed back: Apartment key. Left sitting on the table. Corvis wouldn't be back to New York in a week, he knew. Or even a year.

Once they were over the turnpike, again, Jake turned on his headlight. Singular. The other was burned out. They had passed high over border patrol without headlight and without stopping.

Jake is very careful. He wouldn't take any unnecessary chances with the authorities, Corvis thought.

Jake relaxed visibly. So, did Corvis. Traffic below was at a complete standstill. On the way back to Kinshasa, Jake outlined Corvis's mission. "The children you met tonight? You're taking them to Enceladus."

"The colony that doesn't exist?"

"It's supposed to be super-secret. But thousands of people have disappeared. Someone was bound to tell a loved one. Officials continue to deny that it is anything more than an urban legend. Enceladus is one of the few places where humans will survive the nuclear war. That's been its reason for being, from the very beginning."

"I watched the news while waiting for my flight. It's getting brutal everywhere!"

"Do you remember President Gbonkta?" Jake asked.

"The name is vaguely familiar."

"He was Representative Gbonkta when you met him."

"Oh, yes," Corvis said, "I remember that he was very charismatic."

"He learned about these children a month ago. Warlords have taken over many jungle villages; subjected women and children to torture, arson, rape, and murder. Gangsters have kidnapped many girls to be 'brides' for soldiers; many boys were taken to be trained as boy soldiers. The three hundred or so orphans you met this evening managed to escape. They gathered, little by little, village by village, kept walking and finally, they found their way to Camp Lakoko."

"What incredible courage..."

"Meanwhile, for more than two years, Valhalla II has been parked at Pointe Indienne Spaceport. It was built to replace the *Valhalla*, a luxury cruise ship. Cruising in space was very popular as recently as a couple of years ago. But then the diseases endemic to cruise ships discouraged clients. No sooner had effective antiseptics been developed than pirate ships from the Moon started attacking cruise ships. Norge Cruise Line went out of business just before *Valhalla II* was to have made its maiden cruise."

"Bad luck," Corvis said.

"Valhalla II would have accommodated four hundred and fifty passengers in luxury and a hundred and fifty crew," Jake continued. "It's been reconfigured for more than three hundred and fifty children and ten adult crew. Storage fees and taxes have mounted on this ship, and the company that owned it is bankrupt. Congo wanted to sell it, but between court litigation and a lack of buyers, *Valhalla II* remained in its berth.

"President Gbonkta knows he will face backlash, even prison time. Not only does Congo not have a clear title to the *Valhalla II,* but also there are certainly three hundred and fifty citizens of Congo who are equally needy and equally deserving, but these Gabonese children have shown incredible courage and ingenuity. Purely by chance, their numbers fit, almost exactly, the capacity of the ship. And they have been together as a single group for some time now."

"Still, he will face the rage of some of his supporters," I said.

"Right. Here we are."

Before Corvis knew it, they were landing in front of a magnificent, well-lit pink hotel. It looked like a tall cake with scalloped icing on top. The side trim of wavy pleats reached down to ground level. It seemed to be made entirely of whipped cream. The entrance doors were two stories tall. Corvis was admiring the illusion of softness as he got out of the float.

Jake, again pressured for time, said, "Your room is prepaid in your name, placed by Jake Erlmutter." The float started rising, as Corvis banged rapidly on the door.

"My bag!" he shouted.

Jake landed again and handed it to him.

9
Hotel Lumumba

Stunning on the outside, what had obviously once been a truly grand hotel had seen better days inside. Corvis's suite was twice as large as the efficiency he left in New York. It smelled sweet and flowery, but then the smell quickly overwhelmed. He started coughing. The bathroom was enormous, and it had hot running water. Heavenly.

But then there were subtle signs that the room was not very clean, like the dirty sock on the chair. When Corvis turned down the bedspread, the pubic hair on the pillow did nothing to reassure. At 2329, hours he phoned the front desk. He let it ring for a full minute. *Maybe the receptionist is busy*, he thought. He tried again at 2335. Still no answer. Corvis gave up; threw all but one of the pillows in a corner, stripped the sheets, and took the linens and one pillow out into the hall and shook each item vigorously.

Exhausted. A long, warm shower gradually eased the tension out of his sore though well-developed muscles. Famished, he put on fresh clothes and went down to one of the four bars.

Only one was actually open, as it turned out. It could easily accommodate fifty patrons but was occupied by just four people, counting the bartender. Corvis ordered a beer and a bowl of lamb stew. He took his beer, a couple of cocktail napkins, and a handful of nuts and headed for a table in the shadows.

As he approached an attractive woman patron, he walked through an invisible cloud of expensive perfume. Sitting alone, she looked at Corvis expectantly. Her scent lingered with Corvis, even though he indicated that he preferred to be alone.

Twenty minutes later Barkeep held up a bowl, and Corvis retrieved his dinner: bite-sized chunks of mutton, cassava, onions, and carrots swimming in a gravy that smelled faintly of mint and garlic. A fresh pita was on one side of the plate and a quarter of a lemon on the other. The meat wasn't lamb, but not leather, either. To most, it would have seemed like an ordinary meal; but on that night, after such a long two days, it was a feast. Now to bed.

Corvis cringed as he crossed the threshold into my suite. At least the sickening rosy disinfectant had dissipated. The room was warm. I wouldn't need a blanket. *Don't think about the mattress or what might be under it. Just relax and sleep,* Corvis thought/

He closed his eyes, and instantly, he was back in Camp Lakoko. He saw maimed little bodies with hopeful eyes. He imagined a long trip cooped up in a spaceship with all these needy little children. How long would it take to get all the way to Saturn? Three years? Five years? He didn't know. *How will they cope? How will I cope?*

He rested. His queen bed was infinitely better than being shoehorned between two huge men on a plane. Surprisingly, he did eventually doze. When he woke up the clock said 0507. He could have slept a few more hours. He wasn't exactly refreshed, but he felt more human. He wanted to get moving.

10
Breakfast at Lundula's

As HE STEPPED OUT of the bathroom the phone rang. Only one person would be calling him at 5:35 AM in Kinshasa. "Good morning, Jake!" he answered.

"Where have you been?!" Jake demanded.

"What do you mean, 'where have I been'?"

"I mean, I've been calling your room for half an hour..."

"I went out for a run. Is that illegal?"

"Before sunrise? In Kinshasa? You're taking your life in your hands. Anyway, now that you're back, meet me in the lobby," Jake said curtly. "I'll buy you breakfast."

Their restaurant beckoned with the smell of fresh-baked cinnamon rolls. The sign, in English, French, and Arabic, invited us to 'seat ourselves.' Coffee arrived at our table just ahead of the waiter. I was hungry.

"Would you like to see the menu?" the waiter asked in English.

"I know what I want," Corvis said.

"Me, too," Jake said.

Corvis ordered two eggs, basted, two slices of bacon extra crisp, and wheat toast, dry.

Jake ordered a Spanish omelet and an English muffin, extra butter.

The waiter disappeared into the kitchen. Corvis liked the restaurant. It was spacious and elegant, walls painted light eggshell with gold trim, white linen tablecloth and napkins, gold-plated silverware, and thin white china.

"Here's the plan," Jake said, after looking around suspiciously. "We'll meet Svetlana. Then we'll go to Pointe Indiene Spaceport and look over the ship. Then we'll come back..."

"Wait! Who's Svetlana?"

"Oh, you don't know," Jake said, placing the heel of his hand on his forehead. "She'll be your Chief Operating Officer, while you'll be Captain, Chief Medical Officer, and Pilot. After we meet her, we'll come back here..."

"Sorry! But I'd like to know more about Svetlana. What qualifies her to manage a complex ship's day-to-day operations?"

"She was chief graduate resident assistant in the largest dorm at Russia's most prestigious college, Tomsk State University, and then she succeeded as managing director of the same dorm. She is twenty-three years old, very smart, an excellent motivator, and... "

"She sounds perfect. How long will the trip take?"

"That question will be of interest to Svetlana," Jake said, "When you're finished eating, I'll call and see if she is up yet."

"Do you think Gabon will get involved in the war?" Corvis asked.

Jake scanned his surroundings again. "All countries will be involved in the coming war, like it or not."

When the waiter brought the bill, Jake ordered a cinnamon roll... "to go."

Breakfast was heavenly.

Meeting Svetlana

Svetlana was awake when Jake called. She offered to come down.

Jake asked, "Can we come up? We need to talk."

She agreed.

"I brought you a pastry," Jake said at the threshold of her room.

He introduced Corvis to her. Corvis had to look up slightly to meet her eyes. She wore a brown suit, white shirt, and tie. Her shoes were sensible pumps. *Dorm mother attire. Children will respect her. But she's not very cuddly.*

She had a healthy, clear complexion, and brown hair. Corvis couldn't read her emotions.

He noted that Svetlana was sizing him up, as well.

"You'll have a long time to get to know each other on your trip," Jake said. "Let me answer your questions about your mission on our way to Pointe Indiene Spaceport. Nearly every inch of this hotel is bugged, and we have some sensitive things to discuss. We don't need little ears listening."

Valhalla II

Pointe Indiene Spaceport

Overnight, Jake had cleared a little space in the back seat. It reminded Corvis of his recent seat on the freighter. His butt fit barely, but one arm hung out the window and the other rested on top of junk.

"Your trip will be almost exactly 1 billion miles," Jake said, as we floated over the gridlock. "Your average speed will be about 560,000 miles per hour. You'll be halfway to the Moon by the time the secondary booster burn ends."

Corvis looked at the back of Svetlana's head. *What kind of personality do you have? How will we get along during this long trip?* He wondered.

"There are four times you will experience the effects of acceleration: when you first blast off, then when you exit our Moon, and when you whiz past Mars. Your ship will come close to the Moon to use its gravity to fling you faster on your way. Like a slingshot. You'll use Mars in the same way. The last time you'll feel acceleration is when you begin slowing down to land on Enceladus."

As they approached the spaceport, rockets at three sites spewed white clouds, indicating that blast-off approached. Corvis's pulse speeded up on seeing them. They parked near Valhalla's hangar. Coming from New York, big buildings didn't normally impress Corvis, but this building wowed by its enormity. His entire apartment *building* could fit inside, its footprint at least a city block. No divisions within, either vertical or horizontal, and its volume immense. Inside, what looked like a giant soufflé dish was balanced vertically. Tilting my head, it appeared about five stories high and more than a hundred yards in diameter, sitting on four giant cones. Around the circumference, four evenly spaced blebs protruded.

A man in coveralls, the same one Corvis had seen on Jake's small screen, approached. "Hi," he said, "I'm Max Velter, the general contractor for this project. Sorry I can't give you a tour of the interior. As you can see, people are working on it inside and out, under a tight deadline, so visitors would get in the way, but I'll be happy to answer questions."

"I'll start," Corvis said. "What are those blister-like things around the middle?"

"*Valhalla II* was built as a luxury liner. It wouldn't have windows; those blisters are alcoves. They are seven feet high and jut three feet out from the ship. People can sit in them and feel like they're floating in space."

"They definitely don't look like portals," Corvis said.

"Air resistance is a major problem in launching the ship," he said. "The *Valhalla* is covered with a thin membrane that reduces resistance. Surface area is another problem. What you see here is one-fourth the volume of the ship after it expands."

"How will it do that?" Corvis asked.

"After you leave earth's atmosphere, mass is the only resistance to acceleration. Valhalla has three layers of very tough, very thin plastic sandwiched between two metal mesh walls. The metal is microscopically crinkled and then pleated. The three decks are now three meters high now; they'll each be ten meters high in space. The volume inside the Valhalla will be mind-boggling."

"The four cones contain engines, correct?" Svetlana asked.

"Yes," Velter said, "we switched out two of the four original magma-plasma engines for two new compact hydrogen ion fusion engines. They produce large blasts of non-continuous propulsion. But because you will have two of them, one will fire while the other is charging, so it will feel like smooth continuous acceleration. Like two gigantic, coordinated pistons."

"Until we are free of Earth's gravity, the children will be confined to the cabin, I presume. What is the size and layout of the cabin?" Corvis asked.

"Even before blastoff the cabin will be larger than you need," Mr. Velter said. "It is shaped like a curved hotdog, thirty meters long and ten meters wide, with headroom of nearly three meters. It had four hundred and fifty seats, each large enough to accommodate a 360-pound, or 164-kilogram, person. Children will swim in such large seats, but most will have child safety insert seats. We were able to remove a hundred and twenty-six seats, and still leave you ten empty seats. They can come in handy. Personal carry-on items are placed on the floor in front of the seat. Seconds before blastoff floor segments drop half a meter, and new floor segments slide into place, stowing the carry-ons under the floor temporarily. The seats are arranged in twelve rows, with two center aisles, and the ends of each row are wide open due to the seats we removed. There are six restrooms, three on each wall at the ends of the rows."

"How is the g-force of acceleration accommodated?" Corvis asked.

"Comfort restraints will close around each body. Gel under the fabric covering will first support and then 'give' as gravity increases, preventing injury, especially to the neck and spine. All seats recline fully during takeoff." Mr. Velter said.

"Where sits the COO?" Svetlana asked.

"The COO 'booth' is at the front of the cabin, facing the passengers, just to the left of the Lobby portal. You'll see every seat from there. No walls surround the booth, except for the COO's private restroom. The booth contains a communications deck so that large screens show the COO's image, or whatever the COO chooses to project. Speakers in each seat, and the PA system always carry the COO's audio to all passengers and the pilot. The small private restroom can be used by a passenger in an emergency."

"When is planned the blastoff?" Svetlana asked.

"Ready or not," Velter said, "the payload moves from this little workshop, here, to the launch pad at 2100 hours."

"Tonight?!" Corvis exclaimed.

"Tonight," Velter said. "Beyond that, it's out of my hands." Turning to Svetlana, "A lot of things can affect the actual time of launch."

"Oh my God, Jake! Is that true?" Corvis asked.

Svetlana said, "No way! We can't possibly leave that soon."

"We'll talk about it on our way back to the hotel," Jake said, turning toward his float.

Svetlana and Corvis said, "Thank you, Mr. Velter," in unplanned unison.

Tonight! We're leaving Earth tonight! It's too much. I'm not ready! Corvis thought.

11
Goodbyes

Congo, Africa

JAKE WAS SAYING, "TONIGHT, General Kasavubu will introduce you to the children..." We weren't listening. We had to say our goodbyes.

Svetlana was already dialing. "Mama," she said, while Jake continued talking, "How are you? ... Yes, I'm well. How about you? Have you found someone to help? ... I told you. You *can* afford help, and you need it. You're almost 90, and you have Oksana to take care of... In Africa for now... Listen, I'm going on a mission. I'll be gone a long, long time. Mama! Stop! ... I'm not in any trouble. I'm *not* being *disappeared*. I know she needs me, but I have to... I want to go... To fulfill my destiny. Mama, please stop crying. You would be proud of me. I can't describe the mission. Could you put Oksana on, please? ... Kseniya! My little dove! How are you? I'm going far, far away to help lots of children. No, you can't come help, but thanks for offering. Listen, sweetheart, I won't be home until you are an old, old lady, but I will think of you every day. They don't have phone service there. Be good... I know, you are always good. You are the light of my life. I know you love me... You have a boyfriend?! How wonderful! What is his name? Should you marry him? Maybe you would like to get to know him a little better, first. Oh, how I wish I could meet him, too.

Whoever loves my little... Yes, you're all grown up, but you will always be my little Kseniya."

I was eleven. Folding my clothes, packing my toothbrush, and rolling up my sleeping bag. Nervously anticipating my adventure. Mom was sending me off to summer camp for the third time. I always expected her to be sad. But she never was. More like eager.

Arriving at camp, I pass boys slouching under smelly, muddy clothes stuffed into backpacks on their way to board the bus that would take them back to reality. For a millisecond, I feel sorry for them, knowing that I will look the same a week from now. But I have four fresh tee shirts neatly folded, and my adventure is just beginning, Corvis remembered

Who would he call? Co-workers? Mom? She wouldn't recognize his voice, and he would have to remind her a minute later. More to the point, a week from now who would he wish he had called? Dad! The one person he still loved and respected. But he hadn't called him for months. *This will be hard, but I really must,* he thought. *Hi, Dad. This is Corvis.* Probably better not to rehearse.

Ringing forever. *Maybe he's deciding whether to answer or listen to a message.* "Dad! It's Cor. I haven't called for a while." Corvis's voice cracked.

"You've been busy. Another pandemic!" he said.

Pause. "How are you?" Corvis finally asked.

"I'm fine." Pause. "Take your time," he reassured.

"I'm going away," Corvis said, "and I won't be coming back." *There. It's done.*

"Are you depressed?"

"No, Dad. No! I'm not thinking of suicide. It's something good."

"Enceladus?"

"How did you know?!"

"I keep up on gossip."

"I won't be able to call."

"I understand. I'm glad for you. War is coming."

"I wish you were coming with me."

"So, do I!"

Pause "There's so much I want to say." Pause. "And nothing I can say."

"Your silence tells me all I need to know," he said.

"No, Dad, I need to tell you." Long pause. "I love you, and I truly respect you."

"And I love you. And I am so proud," Pause, "of you."

"From this moment, Dad, even though you won't know what I'm doing, I will try to earn your pride."

Jake was still talking. Svetlana had made another cal. Perhaps he was pretending not to hear our private conversations. Maybe his heart was breaking, a little too. "So, pack your things. Then we'll have lunch. And head back to the spaceport." He landed the float in the lot.

I hadn't really unpacked. I threw in my dirty clothes from the previous day. I pulled the string on my bag. *All my earthly belongings. Stuff. What stuff do I want, or need to take with me from Earth? I won't be coming back. Where will I be living the rest of my life? On a ball of ice.*

12
Swarm Concept

BROBDING · MONTENEGRO, EARTH

THE GHASTLI FAMILY HAD an arsenal of tanks, cannons, troop carriers, speed boats, and planes that small nations envied, and he had just acquired 50 space fighters. In fact, Brobding Ghastli had been hired just two months earlier to prop up the despotic, but not well-armed Popovi regime, in Montenegro. What did Brobding charge Popovi for protecting him? Nothing.

In fact, the dictator would grow richer since Brobding had moved his base of operation there. He hired workers who bought goods. Brobding had annexed Montenegro to his growing empire. But he wasn't interested in governing, just conquering.

Every crime family on Earth paid tribute to Brobding. He was by far the wealthiest man on Earth. He had an army of financial advisers constantly researching legitimate investment opportunities. If money could buy it and Brobding wanted it, Brobding bought it. The Ghastli family had a five-story underground bunker complete with air and water purification, an aquaculture farm, a communications center, and, of course, above-ground warning and defense. He believed, and his advisers trusted, that they would not only survive but profit from, the coming war.

With nuclear world war a certainty, Brobding could smell money in outer space. When he learned that ConShip had replaced its orbiting control center with a newer, larger center, he jumped at the chance to buy the old one. It came with six tenders, each having the capacity to shuttle between orbiting ships of the line. Having built a spaceport in Montenegro, he had no trouble commuting to and from his office more than 100 kilometers above. He bought two "off-the-shelf space fighters" on the black market. Brobding's spaceport monitored traffic, watching for any opportunity to hijack a valuable shipment. On November 20, 2099, an opportunity of unbelievable proportions presented itself.

He was eager to capitalize on a new frontier. On November 21, 2099, Brobding intercepted a shipment of 50 fighters manufactured in the Southern Alliance being shipped to Moon Base. These were large, heavy craft, and each one required massive quantities of fuel to escape Earth's gravity. They flew in tight formation toward their intended new home, Moon Base. In battle, they would have great momentum but poor maneuverability. Ghastlich Orbiting Space Station was now as secure as any of the many international space stations. Brobding had heard rumors of a colony in the outer solar system. On May 2, 2099, Brobding hired Dr. Gerhardt Karlson, an aerospace engineer, to design a large fleet of small, nimble, long-range space fighters capable of reaching the outer planets.

He intended to add Enceladus to his growing personal space empire.

13
Blastoff

CORVIS • POINTE INDIENE SPACEPORT, CONGO

As soon as they walked into the auditorium, General Kasavubu stopped what he was saying. He pointed in the direction of Corvis and Svetlana and said, "Here is the man who put this whole project together, Jacob Erlmutter! Come say a few words to the group."

Jake walked swiftly to the podium and immediately started speaking. "I want to thank all the adults who helped bring this mission to fulfillment, and I want to thank all the adults who have been helping children get ready for this exciting voyage, but mainly I want to talk to the children. You are in good hands during this trip. Your Captain is Corvis Santos, and Svetlana Turgenev will be your Chief Operating Officer, kind of like your mom for the next three months. Both Captain Santos and Ms. Turgenev will be with you tonight..." Jake could see the kids getting antsy, so he concluded, "I wish you a pleasant journey and a wonderful life in your new home."

Gen. Kasavubu took the microphone and turned to Corvis, "Would you like to introduce yourself?"

"Yes. Hello," he said, "I'm Corvis. You can call me Captain Crow." The children laughed. "We'll get to know each other well during the trip, so that's all I'll say for now." The children clapped. He watched as Jake stood by the exit. Jake looked sad as he scanned the crowd one last time. Then he stepped out the door and was gone.

Svetlana was next. "Hi, I'm Svetlana," she said. "You can call me Svet. English is my second language also, like you, so we'll all help each other durink zee treep." She handed the microphone back to General Kasavubu.

Adults had to break up a minor scuffle in the middle of the auditorium.

General Kasavubu picked up his long, technical talk where he left off. Even the adults didn't understand, and the children weren't listening. Some children were playing tag. Others were crying.

Ms. Kongo, the National Director of Education, tried to get the general's attention discretely. When that failed, she marched up to the podium and tapped him on the shoulder. He handed her the mike. "Let's all wash our hands on our way in for supper. Who's hungry here?" she asked.

"I am!" all the children exploded.

Children filed into the large hall, carrying plates laden with traditional treats, older children carrying their own plates, younger ones assisted by adults. General Kasavubu took Svetlana and Corvis to a small private room where they ate during his briefing. "At 1600 hours local time," the general began gravely, "Nicaragua detonated a nuclear bomb in Tegucigalpa, Honduras. At 1630, South Korea dropped a nuclear bomb on Pyongyang. World War III has begun."

"But those aren't large powerful countries," Corvis protested.

"Right. They're puppet states. Expendable pawns of the Northern Confederacy and the Southern Alliance. Each whole block has vowed to come to the aid of any member state. It could be an hour or it could be a month but war will spread throughout the world."

"Vat does this mean for our mission," Svetlana asked.

"Normally, it would mean that the mission would be scrubbed. Now it means the ship must be launched as soon as possible," Kasavubu replied, "tomorrow noon, at the latest."

After supper, while the children showered in disinfectant, their clothes were washed, dried, and irradiated. Earlier in the afternoon their names had been enrolled, cheek swabs were taken, and their DNA recorded in the ship's manifest. There was no time to fit children with spacesuits. Rather, an assortment of various sizes was loaded onto the ship, with a ratio of two suits per child. Engineers put the finishing touches on the spaceship and rockets while the children bedded down for the night.

Corvis hadn't slept for three nights. Kasavubu showed him to a janitor's closet with a cot inside. It smelled so strongly of cleaning solvents and insecticide that he didn't think he would be able to sleep. Svetlana had a different closet of the same size.

Sleep Corvis did. But at 0200, Kasavubu whispered something in his ear. Totally disoriented, he jumped and almost hit the general. "What?!" he shouted.

"Congo has been attacked," he repeated. "You must board the ship and launch immediately."

The auditorium was 250 meters from the launchpad. A long tram stood ready at the door, but the children had to walk or be carried about 20 meters to the door. Bleary-eyed, the children in their new pajamas marched like little robots across the auditorium, down a hall, to the tram. Those too young to wake up and walk were carried. Svetlana and Corvis quickly helped ferry them to their seats on the tram and buckled them in. About twenty adults accomplished the operation.

The tram ride took five minutes. Fifteen children, Svetlana, another adult, and Corvis then entered the elevator, which ascended seventy meters to the loading deck. They walked ten meters from the deck to the main portal. Svetlana and Corvis were on their own from that point, as only passengers were allowed onto the ship. They each carried a sleeping infant in each arm across the gray threshold into the light green interior of the Lobby. The older children who entered with them helped tend to the younger ones. Temporary stairs snaked down to the doorway that led into the light blue cabin. Svetlana laid her two babies in bassinettes on each side of the left aisle while Corvis tucked his into the seats beside the right aisle. They stirred but then drifted right back to sleep.

They seated older girls between the infants. Seconds were ticking by in Corvis's mental clock. *Nineteen down and only two hundred-ninety-five to go and the spaceport could be bombed at any minute*. A few seconds later, another batch of twenty children walked through the door into the cabin and were quickly directed to their seats. Over the next fifteen minutes, fourteen more groups of children filed onto the ship and found their seats.

The window for safe liftoff was closing rapidly.

Even as the last children were being seated, Corvis went up to the Lobby, where a chair attached to a small crane lifted him twenty meters up into the bridge. It stopped next to the captain's seat, which was at right angles to the chair on the crane. The chair reclined ninety degrees, so all my weight was now on his back. Gravity made it slightly difficult to scoot himself into the large seat, but then, comfort restraints, sensing his weight, filled into the contours of his body, with extra support around his neck. That he could hardly move was comforting. From the top of the headrest, a tiny arm emerged and gently placed a headset over his head, a bud finding his ear, the microphone positioning itself perfectly below his mouth. Everything was disorienting. The control panel was above him, like a very close ceiling. He faced a dazzling display of knobs, lights, and dials none of which made any sense whatsoever. But on one monitor, he watched the cabin and saw the children settling in.

Most of them were sound asleep again when the final countdown began. "Ten... Nine..." the PA system announced. The ship began vibrating violently. His seatbelts deployed as he watched those in the cabin also automatically fasten themselves.

The shaking woke all the children, and they were terrified to discover that they were trapped by safety restraints.

"Three, Two, One. Blastoff. Godspeed, *Valhalla II!*" the engineer said.

G-force pushed Corvis hard into his seat. Children screamed. None had ever been on a plane, much less a rocket and it all started before they were fully awake! Svetlana could do nothing to comfort them, and nothing they could do helped them escape the crushing weight of their own bodies. Belts and strong gravity held them in their seats, but gel protected their little bones and fragile organs.

Nine minutes later, it seemed like an hour; the shielding membrane dissolved, blinding sunlight shone in some of the alcoves; the blackness of space punctuated by tiny stars was visible through other windows. Seatbelts automatically retracted and stowed themselves. A few children floated out of their seats.

Corvis picked his words carefully. "We have blasted off, little ones."

As he spoke, the ship began to expand in every direction. "You can get up and explore." They all experienced near-zero gravity for the first time. Corvis felt slightly light-headed, and his stomach wasn't sure it liked the new freedom.

Nursery

En route to the Moon

After four nights without decent sleep and a panicked prep for liftoff, Corvis was finally floating in front of the control panels. Plural. There were panels to control flight, to control internal temperature, pressure, oxygen, light, water flow, sewage, and on and on, and then there was the master control to control whole groups of controls. Vibration during blastoff made the blur even blurrier. *Now I can relax and learn about all these gadgets.*

He was wrong.

Mere seconds into blastoff he started getting calls: "Vessel number 137df8gk3y4, identify yourself!" "Vessel number 3y4, you are flying over sovereign territory!" "Vessel number 3y4, this is your last warning..." He had no clue how to work the radio to respond or how to select a channel and no idea what to say if he had.

On his monitor, Svet was addressing the children. *"Valhalla II* isn't a fun name for our ship, is it?" We were still accelerating, so there was a bit of toward the floor. "Let's go to the cafeteria and think about a better name for our ship."

It looked like they tried to eat breakfast after a stomach-turning blastoff. "Let's have a little contest to name our ship." She had learned the names of the four largest girls. "Rose, Lucy, Gabriella, and Charity will help you write down names you think our ship should be called, and then they'll decide which name wins."

"Valhalla II, you will enter the Moon's gravity in 12 hours," a friendly voice informed us.

Corvis found a tiny button hanging from his headset and tried both the button and his limited military lingo. "Roger that. Over."

A half-hour later, as the children, who had changed into their jumpsuits, were finishing their meal. He heard a girl read the names that had been suggested: "Love-dove, Big Ship, Sky-Hawk, and the winner is... ta tum... *Nursery!"*

It took fully five minutes for the various nations to decide whether or not to fire on their ship or not. Several missiles whizzed past, not even close. Then their aim improved. Missiles came closer and closer. Corvis saw a button marked "Shields" and pressed it just in time. One missile lightly grazed a shield to starboard, but it caused no serious damage. The Stage II rocket was still propelling them, so Corvis had no control over their course.

Svet brought the new name of the ship to Corvis in the cockpit while he was watching all the external monitors. She froze when she realized they were in trouble. Two more missiles narrowly missed them as she watched.

A minute later they heard, "You're above the range of most missiles now, *Valhalla II*. So, you won't have any more trouble...from Earth."

"What does that mean?" Svet asked.

"It means we could have trouble passing the Moon."

When he exhaled, he realized that he hadn't been breathing. He took the note from Svet.

"Pointe Indiene, this is *Valhalla II*. Our new name is *Nursery*. Over."

"Copy that, *Val*..." the base officer checked himself, "... *Nursery*."

"Heading for the Moon next," Corvis said.

"Roger. We are coming under heavy fire now. I don't know how much longer we can..." A distant explosion temporarily interrupted his transmission. "The Moon is Southern territory. They'll be gunning for you. Keep your head down and get past quick."

"What do you mean 'keep your head down'?"

"There's a little button marked 'Shields'..."

"Found it. Thanks. It already saved our lives once."

Corvis's heart rate and blood pressure gradually returned to near normal. He started reading and making sense of the controls. He lowered the shields.

"Are we safe now?" Svet whispered.

"Yes... For a few hours," he said.

The Moon

Two hours later Svet floated back into the large bridge and sprawled in the copilot's seat like a tired rag.

"We're getting close to the Moon," Corvis said. "The Southern Alliance won't be happy with us approaching. We may take some enemy fire."

Her body straightened as if electrified. "Why can't we just avoid the Moon?"

"Because we need the boost the moon's gravity will give us."

"Is it worth the risk?"

"Yes, because we don't have enough fuel to get us to Saturn without it. I'll raise the shields if it looks like they'll shoot at us."

Svet floated above him, hands on her hips, looking down at him. "I don't like it, but you're the pilot."

"Yes. I take full responsibility. But if they fire on us. The children will be frightened."

"Frightened? They will be terrified, and *I'll* be terrified!"

"I'll be scared, too, but we have to be the adults onboard. We need to keep the children under control to get through this."

"You're the pilot. You decide where we fly, and we have no say in the matter," Svet spat through clenched jaws. "But if the ship's damaged... if children die, if they never arrive at Enceladus..." Svet brooded, silent. Her fingers tapping on a control panel, her body quaking with rage, she continued, "I'll do what I can, but there's no telling what people will do when they *really* fear for their lives." She turned swiftly and pulled herself out of the cockpit.

Corvis realized that he was shaking, too. They were flying directly into danger. *I could soon be dead. Given World War III, the only chance these children have for life is to get to Enceladus.* And Corvis was furious with Svet. And then he realized, *I'm defending myself against what Svet said. She must have been right, at least partly.*

He took a breath and reassessed the situation. *Fear can kill just as certainly as a bullet. I need to reassure the children and at the same time give them safety instructions*, he told himself.

Over the public address system, he made an announcement. "This is Captain Crow." Microphones in the auditorium picked up scattered laughter. *They're laughing at <u>me</u>, the captain of the ship!* But he continued, "We're getting close to the Moon. But you probably won't see it when we get very close."

Children were talking while he was making an official announcement. *Can they even hear me?* Fuming, he maintained an even tone.

"There may be some bad guys who may try to shoot at us." The children went silent, listening. Finally!

"I will raise the shields so their shots can't hurt us. We'll pass the Moon really fast and we will continue to Mars and then to Enceladus, our final destination, which will be your new home. While we are close to the Moon, you need to stay in your seats for your own safety. Please use the bathroom now because while we are close to the Moon, the bathrooms will all be locked."

The children started whispering. While he was trying to hear what they were saying, the transponder came to life. "Identify yourself!" a voice commanded.

"This is the *Nursery*," Corvis said. "We have no weapons. We're going past the Moon."

"Divert, *Nursery*. You do *not* have permission to land, and you're forbidden from approaching Moon Base any closer. I repeat, *divert!*"

"We have no intention of landing, but we need to use the Moon's gravity as a slingshot maneuver. Otherwise, we won't have enough fuel to reach En...to reach our destination."

"Divert at once, *Nursery* or your ship will be destroyed!"

"Listen to reason," he pleaded. "We have more than three hundred innocent children on board. We will not land, but we *must* approach the Moon at a high velocity."

Dozens of tracer beams immediately whizzed across the bow of the ship. Stricken with terror, he was paralyzed. Amazingly, none of the beams found their mark. He quickly raised the shields.

A huge ordinance exploded to the port side of the *Nursery,* and very close. They listed, and his ears registered the concussive force through the hull. On his monitor, he saw and heard children screaming and vomiting. Sweating profusely, he managed to right the ship. Bracing for a direct hit and the total destruction of the *Nursery*, he noticed that gravity increased. Laser beams slowed. The *Nursery* accelerated toward the Moon. More shots came at them, all missing the ship.

The Moon suddenly filled his entire view as they accelerated even more, and he realized all on board felt the heavy tug of gravity. They whipped around the Moon and, half an hour later, shot out of the Moon's gravitational field, moving significantly faster on their way to Mars. As suddenly as it had all begun, it was over. No more explosions, no more threats, no more gravity, just a mess to clean up in the auditorium, both emotional and physical. Corvis lowered the shields so the children could see out the observational alcoves again.

He didn't bounce back instantly. Emotional chaos reigned in the cockpit, as well as in the rest of the ship and he resolved that no one must ever know how terrified the captain had been, much less help him recover. He was shaking uncontrollably. If he had tried to press a button, he was sure to press the wrong one. He was breathing fast and shallow, and he felt faint. *What's happening to me? If I die what will happen to the ship? The kids?* He recognized panic in his thoughts and in his body. He forced himself to breathe more slowly. *The danger's past, at least for the moment. The ship is perfectly on course, having executed a tricky but essential maneuver.*

His monitor showed the teenagers and Svet methodically cleaning up the children. *I lost control of the passengers, but they seem to be doing fine, now,* he thought.

"We still have to get past Mars," he said to the empty cockpit. *Next time we may not be so lucky. I need to talk to Svet, but she's busy.*

He knew the ship could fly itself, so he went to the auditorium. Suddenly he was aware of the sweat stains around the armpits of his shirt. He was already painfully self-conscious when young voices bombarded him. As he floated through the door children called out, "Cap'n Crow, the bad guys were shooting at us!" "Cap'n Crow, they tried to kill us!" "Cap'n Crow, I want my mama!" Every statement seemed like an accusation, but he had to be the adult. Anything he tried to say sounded defensive in my head, so he just said, "I know, I know. We're safe now." He patted heads and rubbed little hands. "Would you come to the bridge when you have a chance?" he asked Svet.

She didn't answer, but an hour later, she pulled herself into the cockpit on the handholds, her body rigid. "Was good what you did, comforting the children," she said quietly, repeating obviously rehearsed words, her face both sad and stern.

"We need to talk," he said, trying to keep his tone conciliatory.

"Yes, we do," she said, more firmly than he liked.

"We need to discuss discipline..." he began.

"Discipline!" she exploded. "Discipline! At a time like this...when you have just taken us to death's door!" She shouted for all to hear, "You want to talk about *discipline*!?"

Her anger hooked his. He was enraged, but with great effort, he controlled the volume of his voice. "This time we were lucky..."

"Lucky?" she replied, her volume mirroring his now. How were we 'lucky'?!" she demanded.

"They missed," he said, amazed that she hadn't noticed, "Every single shot they fired at us entirely missed!"

Svet shook her head in disbelief. She buried her face in her hands. When she looked at me again, she was more composed, more confident. "You seriously think it was luck? That the best sharpshooters in the Southern Alliance could fire all those beams and a couple of huge laser-bombs without inflicting even a scratch on this gigantic target?" Pause. "By chance?" She paused again. "They were warning shots! Very. Carefully. Placed. Warning shots!" she concluded softly.

He floated over and hugged Svet's rigid body. He guessed they were both surprised by his action. "You're right," he said, laughing and looking her in the eye. He repeated, "They were warning shots!"

Svet appeared to be pondering something that she didn't voice. After a minute, she said, "I have to get back to the kids."

The moment Svet left the cockpit, he felt heavy. He realized they were in zero gravity, but he felt like he weighed a ton. *All those nights without sleep, followed by an adrenaline peak higher than Everest and then a valley deeper than the Grand Canyon, have left me very, very tired. I needed some sleep. Is that all I need? No. I need to sleep every night for the next three months, or I'll be of no use to anyone. I need a copilot!*

Lights were starting to dim on the ship when he glided out to the auditorium again. Svet and the older girls were organizing the next day's activities. Corvis took the two biggest boys into the hallway. "How would you like to be Cap'n Crow's assistants?" he asked.

Both boys eagerly assented. Taking them with him, he found a handhold close to Svet and told her, "I'm commandeering these two boys to help out in the cockpit."

"That's a good idea," she said, "but they will need to attend school and do their homework, just like all the other children."

"Understood," he said, "You'll be good students, won't you?"

They nodded.

"*And* they must eat with the children," she called after me.

"Yes, of course!"

When they arrived in the cockpit both boys looked awestruck. Three large seats faced the control panels, which spread out both below and above the observation windows, with hundreds of dials, knobs, switches, and monitors showing many parts of the interior of the *Nursery*, as well as half a dozen exterior views of the surface of our ship.

"Who sits there?" the small boy asked, referring to two more large seats that faced the rear wall of the bridge, each with its own set of computer panels.

"The one on the right is for the navigator, and the one on the right is for the chief engineer," Corvis said.

He told the taller boy, "Why don't you sit on my left," and to the shorter one, "and you can sit on my right.

"Way up here are clocks. The green one is the ship's clock. Our days are getting a little longer so that we will be ready for the thirty-three hours long days on Enceladus. The blue clock is Earth time in Kinshasa. The white clock is the time on Enceladus. The other clocks don't matter for now. You can help me by taking turns watching all the dials and numbers on these three panels. One boy watches the panels for an hour. Then the other boy watches them for an hour, back and forth. Do you think you can do that?" he asked.

"Yes," the tall one said.

But the short one asked, "What does the other boy do while he isn't watching the panels?"

"That's a great question," Corvis replied, "There's a whole set of video games that you can play on your monitor, this monitor, right here. Also, you can look out at the stars. Here is a star map that tells you the names of the stars and their distance from the *Nursery*.

"Now, the most important part of your job. If either of you sees a flashing red light anywhere in the cockpit or if you hear a bell ringing, you must wake me up right away."

Both boys were attentive.

"Can you do that for me?" Corvis asked.

"Yes," they chorused.

The huge bridge had all the amenities of a home. One of the four hammocks, anchored to the port wall, floated four meters above the floor. He told his alarm to wake him in one hour and zipped himself in. He thought he was asleep before he stretched out.

When the alarm woke him, both boys were asleep, of course. He checked the panels. They were still on course and nothing was threatening them. He gently guided the boys to the dormitory, and they found their beds and zipped in.

Tomorrow, he would give them more tasks. Maybe they would stay awake a little longer.

14
Spotting

Svet floated into the cockpit, Corvis's two assistants in tow. "Calling, Nurse Crow," she said, smirking, "you're needed in the infirmary."

"OK, boys," Corvis said while mentally noting that he needed to learn their names, "This is my buzzer." Corvis handed the tiny device to the tall boy. "Now it's your turn to really work. Remember, buzz me if any red light flashes." Corvis turned to leave.

"Or a siren sounds," short boy added.

"Yes!" Corvis said at the door.

Svet explained the problem. "These girls have been living together long enough that their periods are coordinated. It's probably just their normal flow."

They were followed by three teenage girls as they glided through the ship to the Sick Bay. Corvis hadn't visited the Infirmary yet, so he didn't know what to expect. When he opened the door, he was flabbergasted. Instead of two little gurneys and a medicine chest, he found a huge, light, airy, fully equipped trauma clinic: six bays, with two beds separated by a curtain in each bay, along with oxygen and suction in the wall. Six more hammocks hung in the waiting room next to a crash cart with a defibrillator, airways, and epinephrine. Central Supply was a large walk-in closet with net-pockets covering twenty-seven square meters of the walls. It had IV fluids, catheters, tubing, splints, cervical collars, sutures, and everything else a nurse could need. There was a freezer for cold packs and a heater for warm blankets. Over-the-counter drugs, tongue depressors, swabs, and bandages of all sizes were in an unlocked cart, while controlled substances were in a locked electronic dispenser. Wondering how to unlock it, he peered into a small peephole. Suddenly it turned red, then green then red again. Just like at work, it was reading my retina. *Click.* A touchscreen appeared. He tapped on the list, and over two hundred drugs scrolled down. "I have died and gone to heaven," he said to Svet.

She replied, "It smells like... a doctor's office."

"That's a good thing," he asserted. "Don't you think?"

"I just want to do what we have to do and get out of here," she said. "It makes me feel like I'm about to get a shot."

"What are you here for?" he asked one of the girls.

"They're spotting," Svet said lightly, answering for all of them.

Corvis knew they were all pregnant as a result of being raped by the same gangsters who had murdered members of their families before their eyes.

Corvis showed each girl to an exam room and demonstrated how the controls worked on their entertainment devices. "You can lie down and zip up or sit and watch a show, whichever you prefer."

"I will need a chaperone with me while I examine each girl," he said. "Can you stay with me?"

She cringed visibly. "I guess so."

Corvis washed his hands and laid a fresh gown on each of the three hammocks. He asked each of the girls, "Please put on this gown. You can float out of your hammock whenever you want," he said. He remembered again that he was going to try to learn the names of each of the passengers.

With Svet beside him, he spoke with the first girl in her private room. "I'm Captain Crow," he said, "What's your name?"

"I'm Rose," she said, "Rose Koko." Rose was 17.

"What do you think is going on?" he asked.

"I'm afraid I'm losing my baby," she said, beginning to cry silently.

"May I feel your abdomen?" he asked.

She nodded and laid on her back and put her feet in the elastic stirrups above her hammock.

Her abdomen was soft at first, but when he felt it tighten. "You're having a contraction," he told her.

"I'm definitely having cramps," she replied.

"May I look between your legs?" he asked.

She nodded.

Corvis pulled down an operating light hanging from the eight-foot ceiling. She was bleeding with a moderate flow.

"I think you're right. You seem to be having a miscarriage," he said regretfully while charting his findings.

"Rose, I know this is hard for you. Please stay here and rest while I examine the other girls." He put a pad under her to absorb the blood. "I'll be back soon." He removed his gloves and washed his hands.

Svet went with him to the next exam room.

"I'm Captain Crow," he said to the second girl. "What is your name?"

"Mary Ndong," she said without elaboration.

"I notice you have scars around your eyes, and you appear to be blind," he said softly. "What happened?"

"While the soldier was raping me, I said, 'I will remember your face, and you will pay.' When he was finished with me, he splashed acid in my eyes, saying 'You will never see me or anything else again.' Now I am blind and bearing his seed." She spoke without emotion, in an almost mechanical voice.

Corvis felt chills. *What horrible torture this girl has experienced in her short life. And what incredible maturity she has.*

"That was a terrible experience. I'm inspired by the way you have overcome this assault. You seem to function very well."

"I'm stubborn!" she said, half smiling, "I don't intend to let him take any more from me than he already has. I have even forgiven him, not for his sake, but so that I don't carry even the slightest bit of anger toward him. Death is ahead for him, life for me."

"That's a good attitude. Unfortunately, you seem to be having a miscarriage," he said.

"God's will be done."

Corvis looked at Svet. He saw tears rolling down her cheeks.

"Here's the remote," he said, placing it in Mary's hand.

Mary said, "Thanks, but I'll continue with the book I was reading."

Corvis noticed the earplug. It was an audiobook she was reading. "I'll be back after I check on the others."

He took off his gloves and washed his hands again.

"Are you ready for the next one?" he asked Svet.

She looked pale but said, "Let's go."

Again, he introduced himself. "What is your name?" he asked.

"I'm Charlene Koumba," she said. Like the others, she was having a miscarriage and had a moderate flow of blood. The soldiers raped my mother in front of me. Then they raped me. I don't even know which one of them is the father of my baby. But I want to hold my baby," she pleaded.

He glided with Svet out of the infirmary. "Three girls, three miscarriages. Damn," he whispered. "All three of these were probably precipitated by a combination of blastoff and the trouble at the Moon." It had taken them an hour to make the first round, so it was time to check on Rose again.

He noticed that Svet looked tired, and she grasped a handhold to steady herself. It was going on three days since either of them had really slept.

"Can you make one more round?" he asked. "Then we can ask three other girls to come and sit with them."

She swallowed hard and straightened herself. Finally, she said, "I'm ready."

They returned to Rose's bay. "When did the spotting start?" Corvis asked Rose.

"I started feeling cramps when shots were coming at us from the Moon."

I'm an ICU nurse, not a psych nurse. I stay as far away from emotional counseling as I can, Corvis thought. His chest felt tight as he began talking to Mary. "I know that you got pregnant in a bad way, and I know you have very mixed feelings about losing your baby. To make matters worse, strong hormones will flow in your blood because of losing your baby. It will help if you talk to someone about your feelings over the next few days."

He asked Charlene, "Would you like one of the other girls to sit with you?"

Each girl agreed that they would like to have a friend sit with them, and each named the person she wanted. Svet was only too happy to go out and find the three companions.

When they were all settled, Corvis suggested to Svet that they go to an officer's quarters to debrief. "That was uncomfortable for you, wasn't it?" he asked.

"I don't like anything medical," Svet said. "But these girls are so young, and they have already suffered so much... I can't help feeling their pain. It made me feel so sad that I was almost ill. Not to mention that all the blood made me feel like throwing up."

"You made a big sacrifice. It's good you were there for them. They know you care. Are you going to be OK? Do you need to take a rest?"

"Of course, I need to take a rest! But I'll be OK. Thanks for talking to me about it."

On his way back to the cockpit he paused to watch three toddlers playing. One was especially cute with her hair neatly braided and her little pink jumpsuit just so. One of the older girls said "That's Lisbet Koko. Isn't she pretty?"

"Yes," he said, "she's sweet."

As Corvis entered the bridge, he said, "Thank you for watching the controls. Were there any problems?"

"None," the tall one said.

The short one added, "no alarms." He handed me the buzzer.

"Breakfast will be ready soon. Why don't you join the other children?"

Corvis needed to be alone. As soon as he sat down in his seat, he imploded. *Billions of dollars have been spent on this mission. Moon defenders shot at us, and now there are three miscarriages in progress. All this, and we're barely a day into our trip. It feels like this mission is doomed.* He wanted to cry felt he had to stay in control. *This mission is seriously compromised. Having a bawling captain won't help,* he told himself.

Next, he realized he was hungry. *Really* hungry. He hadn't eaten since dinner the previous night, and he'd been working hard. He checked all the controls and glided back into the auditorium. The children had finished breakfast. He met Svet and asked, "Where's the galley?"

"It's just beyond the cafeteria," she said, "but if you're looking for a snack, it's not what you're expecting."

"OK," he replied without asking her to elaborate.

The kitchen he entered was bigger than a hospital kitchen; it was a huge industrial kitchen. Spending a few minutes there, he realized he was actually seeing *four* industrial kitchens: Pods A through D with a central command pod with one computer terminal controlling each of the four pod computers. Each computer displayed "Status: Lunch," showing the menu and the phase of preparation for each item, and a countdown timer for serving it.

He came looking for food. He saw spotless counters that spread out over many square meters, with dozens of mixing bowls, pots and pans, all large but no food. He opened drawers, hoping to find chips, at least, and saw neatly divided spaces. A silhouette under the whisk prescribed that a whisk be placed there and nowhere else, and so for every different type of knife and spoon.

Each pod had nine warming ovens and nine refrigerators, identified as A1, A2, A3, etc. Surely, he could find food in one of those. He tried the closest refrigerator. It probably held food, but it was locked.

Frustrated, and hungry, he found Svet in one of the classrooms. "I'm hungry," he said, pitching his voice in a high register, "Feed me!"

Svet laughed. "Your hot food is in C7 warming oven, and your cold food is in the C7 refrigerator. Look into the peephole, and the computer will read your retina and unlock the doors for two minutes. Children have access to food at mealtime and three snack times each day. The engineers didn't want us eating out of boredom and getting fat."

"How do you find time to cook?" he asked.

"We don't," she said, "the fully automated food factory is behind the two pairs of double doors at the back of the kitchen. Humans only use the kitchen for special orders."

Svet was right. Corvis found all he wanted for breakfast and returned to the bridge. The "scrambled eggs" were rubbery, the "toast" was flaky but didn't taste anything like bread, and it didn't taste toasted. *Don't think of it as toast and scrambled eggs and toast. Let me think of it as a culinary adventure.* It did satisfy his appetite, and he fell into a restful sleep after eating.

Mbiximia Pestis

Bringing his assistants again, Svet floated into the bridge with one of the older girls. "Honesty M'ba, here, woke me up at 0637," 'Rose needs you again,' she whispered.

'Is she bleeding again?' Corvis asked.

'No, it's Lisbet, her daughter,' Honesty said.

"Lisbet has a large red welt under her arm, and she's feverish," Svet said.

Corvis felt a chill. "That doesn't sound good at all."

"It's worse," Svet said gravely. "Two other little ones have similar problems."

"Please have them meet me in the infirmary," he said immediately. "OK, boys. I need to learn your names."

The tall one said, "my name is David."

"I'm John," the short one said.

He handed the buzzer to David. "Call me if you need me. I noticed you didn't fall asleep last time. Good boys!"

Honesty and Svet were already in the infirmary with the other girls when he arrived.

"We can't stay," Svet said as she and Honesty left.

When he saw Rose and Lisbet together his heart felt like lead. The sweet, happy little girl he'd met the day before was cranky today. Rose lifted Lisbet's arm so he could see the welt, but Lisbet resisted "It hurts, Mommy!"

This can't be happening. Fever, welt, irritability. I'm not getting anything. Stress and exhaustion prevented his brain from working properly. "Let's take her temperature," he suggested, pointing the thermometer at Lisbet's forehead. He glanced at the readout. "It's 103° F. But little children spike fevers easily. She'll be OK, but she should lie down with a cool cloth on her forehead. I'll be back after I look at the others."

He washed my hands before leaving.

Putting on gloves, he looked at Anabelle, the 18-month-old daughter of Charity Segy. She had a welt in her groin, bad body odor, and her temp was 102° F. "I'll stay in the infirmary until she starts getting better. Meanwhile, please keep a cold cloth on her forehead," he said, handing Charity the rag.

Same symptoms. It must be the same disease. What could it be?

Clement was the 2-year-old son of Gabrielle Gondjout. He had a lump on the back of his neck. He held his head extended in what appeared to be an uncomfortable position.

When Corvis asked him, "Can you touch your chin to your chest?" He didn't reply. When Corvis tried to help him, he cried. Although he thought it would relieve pressure on the knot, he couldn't move his head forward at all.

His fever was 104° F., he smelled awful, and he was lethargic. Corvis put all the data in the computer, hoping it would instantly spit out a diagnosis. While the computer analyzed the data, he told Gabrielle, "I'm going to start an IV on Clement so that I can administer medications."

He had no idea what they were suffering from, and he felt frustrated and helpless. *Time is of the essence, and the computer isn't giving me what I need!* He started Lactated Ringers IVs on all three of them, gave each a fever reducer, and took blood samples for the automated lab analysis. *I think they have a bacterial infection, but I don't want to start antibiotics until I know which one to use. Thank God for the computer, but where's the diagnosis?* His heart was racing.

Rose looked worried. Corvis hoped she didn't read the concern on his face. She tried to distract her daughter with a fuzzy stuffed lion. "Lisbet is getting worse, Cap'n Crow," she said in a quiet, tense voice.

"I know," he said. "I'm waiting for the results of her blood test."

"Help my baby!" Charity begged. Anabelle was hugging a fluffy zebra. Her condition was also deteriorating.

He felt totally weak. He considered picking a strong antibiotic without knowing whether it would work or not but decided to wait in order to use the correct one. "I'll be able to give her some antibiotics as soon as I get a diagnosis from the computer."

Clement clung to a short-haired toy giraffe. "Do something! Quick!" Gabrielle demanded. Clement had gone from lethargic to deep sleep, occasionally twitching. His temperature was 106° F.

Oh God, please help us! "I should be able to get him some antibiotic in just a few minutes," he said hopefully. "Try to keep him cool."

Lisbet temperature was also 106° F.

"Your child is seriously ill," he told Rose. "Try to keep her quiet."

"I know she's ill. Can't you help her?"

The antipyretic obviously wasn't working, and he felt increasingly hopeless. *Is this a childhood disease? Why aren't others getting sick? Or are they?* He was light-headed, near panic.

After five full minutes, an eternity for a computer, there were still no results, so he started visiting each child yet again.

Lisbet started seizing during my visit. He wrapped her in a cold blanket, then checked the others. By then, the other two children were also having seizures. He put cold blankets on each of them. "Make sure the cold blanket stays wrapped around your child, even if they try to kick it off," he advised each mother.

Is the computer broken? Where are the damn results? He wanted to scream. *I can't treat what I don't know!*

All three children were unconscious when the diagnosis finally came back: Mbiximia pestis. Bone plague. He pushed massive doses of curcumicin, the best antibiotic for bone plague, through their little IV lines. Without the computer, he would never have thought of curcumicin. Under better circumstances, this medicine would have killed the bacteria. But their little hearts failed before any substantial amount of antibiotic was delivered.

"Mbiximia pestis, or bone plague," the computer reported, "was first discovered in 2067 in Gabon. It was carried by fleas. A vaccine wiped it out, and the last case was seen in 2070." *Even computers are sometimes wrong! No wonder I'd never heard of it.* And then, with a shock, *Bad odor! I should have thought of plague.*

Now comes the hardest part. He had plenty of experience comforting loved ones after a death, but never like this. These had been living vibrant children, cut down suddenly. *My mission was to deliver them to Enceladus.* Charity had lost Anabelle, Gabrielle had lost Clement, but poor Rose had now, not only lost a fetus but also, a beautiful three-year-old daughter.

Guilty as charged, his internal judge declared. *I should have been able to save them!* Pain in my chest forced me to hang on to a hammock. *You can have your meltdown on your own time. Right now, you need to remain professional and compassionate for the mothers.* He forced himself to push off and visit Rose. He handed her a birthing blanket. "Would you like to wrap Lisbet in this? I'll be back in a minute."

Then he went to Gabrielle. "Would you like a blanket to wrap Clement in?" Gabrielle angrily grabbed the cloth without a word.

Finally, he visited Charity. "Here's a baby blanket for Anabelle. Her body must remain in the infirmary but take as long as you need to say goodbye."

He returned to Rose and said, "Stay as long as you want to with Lisbet." He said the same thing to Gabrielle.

The minute he left the infirmary, he realized the magnitude of the crisis the *Nursery* now faced. He was terrified. *We have Mbiximia pestis on board.* Others could be infected. *How in the world do I tell others to keep calm when I, myself am panicking?* Then he realized that they were in an entirely different situation than just an hour before. They knew where the plague was coming from, and they knew how to treat it.

He found Svet and explained. "Somehow, despite all the disinfectants and irradiation of everything that entered the ship, we have fleas carrying bone plague aboard. We have to check every child and caution them to watch for warning signs of the disease, and we have to do this quickly but without causing panic."

"We're locked in a ship with a plague, and we're not supposed to panic!?" she retorted.

"Think, Svet," he said quietly but firmly, "Think about the children. It's not going to help them if *we* panic."

She started crying. He held her. "We're only two days into a *three-month* journey," she sobbed, "and already I'm sick of this ship!"

If only you saw the news from Earth, that a full-blown nuclear war is raging, you would know what a blessing this ship is.

As her body relaxed, he drifted back. "Ordinary shampoo will kill the fleas. After each child showers, we need to check them for fleas and flea bites. Stuffed toys, especially, need to be washed. Antibiotics will kill the plague if we recognize it in time.

"So, others may also die?" she moaned.

"We weren't looking for symptoms until now, and the little ones didn't know how to complain. But now that we know what we're up against, no one else needs to die."

Svet said, "They must all shave their heads!"

"It's not necessary, ordinary shampoo..."

"You're the Captain and medical officer, but I'm COO. If I say they shave, they shave. End of discussion."

Boss lady Svet is back. "OK," he said smiling, "I'll shave my head, too."

Her hands went to her head. "I guess I'll have to shave mine. I don't want to look odd."

"I've got to check on the bridge," he said. "Are you OK?"

She nodded.

And me? Am I OK? I've got to be. I may be an utter failure as a nurse, but I'm the only captain this ship has got. Stiff upper lip, Corvis!

Entering the bridge, he smiled and asked, "How is *Nursery?*"

"*Nursery* is fine, Captain!" John grinned. David smiled, as well.

Corvis smiled, but he had severe pain in his chest. "I have a little more business to take care of. Then you can brief me on what has been happening up here."

It was a short distance back to the infirmary, but even in zero gravity, his body felt like it was made of lead. His mind told him he'd done everything he could to save the children, but his heart still accused him of failure. So many times, he had comforted survivors. Why was he so dreading this? Perhaps because they were on a ship together. When he finished talking to them, they couldn't just go their way and he go his.

Svet saw him heading for the infirmary, and she joined him.

The infirmary should have smelled like death, but it smelled much worse. It smelled like rotting flesh, even with the filters working. Corvis approached Gabrielle Gondjout. Her bundle of sorrow looked so tiny lying inert in the adult-sized hammock. "I, I'm so sorry for your loss."

"My loss!" she said quietly, her lips barely moving, her jaw locked, "He has a name! His name is Clement. You are the doctor. You were supposed to save Clement's life."

"I'm not a d... If I had identified the illness sooner, I'm sure I could have."

After a long silence Gabrielle asked, "Could I be alone with my son, *please*."

He felt appropriately chastised.

In the next bay Charity Segy looked so alone in such a large room. "I'm sorry about Anabelle."

She was slow to answer and didn't take her eyes off of the shrouded toddler. "I loved her. I wish it could be me lying there dead and her playing with her friends right now."

Corvis didn't know what to say. Finally, he said, "It must be very hard." He wanted to add that he was available if she wanted to talk, but he figured she knew that.

Then he entered Rose's bay. She was sitting on the edge of the hammock, cradling Lisbet, rocking back and forth. "I'm sorry," he said.

A minute later, she looked at him. "Her father took me by force. I hated the thing growing inside me. Every time she moved, it was like he was inside me again. When I was delivered of her, I realized how wrong I was to hate her. She was love incarnate, and I was the center of her universe."

"You loved her. She was so sweet," he said, tears in his eyes.

"I don't know why she had to die," Rose said, "but I refuse to be angry with her or with you. She was the light of my life. She was love. That's where it was, and that's where it will stay."

Corvis actually managed to smile. Then he nodded and floated out of the room.

Svet was waiting outside the infirmary. "I don't think I could have done that."

"Done what?"

"Talked to those poor women."

An hour later, he returned to the infirmary. He asked each mother if he might take her child. "Your baby will be kept safe until we arrive on Enceladus."

All were ready, and he took the little bodies to the freezer.

Bald

Corvis watched as the older girls repeatedly embraced Rose, Gabrielle and Charity. They seemed much better even by the next day. On Sunday, we memorialized the three small children. The service was short but beautiful. Lucy Aubameyang read the poem she had written for the occasion

When will we return to
Shimbezu?
We left Shimbezu a land of
hunger, a land of pain
We left Shimbezu our beloved
homeland
But Shimbezu lives in our souls
We took flight to the heavens
In the ship was a little flea
A little flea bit our little cousins
Their bones ached, their ribs
cracked
Where did you go little cousins
Have you returned to Shimbezu?
Far from home we shaved our
heads.

*Our heads bowed low with
sadness.
When can we return to you,
Shimbezu?*

Vivian Anikor had promised to set it to music.

The three tiny bodies would lie frozen in storage until we reached Enceladus. The mood was somber for a day or two, but death is a part of life in the jungle, and children are amazingly resilient.

Their life on *Nursery* settled into a regular pattern. Children had school five days a week. Their developing minds were hungry. Robots did a wonderful job of sensing the attention span of children, varying the content, illustrations, and audio every five minutes at the most. School attendance added daily routine and provided structure. Weekends were for fun, chores, and rest. Svet consulted with the older girls to plan activities like ones they practiced in Shimbezu, the district of Gabon they came from.

Svet started introducing algae into their diet on the first day. Green "rice" tastes nothing like white rice. It has the same size and shape, but the flavor is, well, different. It was very nutritious, but it was still algae. On Saturdays, older girls taught children six and older to cook traditional Gabonese dishes. They had no fresh fruit and few vegetables but made do with the almost infinite variety of textures algae could be formed into, and flavors that could be added. They also greens grown in the greenhouse, as well as mushrooms and other fungi.

A dozen large bolts of cotton cloth, each dyed in a different traditional pattern and color, had been loaded on Nursery before blastoff. In math class the children calculated the number of square inches of cloth. It came out to almost 1,300,000 square inches. Divided by the number of Gabonese children on the *Nursery*, now three hundred and eleven, meant we had almost three and a quarter square yards per person.

Corvis dreaded the day when he would have to start preparing the children for our approach to Mars. Svet didn't bring up the topic, so he didn't know what she thought or felt.

15
Two Armadas

JiAnn

WEARING A THREAD-BARE BUT comfy robe, JiAnn was enjoying the scent of bacon frying and anticipating a peaceful breakfast at home 'in retirement" when Malcolm's message arrived. "I need to stay in the Bubble, but I would like to get the word out that two groups of ships have left Earth."

She quickly turned off the heat under the pan and phoned Convener Cly. "I know, it's early," she said, "but you'll want to know immediately. An armada of five ships launched from Mojave Spaceport within twenty minutes of each other last night. One hour later a large rocket launched from Jiuquan Spaceport, China. An hour later still, the payload separated into five parts consisting of a large ship and four fighters. The satendrites believe Northern Confederacy and Southern Alliance each intend to invade Enceladus."

"Thank you for calling, Madame Dragomark," Cly said, "Our generals will be interested to know this."

JiAnn had just finished eating, and less than an hour later, at 0700 hours the Convener called. "The generals want a meeting at 0800 hours. We'll be in the Small Conference Room. Please bring the latest data from the satendrites with you."

All eight generals wore identical Enceladus Colony Defense uniforms, light blue, and form-fitting. Only a tiny insignia on the right lapel indicated the country they represented on Earth, the nations that had contributed the most resources to establish the Enceladus colony: Germany, Italy, the United Kingdom, and the United States, belonged to the Northern Confederacy; China, Russia, Brazil, and Argentina, of the Southern Alliance, had also each sent a general to defend the colony. On Earth these two powerful groups were in the final process of destroying each other and all other human life there, but on Enceladus, they all coexisted amicably.

Ten people sat around a rich-toned, oblong wooden table set in a fake-maple-paneled room. JiAnn contemplated a wood carving of the seal of the Enceladus Colony: a large snowflake with domes in one arm, farmers working crops in another, books in the third, fish in a fourth, lab instruments in a fifth, and symbols of the arts in the sixth; below the snowflake appeared the words "Enceladus Colony Est. 11-19-2073." As she settled in, she noted that the twelve chairs at the table, as well as the four in the corners, were upholstered in realistic faux leather, comfortable but not cozy. The lighting was adequate but not harsh. Microphones embedded discretely in the table reminded her and everyone at the table that their every word was being recorded. A teenager rolled in a cart laden with a large carafe of coffee, ten steaming cups, and pastries that smelled like they had just emerged from the oven. A pitcher of water surrounded by ten glasses sat in the center of the table. The ambiance suggested a warm environment for amiable and above all, professional conversation.

General Dioikis, in his deep voice and precise diction, led off. "The news from the satendrites troubled all of us but surprised none. Each of us has received orders in the past twelve hours. We're told to separate nationals in residences; and to establish martial law, with all civilians to be confined to quarters until further notice."

JiAnn envisioned her colony broken into separate enemy camps. She felt sad. *This isn't the Enceladan way.*

Convener Cly's face grew dark. He leaned forward as if ready to speak but then leaned back.

JiAnn spoke. "That means tearing families apart, punishing citizens of E8 nations, while minor nationals and birth-right Enceladans are free to roam. Have you discussed this among yourselves?"

"We have," General Dioikis replied, "We, each, face difficult decisions. Our national cultures are very different from each other, and yet each of our chains of command has issued almost identical orders. Each of us faces the same dilemma, either we attempt to follow senseless orders, impossible to completely obey, or refuse to obey orders given by duly constituted commanding officers."

"Have any of you made any decisions?" Cly asked.

JiAnn caught herself running her fingers nervously down through the tips of her hair.

"We've come to several decisions after consulting with each other. First, we must and will respond. We will cite the practical difficulties involved in implementing these orders. Second, we agreed we do nothing to implement our orders for 30 hours. We will offer excuses to our commanding officers. Third, we agreed that none of us will take serious action before consulting each other. We also affirmed that each of our missions all boils down to this: protect and defend *all* Enceladans, not just *our* nationals. We all believe that we were commissioned to do this from before we left Earth."

"Well, that's a relief," Cly said and, after a pause, added "I guess. I always thought our defense force was one, undivided unit. It's a bit of a shock to learn you each really do have divided loyalties."

"That's correct," General Dioikis said. "And that fact makes our decisions both more difficult and at the same time helps us recognize that we are all in the same boat... in more ways than one."

"Representative Schwartz leads a caucus of several representatives who are calling for independence from Earth. I told them that with military action at our door, this is not the time to consider such an important question. Maybe I was wrong," Cly said.

Dioikis replied, "We generals differ in our political and economic values, but we have one deeper, common value: to guard a remnant of humans on Enceladus from the annihilation of nuclear war. Still, not one of us is eager to confront our commanding officers on Earth."

"I need to inform the Council about all these developments," Cly said, "You all know a battle royal awaits me in the Council."

When the meeting ended, JiAnn was the first to leave the chambers.

16
Gift for the Pilot

CORVIS · NURSERY

IT WAS AN HOUR past lights out on the 11th Earth day of their journey. Mars was highlighted on Corvis's star map.

We're getting closer to Mars. I need to find out what Svet is thinking, but I dread the argument that we are bound to have, he thought. *She wants to avoid Mars, and I want to avoid the discussion.*

At that very moment, Svet glided onto the bridge wearing only a sheer silk slip. "Special deleevery! A gift has arrived for ze very beesee pilot," she crooned.

He was confused not only by her words but also by her behavior. *Has she suffered a nervous breakdown worrying about what will happen at Mars? This is not the Svet I met in Africa.*

His face must have telegraphed his confusion.

"You're a man," she said, "and I'm a woman. We're both young, and we both have urges. Why shouldn't we satisfy each other?"

At first, he felt relieved. *What she is saying and doing was quite natural.* Then he felt awkward. "I'm sorry," he said, "but I... I'm gay."

Svet deflated before my eyes. She slumped and turned white. Her face contorted as if holding back tears. "That's OK.

You don't have to make excuses. Many men have rejected me," she said while covering her body with her hands.

"I'm not making excuses, and you're a very beautiful woman, but I'm attracted to men," he said.

Svet hurried off the bridge.

Corvis wondered what he could say or do to help her regain face. He considered several options, but he decided the best course was to just continue to treat her as the professional woman she was, the COO of a ship carrying three hundred and eleven children from certain death on Earth to a new life on Enceladus. He would tell her that if the opportunity arose, how much he respected her. *If you weren't such a coward, Santos, this would provide an opportunity to get to know each other better.*

Fire

December 3, 2099

The children had finished lunch and were in their afternoon classes.

I can't put it off any longer. I have to talk to Svet. We will be passing Mars soon.

"Mars Base to *Nursery*. You are on an intercept course with Mars. Provide landing permit credentials."

Blood drained from Corvis's head. *Here we go again,* he thought. Over the PA he said "COO, please come to the bridge ASAP."

Svet floated through the door.

"We're in for trouble again," he told her.

"What kind of trouble?"

"Mars is demanding our landing permit."

"But we're not landing on Mars."

"They believe we are." he sighed. "I have to try to explain. Here goes," he said.

To Mars, he reported, "*Nursery* to Mars Base. We are *not landing* on Mars. We are merely going to use the mass of Mars to fling us toward the outer solar system."

"*Nursery*, if you're not intent on landing, you must divert."

"We would like to approach Mars at the equator. Far from the base and far from any settlement."

"You may not approach closer than 1000 kilometers."

"That will not allow us sufficient acceleration. We need to approach at an altitude of 100 kilometers."

"Negative. That's *much too close*."

"Let's avoid trouble," Svet said to him, "We will get enough fling at 1000 kilometers."

"They called us '*Nursery*,' which means they have data from our approach to Moon Base. Staying above 1000 kilometers would lengthen our trip by over a month, and we don't have enough supplies to survive that long..." After a minute of thought, he said, "But it gives me an idea."

"Understood, Mars," he reported. "We will not decelerate. That way you'll know we have no intention to land."

Svet's face looked hard as a rock.

Oh, my God, how will we ever overcome our differences? I just keep on insulting her.

For the next several hours Svet and Corvis scarcely spoke.

He decided to tell the children, while they were in class, what was happening. "This is Captain Crow. The red planet that you have seen getting bigger is Mars. As we get closer, I'll ask you to stay in your seats for a while. The closer we get the faster our ship will go. Speed will push you back into your seat. But this will last only a short time..."

He noticed a red light flashing. And then the PA system came alive with a robotic voice: "Fire! Fire! Report to your stations. This is not a drill. Report to your assigned fire stations." Then a shrill siren blared, and the message repeated.

Corvis's safety monitor showed that the fire was in Dormitory C. *This can't be happening. A fire on board just when Mars may attack us at any minute.*

He couldn't finish what he was saying to the passengers. "I'll have more to say later," he tried to shout over the siren.

He thrust himself, full speed, off of the Bridge, and through the dining room. Another push sent him speeding down the forward portal, thought the gym, to Dormitory C. Fire alarms were blaring. Terrified children screamed. Smoke filled the dormitory, and all the passengers coughed trying to breathe, but he didn't see any flames. A glob of ashes floated near one of the hammocks; black smoke continued billowing out of it.

Svet held nine-year-old, one-legged, Erwan. Months earlier, soldiers had hacked off Erwan's right leg. Nothing Erwan could have done would deserve that.

"Erwan was calmly adding strips of cloth to the fire," Svet told Corvis.

He looked at Corvis and smiled. Svet carried Erwan and his crutch, and they left Dormitory C just as fire doors closed and the room was evacuated of air.

Svet set Erwan free on the float. He immediately pushed off to the opposite wall. Corvis got close to Erwan. Children crowded around, worried, yet curious.

"You're going to need a time-out, Erwan. Please follow me," He ordered.

Corvis started to leave, but Erwan stayed by the wall.

He took Erwan by the hand. Surprisingly, he didn't resist, and he held onto his crutch. They went down the aft passage Deck C and to the Infirmary. Svet brought Rose with her and joined them.

"Tell me how you started the fire," Corvis said to the boy.

As if explaining an interesting toy, Erwan said, "I bent a paper clip back and forth until it broke. Then I put one end in an opening to the electric outlet, and the other into the other opening. It made a spark. Then I used the spark to burn some cloth." He grinned.

"That's very dangerous. The whole ship could..."

Corvis noticed that Erwan was smiling even more broadly, so he discontinued his warning and made the consequences more personal for Erwan.

"You need to stay here for fifteen minutes and think about how dangerous starting a fire was."

Erwan tried to follow them out of the infirmary, but Corvis pushed him back in and held the door closed. Erwan banged on the door and periodically tried to jerk it open, shouting, "Let me out of here!"

"Rose," Corvis said, "will you hold the door closed for fifteen minutes, and then let him out? The automatic light will stay on as long as someone is in there."

"I hope I can," Rose said, "he's such a strong boy."

As Corvis left, Erwan was still crying and begging, "Let me out! Please!"

Mars

December 4, 2099

"*Nursery*! Your angle of descent is too sharp. You must divert at once."

Oh my God, this is where it all ends? But Corvis used his brave soldier voice. "We are not approaching any inhabited area. We have more than three hundred children on board, whose lives depend upon our maximizing the use of Mars's gravity for a boost in speed. We have no weapons, and we are accelerating rather than attempting to land. You have no reason to fire on us."

And then, over the PA system, he said, "All passengers, please take your seats and buckle up. Repeat. Please fasten your seatbelts at once."

He hoped someone was keeping an eye on Erwan.

On the starboard monitor Corvis saw a fighter rocket. Another soon appeared on the port monitor. He expected them to start firing any minute.

"Do *not* change course, *Nursery*," an authoritative voice said.

He felt the increased g-force and knew the children did, too. But he didn't hear any crying this time. According to the view out the front window of the bridge, the Nursery seemed about to crash directly into the planet. He couldn't breathe. Either they'd be smashed into atoms on impact with the Red Planet or lasered into nothingness.

He waited.

The fighters fell away. *What? Nothing? All that fear for nothing?*

Mars was under, rather than in front, of them. The sound of distant thunder alarmed him. Another strong jolt pushed him, unexpectedly, deeper into his seat. Corvis had forgotten that the two hydrogen-ion fusion engines were programmed to fire up as they passed Mars. Five minutes later another thunderbolt followed by a long swoosh told him that the news engines were functioning correctly.

In minutes, Mars was behind them. Their speed was now over 500,000 miles per hour and accelerating. The two moments he had most dreaded, passing the Moon and getting a boost from Mars, were now history. As weightlessness returned, he took in a deep breath and exhaled long and languorously.

His own space

Growing up, he'd always shared a bedroom with a brother. His house was so chaotic that from my sophomore year in high school, when he started taking college classes, he did his homework at the public library. Years later, his efficiency apartment in New York, rented when he graduated high school, had been the first space he could call his own.

On the *Nursery*, his "captain's quarters" would have been large and comfortable, even on Earth, but in weightlessness the whole volume, from the floor to the 20-foot ceiling, was usable. Digital wallpaper on large sections of the walls, as well as floor and ceiling, contrasted with each other. He hadn't bothered to change the default patterns. The floor was tan woodgrain texture. One wall had wide stripes of light blue and light green, while a second wall had small amorphous spots of brown on yellow cream, and the third wall was aqua with fine white stripes. His double-wide canvas hammock anchored to the wall at four points was very comfortable. The square-meter table stowed nicely into another wall. From his bunk, or almost anywhere in his room, he could watch 3-D movies on a 2 meter by 3-meter wall screen. He could play games, on the same screen. Most significantly, his chambers were private. He could lock the door that separated his enclave from the Bridge and the rest of the ship.

Alone in his own space, he reflected. *We've passed the two choke points where I expected opposition. I think, or maybe just hope, that life is going to settle into a boring routine for the rest of our long, long journey. I know there will always be maintenance to do, and little emergencies, with so many children on board.*

Although he didn't feel horny, he felt full and needed relief. *I had had a wet dream a couple of nights earlier. I could masturbate, but that never really scratches the itch. We'll be arriving on Enceladus in a couple of months. I hope I will soon find a guy to at least hook up with there, if not marry.*

17
Celebration

Working a crossword puzzle in the parlor of her flat, JiAnn jumped when Convener Cly's voice interrupted the calm classical music she had been listening to. He'd preempted all media to address the entire populace of Enceladus. "Gentlepeople, December 4, 2099, will go down in the history of Enceladus. At 1000 hours this morning, the Colonial Council voted unanimously to declare independence from Earth. From that moment and forever after, we are no longer Enceladus Colony, but the independent and sovereign Nation of Enceladus."

JiAnn held both hands over her heart. *I never thought the Council would have the courage to do it! This deserves a glass of my* special *tea.*

That night, The Caverns, like all the residences, erupted into spontaneous celebrations. JiAnn surprised her neighbors with a raunchy old sea shanty she had learned on Earth. By then, she had drunk more alcohol than she considered decorous. Even her friend Millicent, who had loudly worried about the consequences of breaking with Earth, feasted with abandon.

JiAnn walked unsteadily down the sidewalk of her neighborhood. Every residence was fully lit. People were dancing in the streets. This was a night to remember.

18

Birth

CORVIS • NURSERY

As HE FLOATED, UNHURRIED through the common areas of the *Nursery*, he noted that, even without knowledge of the billions of deaths on Earth, the atmosphere on the *Nursery* was somber. Their own losses due to plague had cast a pall over everyone.

Svet was amazing. He watched her take time with a 3-year-old. "Oh, look at you, Christopher!" she said as the toddler pushed off and somersaulted six times before grabbing a handhold on the opposite wall. He laughed and accepted her high five. Later, she stopped by a six-year-old with a book. She sat with the girl almost in her lap and said, "Will you read it to me, Mary?" And he saw her meander around art class calling each child by name while admiring their creations. The effect struck me as magical.

In the fitness gym he watched children tumble, and bounce into each other harmlessly, flying through the enormous space like big, pudgy, wingless birds.

When Jake called me, what was it a month ago? Seems like it. I never imagined the joy I feel right now. Finally, our trip is going the way it should. If it continues like this, the remaining time will fly.

At 0445 hours, December 6, Svet asked him to visit Lucy Aubameyang in the infirmary. Lucy was in labor. Labor and delivery had always been risky among her people, especially in the refugee camp, and Lucy was afraid.

Corvis was afraid, as well. After three miscarriages and three toddlers dying in the infirmary, his heart raced as he entered Lucy's exam room.

She progressed rapidly, and delivery started at 6:55. Without gravity, Corvis anticipated that a gentle suction cap applied to the baby's scalp might help to draw the baby out. It worked perfectly, and Paul Aubameyang was born at 0659 hours, the first and only live birth on the *Nursery*. The baby cried lustily.

With a soft towel Corvis vigorously rubbed Little Paul's body to stimulate circulation, applied a diaper, and then laid him on Lucy's naked chest and covered them, up to the newborn's face, with a sheet. Mother and baby gazed into each other's eyes bonding instantly.

It's odd that our consumption of paper products came to mind, probably because of the tiny newborn diaper. *The 317 of us will have gone through a lot of toilet paper, facial tissues, paper towels, and napkins during our three-month journey. All of it will go into the vat along with enzymes to facilitate digestion and come out as fresh thin mats of clean, white paper. It will be layered and textured for napkins or toilet paper, then cut to the correct size. Diapers will have three layers, an inner one that wicks moisture to the middle, an absorbent layer, and the outer layer will be waterproof.*

Svet took to the PA system. "Once again we have seen the miracle of new life," she said. "For our community has seen more than its share of sadness, but Little Paul is the baby of all of us!"

19
Threat and Response

JiAnn • Enceladus

GENERAL DIOIKIS HAD INVITED JiAnn to attend the evening meeting of the generals to answer questions about the progress of the two armadas dispatched from Earth. She found her usual seat at the large conference table in the wood-paneled room. As usual, coffee was served, even though none of the generals took any. Chit-chat continued until the last of the generals arrived.

"Just in case the armadas come this far" General Dioikis said, addressing the other generals, "we need to have a plan."

"In the..." General Clark paused for emphasis, "...*highly unlikely* event that the armadas come this far, we have twenty-five fighters to their, what? Ten?"

"We still need a plan," Dioikis said. "The long-range squadron is likely to encounter them first. Our best pilots need to be in that squadron."

"Elite Squadron is led by Captain Ramos, with wingmen Davis, Washington, Reitmann, and Pistis. They're the best we have," Clark replied with finality.

"When were they selected?" General Dioikis asked.

Clark answered, "Eleven months ago"

"We need to be sure they're still our best. All pilots need to be re-tested."

Clark glared. "That could cause serious morale problems."

"Pilots understand that there will be periodic competition for the top spots. It's important to have our best pilots in those positions. I recommend testing all our pilots."

Squadron Leader

General Dioikis had committed to keeping JiAnn informed of anything that involved Billy Birchfield since Billy was now Apprentice Dragomark.

He sent her the results of qualification trials; Tyler Washington had tied with Billy Birchfield each with a total score of 97%. Pistis got 89%, followed by Soliva at 85% and Reitmann at 84%. Ramos came in a distant sixth.

General Dioikis assembled the new members of the elite squadron and told them, "You have shown superior ability to defend Enceladus. Now you must elect your leader."

Tyler received two votes, Billy three. Tyler immediately submitted his formal resignation from the Elite Squadron to General Dioikis. Dioikis shared the bad news with Billy. "Talk to him, Will you?" Dioikis asked.

Billy reported back the next day. "I invited Tyler to have a beer, and he accepted. 'I need you,' I said, 'Actually, Enceladus needs you, Tyler.' Tyler looked really down and didn't respond. 'And if it comes down to life on Enceladus, it may hang on the best people defending us,' I went on.

"Tyler still looked sad and didn't say anything.

"'We're not just friends,' I said, 'we're each other's best defense. We belong in the same squadron, especially now.' After a moment Tyler just moaned, 'I wasn't elected.'

"'I voted for you,' I told him.

'You really think I should stay?'

"'I *want* you to stay,' I said.

'OK.'

"'Yes!' I shouted. We clinked mugs and laughed.

"Tyler's definitely back in the squadron."

20
24th Birthday

CORVIS · NURSERY

CORVIS STARTED HIS DAY with some light flaky algae crackers that he had learned to like and some light brown protein drink that didn't have much flavor. It was my 24th birthday. Even though his birthday was so close to Christmas, his mother always arranged some sort of celebration. She did something special when any of us had a birthday. He wanted to celebrate, but how? Go to the gym? *Need to do that, anyway. Maybe I'll watch one of my favorite movies.*

He always thought of his family on his birthday. He had two brothers and four sisters, so his mom couldn't afford anything elaborate, but each of them knew they were special when their birthday came around. Until now, he'd always made it a point to call each of his siblings on their birthday, and most of them called Corvis on his. It's one way they stayed in touch.

His last talk with Nick, his name was Ewing Eduardo; he didn't know how he got the nickname Nick, was typical.

"How's my baby brother?"

"You may be the oldest, and I'm the youngest, but I'm no baby. I have a college degree," Corvis had crowed.

"But you'll always be my favorite brother," Nick replied.

"Ricky's your only other brother, and you probably say the same thing to him," he said.

"I can have two favorite brothers if I want to," Nick said.

"I love you, Nick," Corvis said. "You've always been like a dad to all of us."

"I love you, too," Nick said, "and you've always thought more highly of me than I deserve."

Nick was an oncologist up in Maine, and he had far more patients than he would like to have had. "Too much cancer these days," he would always say.

Today Corvis pictured his mom and each of his siblings and wondered how they were doing. Wondered if they were still alive. Considering the last news broadcast that he'd monitored from Earth, he suspected they were probably all dead. He wished he could just call and check on each of them.

He was feeling profoundly sad when, at 1830 hours, Charity, one of the older girls, appeared at the door of the bridge. She looked worried. "Svet needs you, urgently... in the dining room." She took him by the hand and with a strong grip, urged him there.

"What's going on? Is someone hurt?"

Oddly, all the children were sitting at tables watching Corvis intently. Most were smiling, and some were even laughing. He didn't see Svet anywhere.

"Seriously, where's Svet?"

Charity silently but persistently pulled him to the front row of tables. Svet jumped up and shouted "Surprise!"

And all the children shouted, "Happy Birthday!"

"Charity," he said, "you are a good actor! I really thought something terrible had happened to Svet!"

Robots had already started serving dessert. Svet led the children in singing "Happy Birthday to Corvis."

John offered to go to the bridge so Corvis could sit with the children in the cafeteria for a while.

Christmas Eve

Corvis wandered through the ship and noticed the decorations the children had made for Christmas. When he found Svet in a classroom, he asked, "What religion are you?"

"I'm Russian Orthodox, but I haven't been to church for a couple of years. How about you? What is your religion?"

"I'm Roman Catholic, but, like you, I haven't been to church for a long time. What about the children? Do you know what religions they follow?"

"The toddlers and infants, I don't know unless they have older siblings that can tell me. Among those who are old enough to tell me, most are Christian of some sort. Only three or four are Muslim," Svet said.

"So, they're decorating for Christmas."

"Yes, they all love Christmas, regardless of their religion."

When he returned to the bridge, he thought about feeding 315 people, not only for the holiday but for three more months. It weighed on him as a huge responsibility. Food is heavy. The ground crew had loaded two day's-worth of ready-to-eat food. For the rest of their three-month trip, they had to grow their own food on board. Algae was just about their only food. He rechecked the status of the 30 tanks, each containing 50 gallons of growing medium. Nutrients, acidity, oxygenation, and density for each tank were all well within the optimal range. Simulations of more than 500 foods were preprogrammed into the fully automated texturizer. Different proportions of each alga, flavoring, and tooth resistance produced a fair approximation of nearly any food one could ask for. Svet punched in the menus, and computers directed mixers, texturizers, ovens, and freezers to produce finished, nutritious meals.

His computer showed that they had 37 days of mature dry algae. Several days' worth was on the drying racks, and six tanks were being harvested at that moment. They had plenty of nutritious food, but Christmas was coming. It would be nice to have at least a little real Earth food for a change. He was curious whether any of it was left.

He couldn't believe his eyes when he saw that they still had 1.9 days of Earth food on board.

The next time Svet came onto the bridge he said "Thank you for preserving the Earth food. It will be a nice treat for the children."

"I've been thinking about other ways to make Christmas special for them," she replied. "Tens of thousands of bright beads of all colors of the rainbow are also on board. I randomly assigned each child a secret friend. Children have strung beads into jewelry as Christmas gifts for these secret friends. In school, they have also learned several Christmas carols."

The atmosphere on the *Nursery* was truly festive on Christmas day. The children ate Earth food for breakfast, lunch, and dinner. Corvis spent half an hour on Christmas day with the children in the common areas. Children crowded around Little Paul wherever his mother took him. While he seemed delighted by the colorful paper, cloth, and bead decorations, he didn't understand Christmas, of course.

Nevertheless, a four-year-old, Sandra, explained to Little Paul "Round John Virgin was the father of Jesus." And five-year-old, Peter, told Paul "Baby Jesus didn't cry because he was away in a manger." Four-year-old Patricia said, "Punches the Pilot steered Santa's sleigh."

An hour later, I floated through the auditorium. I heard six-year-old, Thaddeus, say "At home, I would be out fishing now."

Guy said, "I just wish I could go out into the jungle."

Nine-year-old Thomas whom they idolized, advised them, "You know, we will never go home again."

Guy turned away, trying to hide his tears.

21
Brobding's Woman

BROBDING · SOUTH AFRICA

BRO LIVED IN PRIVATE quarters in the recently rebuilt Fort Kosmac. He had clothes, but he preferred not to wear them. With this woman he didn't hide anything. He didn't need to. Not that he was vulnerable to her; quite the contrary. Brobding's current woman was completely expendable, just as Persephata had been earlier.

Persephata had pleasured Brobding, *and* she became useful to the Family.

An extraterrestrial alien once visited them. Brobding never mentioned it because it was nobody's business but theirs. Persephata never mentioned it because people would have thought she was crazy, even though they had evidence to prove it.

Brobding never mixed business with pleasure except when torturing offenders. "You can be my lover or a lieutenant," Brobding had said, "Which is it?"

"Both," she replied.

"No," he said firmly, "one or the other. Chose now."

"I'll be your lieutenant."

"I need someone to go to Enceladus to establish a Family outpost there."

She would miss Brobding, and Brobding wouldn't forget Persephata. On December 13, 2097, after five years with the Family, she joined with the help of the Family the crew of the spaceship *Residuum* headed for Mars. Officially, the ship exploded shortly after liftoff, and all its crew perished. Actually, they landed on Enceladus on March 21, 2098. She immediately got a job as a mechanic's assistant in the government garage. It was a low-paying job, but she would make lots of money moonlighting.

Quitting the Family was not an option. You can't divorce your godfather.

Tom Kearn had allowed Mildred Gillies 24 hours beyond the deadline to pay her debt to the godfather. Tom received the standard punishment of branding with the letter "G" on his right hand. Some thought the "G" was for "godfather," others said it was for "Ghastli." Either way he was marked forever, for all the world to see, as Brobding's property.

Tracy Hanson got caught using drugs. Brobding, himself, clamped her pinkie with pliers, pulled and cut at the first joint. The Ghastli Family physician made a flap of her skin and stitched a covering for the stump.

Major infractions, or more than eight single-finger-punishments resulted in unceremonious elimination.

Every godchild in Family Ghastli "volunteered" as a potential soldier in the Swarm, like it or not. He had more soldiers than he needed; only one in ten would blast off into space, but Brobding needed pilots: 101 of them. Brobding offered a handsome finder's fee and an equally large signing bonus. Each candidate was aware that she or he would get away from the hell that Earth had become, and the signing fee might even secure transit to the Moon or Mars for a few family members. Today, he would interview the first 50 in ten groups of five.

The room was small. No ventilation, intentionally. Warmer even than Brobding's home. The table at the front was five feet long. Five chairs faced the table. A white sheet had been laid in front of the table.

Time to apply his makeup. Two assistants stood ready. A large bowl held a half-gallon of blood from the steer slaughtered this morning for tonight's dinner. He reached back in a well-practiced routine, grasping roughly half of his long red hair and dipping it in the blood until it was saturated. He let the blood first drip down his chest and then down his back. After repeating the process with the other half of his hair, he lowered his chin toward the bowl, drenching his uncut, red beard in the blood. The excess dripped over his belly. Finally, he cupped his left hand, filling it with blood that he splashed over his right shoulder, and repeated the process for the left shoulder. He wiped his wet hands on his forearms.

Warm, drying blood filled the room with the thick, heavy smell of death. Brobding signaled for the bowl to be removed and the full-length mirror to be brought in. Admiring the effect, he stood for five minutes while the blood congealed. Then he motioned for the make-up cloth to be removed. Brobding's nose had, by now, had adjusted, but he knew the candidates would be nauseated.

Displaying full frontal and stretching himself to his full height, he nodded to the doorkeeper. The first five pilots filed in, each escorted by a guard with a gun cocked and ready. He did not hide his delight at the fear and disgust he read on their faces.

"Do you understand that this is most likely a one-way trip?"

All the pilots had been screened for their capabilities, for any liabilities or divided loyalties, and for other weaknesses. All fifty were offered contacts. Forty-five accepted. Forty-five out of the needed 101 fighter pilots. And he still had to hire people to serve other roles, including servants on the mother ship, and technicians, and pilots to man tenders that would service the fleet in the far reaches of the solar system.

At the end of a long day of interviews, Brobding was tired. He took a shower, thoroughly washed the blood away, and donned a pair of shorts. He looked like a different person. As he ascended to the residence, he heard her screaming threats and curses. *Good,* he thought, *she's keeping the help in line.* As he opened the large, ornate door, the shouting stopped instantly. A huge spotless entry hall, with its intricate crystal chandelier and a gleaming table with a four-foot ancient vase filled with fresh-cut flowers, welcomed him home. Flowers filled the place with their fragrance. Woman, the only name he had for her, was dressed in a fine red silk sarong with gigantic lotus flowers worked in metallic gold thread. She stood just shy of five feet tall and looked demure and fragile. He smiled as he imagined her commanding a small army of servants.

Her tiny hands, with nails so long they made practical work impossible, proffered his favorite cocktail. Her arthritic knuckles reminded him that they had been together for more than a couple of years. Brobding lipped and tongued them, and they were transfigured into erotic assets. She purred her contentment. They had not discussed commitment. In fact, they had spoken little, both preferring actions. Lusty actions.

He bent to kiss her forehead and finished his drink. Lovemaking was never routine. Woman's luxurious life and her power within this incredibly wealthy household depended upon satisfying her man in ever-novel ways.

Brobding knew she paid the most expensive prostitutes to teach her. He also knew that her own instincts led her to make every moment seem natural, spontaneous. She bent her body in ways that seemed impossible to arouse and excite her man. Brobding made love vigorously and muscularly. But he was also careful neither to break bones nor to suffocate her. He delayed climax again and again, to make the pleasure last longer.

Brobding's power over "family" and employees was absolute. He had directed, with a small finger movement across his neck, the execution of more than half a dozen of his godchildren. Woman worshipped Brobding as a god. And, though his Woman was outside the chain of command she, knew she lived only because Brobding willed it. She treated godchildren, even high-ranking ones, with utter disdain. Brobding knew she was both hated and feared for it. If she died, no one would shed a tear.

22
Armadas Pass Mars

JiAnn • Enceladus

BILLY REPORTED TO JIANN. "The satendrites directed my attention to the two armadas approaching from Earth. They've just gotten a significant speed boost as they passed Mars."

Concerned, JiAnn immediately reported to General Dioikis.

Dioikis wasted no time. He sent a generic message to the armadas. "Earth-based ships without prior permission to land will be destroyed if they come within 25 million kilometers of Enceladus."

General Lopez's response arrived an hour later. "Five ships of the Southern Alliance are headed to one of the many moons of Saturn with civilians on board. Our mission is entirely non-military. Safe passage is formally requested."

"Our 25-million-kilometer perimeter is inviolable. Be aware that you are considerably out-gunned in this part of the solar system," Dioikis responded.

The Northern Confederacy's armada did not send any message in reply.

He reported all this information to JiAnn.

23
Enceladus?

CORVIS SAT IN THE pilot's seat pondering the strange task before him. *How do I contact a settlement that doesn't officially exist?* He had been thinking about what to say since the first day of their journey. *What if they don't speak English? What frequency do I use? What if they don't respond?...or I can't understand the response? Guess I'll just pick a channel and give it a try.*

"Um, Enceladus?" he transmitted into the black void, "This is *Nursery*. Um, I don't know the protocol, but we are a ship from Earth... We're carrying... 296 children, 16 teenagers, and two adults. The adults are the pilot, that's me, and a Chief Operating Officer. We have no weapons. We are bound for Enceladus. And... even though we are still a month out... we are requesting permission to land... when we arrive. Over?"

He calculated that at the speed of light, it would take his message about half an hour to get to Enceladus, and even if someone there received it, and replied immediately, it would be *another* half an hour to hear back.

That knowledge did nothing to help the time pass more quickly. The minutes ticked by painfully slowly. *Should I try a different frequency? ...several frequencies?*

To his surprise, his monitor lit up 43 minutes later. The hologram of a very handsome young man spoke to him from in front of his monitor. He looked stern and official in his light blue, form-fitting uniform that revealed every detail of his slim, muscular upper body. He spoke over the familiar hum of the hologram image: "*Nursery*, this is Enceladus Base," he began. "Delta one month on your recovery time. What is your name and MOS? And what is that of the other adult? Change to a different channel for each transmission. Over."

"Say what?!" Corvis said without transmitting. *Well, I did get a response, and the soldier certainly is cute. Probably straight. How do I tell him that I didn't understand most of what he said without sounding like a complete idiot?* He decided to be direct and honest.

"I'm sorry, sir, I don't have a military background. Um. The only part I understood was our names. My name is Corvis Santos, and the COO is Svetlana Turgenev. Over," he transmitted.

A kinder, warmer, 3-D bust greeted him an hour later. "These are difficult days for people in the inner solar system," the good-looking face said. "Many want to come to Enceladus; some have bad intentions. I was testing to see whether you're military. We'll need to know a lot more about the contents of your ship and your reasons for coming to Enceladus before you'll be allowed even to *approach* Enceladus. Currently, we're not permitting *any* outsiders to land."

Corvis squirmed in his seat and perspired.

"But for now, I'll cut you some slack," the military one said as if he could see Corvis's discomfort.

"Please upload your complete ship's manifest, with all passengers' and crew's names and DNA profiles. Photos of all spaces within your ship will also be needed at least a week before your planned arrival. Once you actually land, before anyone is permitted to disembark, drones will enter your ship to sniff for disease, drugs, and weapons. My intuition tells me they won't find anything." He stopped and smiled.

Corvis paused the recording and looked at the speaker's image from the right and from the left, and the more he saw, the more he liked.

"Since we will be working with each other," he continued, "let me say, first...I like your face, Santos..."

Corvis's reaction was strong and visceral. *Did I really hear you say that? I can't believe it.* "Wow!" he transmitted, "I didn't expect that! I like your face, too! And your shoulders and..."

Svet floated into the cockpit at that moment. "I heard voices in here, and I wanted to check on you."

Corvis was sure he turned three shades of red and rebooted the transmission. "We've made contact with Enceladus!" he said, "Have a seat and listen."

He noticed details he had missed at first. Behind the handsome young man was a cavernous situation room with large monitors on a distant wall.

"...I like your face, Santos..."

"Well, well, well!" Svet interjected, and then, "You're blushing."

"My name is Lt. Billy Birchfield. I'm a fighter pilot. The title sounds impressive, but it's usually boring, this far from the Sun. That's about to change, I believe. More about that later.

"So, about me, I'm a birthright Enceladan. We call ourselves 'Dans.' Birthright Dans are called Birth-Dans, and naturalized Enceladans are called 'Earth-Dans.' I'm 24, and still single. But I don't intend to stay that way long.

"Now, tell me about yourself and your COO. Over." The hologram flickered out, and the buzzing stopped.

"My, oh my!" Svet said, "We *definitely* have contact with Enceladus. And your face tells me you weren't lying when you said you were gay."

Pushing past his embarrassment, he said, "The children will want to know."

"I'm not sure they should know everything..." she said smirking.

Corvis didn't respond.

Backing away from the awkward moment, she asked, "Do you want to tell them, or shall I?"

"Why don't you tell them?" he said. "They will be excited, too. I want to upload the ship's manifest and other documents and begin photographing the ship."

"Hello, Lt. Birchfield. I'm from New York. I'm a nurse, and I will be looking for a job when I get to Enceladus. Do you have a hospital there? Over."

24
Out of the Cloud of Satellites

JiAnn • Enceladus

JiAnn reported to President Cly: "The satendrites inform us that a large group of objects has departed from the thousands of satellites orbiting Earth. They're moving together at a high velocity toward Mars. The satendrites don't have a count of the number of objects in the group, as they blink in and out of sight randomly."

A regular volunteer at the Butterfly Garden, today she was conferring in verdant surroundings, tending orchids.

"What kind of objects are they?" Cly asked.

"Data are incomplete, but some of them could be fighter rockets," she said.

"What's causing them to blink?" Cly asked.

"The only similar phenomenon is when a celestial body is eclipsed by a dark body," JiAnn replied. "We don't know what might be intermittently blocking their light."

"Please continue researching this," Cly said. "In particular, try to find out the history of this group of objects."

"I certainly will, sir."

It would be hours before Malcolm would have more information, so she continued calmly cross-pollinating orchids, noting each hybrid in her pad.

Crisis

JiAnn had zoned out, thinking about the nuclear war on Earth with a billion people already dead. Coming back to the meeting, she smelled the coffee steaming in front of her on the conference table. Bamboo wall paneling convincingly simulated walnut. President Cly was still speaking. "...these three different groups appear intent upon invading Enceladus."

"Our fighters can enforce a 25-million-kilometer national perimeter, but once an enemy enters that space, it could be just hours before they land if they somehow manage to evade our defenses. We have five fighters with a 100-million-kilometer range, but that number could easily be overcome by the combined forces of the observed invaders," General Dioikis stated grimly.

JiAnn thought about Billy, the Dragomark Apprentice and ace pilot. "The Dragomark and his Apprentice will be in the Bubble to communicate with the satendrites continuously from now until this crisis is over," she affirmed.

"Recall," General Dioikis cautioned, "that the recently appointed Apprentice is also the leader of the Elite Squadron. He may be called up at any time to head off the enemies at the 100-million-kilometer perimeter. If he's off fighting, he won't be available to man the Bubble."

JiAnn's pulse quickened when she thought of Billy flying into danger. *Why Billy?*

History of the Cluster

Enceladus

JiAnn studied the face of General Dioikis from different angles as his hologram appeared in front of her. *He looks determined, not angry*, she thought, *I must find a way to get Billy exempted from this mission*. She reported to Dioikis from the tiny Office of the Dragomark in City Hall. "The satendrites have searched their databases and found a series of more than 20 launches from a spaceport in Montenegro in the 24 hours from November 3 to November 4 last year. The first of these rockets carried a massive payload. All the objects orbited Earth for almost two months. In early January, they formed a tight cluster before departing Earth orbit rapidly. That's all the history I have on them, General Dioikis, but I researched the Montenegro Spaceport, as it seemed like an unusual place to launch spacecraft from. It was built in 2097 by Family Ghastli and is still owned by them. I'll continue digging."

"I'm sure this information will be a big help, Madame Dragomark," Dioikis said, "Thank you."

25
Mission-Ready

CORVIS

BILLY'S 3-D IMAGE SET Corvis's heart racing. His whole body felt happy to welcome him onto the bridge, but his feelings quickly changed as he studied Billy's emotions. There was nothing joyful about his expression.

Over the hum of the hologram Billy said, "General Dioikis has told us to be mission-ready. We could blast off at any moment. Here's the situation. The Southern Alliance armada has returned to Moon Base. However, the other armada is accelerating toward Enceladus. If the Northern Confederacy's armada lands on Enceladus, we expect they will enslave all Enseladuns with electronic brain probes. They can do this quickly and efficiently without laying hands on anyone. Brain probes use remote nanotechnology. We must not let them land. If they continue accelerating at their current rate, they'll arrive at Enceladus on 21 February. We still have time to plan and execute. Elite Squadron's five ships have a range of 100 million kilometers. The effective range of our guided missiles is 30 million kilometers, and that of our other 20 fighters is only 25 million kilometers.

"The Northern Confederacy fleet includes a mother ship and five fighters. The satendrites report that the mother ship has tremendous firepower, so we'll be outgunned at 100 million kilometers out. But we're the best of the best. They'll have traveled a couple of months, whereas we'll be only six days from home. We can do this!

"And, yes, we have a hospital, a small one. Don't worry, you'll find work. Over."

Corvis's joy had long since evaporated. *What if these enemies reach Enceladus before the* Nursery *arrives?* Their arrival at Enceladus was going to be complicated. In spite of Billy's optimism, Corvis was worried.

26
Speed and Vector Change

JiAnn • Enceladus

Malcolm called JiAnn. Only his head was visible, the background completely black. "I need to stay in the Bubble, Boss. Too many things are changing quickly. But we need to get new information to Dioikis. The cluster of objects that left Earth is now heading for the *Nursery*. The satendrites are visualizing some round objects in the group, as well as some fighters. I still don't dull black know what's making them blink out of view so erratically, but it could be these.

"Meanwhile, the Northern Confederacy armada is no longer accelerating. It is not slowing, but it is not speeding up any longer, either. I don't know what to make of this. Data are incomplete, but let's give what we have to the general."

"I'll let General Dioikis and President Cly know," JiAnn confirmed.

Cly with Navajo pots behind him, Dioikis surrounded by huge monitors, and JiAnn in her tiny Victorian parlor met by video conference.

"We need to send shots across their bow," the general said, looking determined.

Cly rubbed his chin thoughtfully. "That will announce to all humanity that Enceladus is inhabited. And it will establish our reputation from the beginning as a warlike nation."

"Earth is radioactive," Dioikis instated. "People are desperate to find a safe haven. The Northern Confederacy wants to bring Earth's war to Enceladus. Confirming what many people already suspect about Enceladus is a small price to pay for our freedom."

JiAnn nodded and took a sip of tea. A minute later she said, "I don't usually favor violence. But in this case, firing a couple of missiles might send a clear message."

Cly looked sad, not angry as he responded. "Limit it to two missiles, at least for now."

"I'll keep you informed," Dioikis said before leaving the meeting.

JiAnn felt deeply disappointed that Enceladus would announce its existence to the Solar System by firing missiles.

27
New Mission

BILLY'S HOLOGRAM APPEARED IN front of Corvis's monitor, strong and handsome, as usual, but looking serious. Half-sitting on the edge of a desk, he was framed by a large monitor. Fighter pilots, two women and two men sat at small tables nearby. Lockers lined the walls behind them. "FYI. I'm transmitting this meeting to the *Nursery*," Billy said, addressing the squadron, "Sorry, all, but we're now on 24-hour standby. Also, our mission has changed. A group of fighters launched from Ghastli spaceport in Montenegro in November. They and the armada are both aiming for the *Nursery*..."

Corvis's mind and heart seized. *They're targeting us now!* he realized.

"...which has no weapons," Corvis continued. "We don't currently know whether they're acting independently or in coordination."

The Nursery! *No! It can't be!* Corvis hardly heard anything else Billy said. His monitor showed uniformed service members who appeared to be mulling these facts.

"If the armada captures the *Nursery*, they will have 314 hostages."

The pilots looked worried. Corvis's own vision blurred, and he found it hard to breathe as he listened.

"Early estimates are that we will be out-gunned at least five-to-one."

The fliers all started talking at once. If he hadn't been weightless, Corvis probably would have passed out. As it was, he felt like he was in a dream, a horrifying nightmare.

"At ease," Billy said after a moment, and the pilots grew quiet. "We're out-gunned, but we are smarter than they are. Remember, you are the best of the best. You're sharp and you're fresh. Let's stay that way."

Corvis pushed off from wall to wall, back and forth on the large bridge, holding his head, brimming with nervous energy. The soldiers continued talking in military lingo that he couldn't understand.

After the meeting ended, Billy remained in the same room, deserted by the others. When he leaned in close to the camera, it almost felt like he would touch Corvis. "That's the bad news, Corvis. The good news is that Enceladus is going to do everything in its power to save the *Nursery*. Over."

Holy shit! Holy, fucking shit! And a minute later, *Good thing the children couldn't read my mind. And now it will be an hour before any of my questions will be answered.*

"Oh, my, God," he transmitted, "We can't protect ourselves! Can't you do something to help us? Don't you have long-range missiles to destroy them? The worst part is what I don't know... I don't know exactly how many ships are bearing down on us. And I don't know when you'll get here. We need help, and we need it soon! Over."

As soon as he had transmitted, he regretted that he had been so emotional. He tried to calm down. He floated back and forth from one side of the Bridge to the other. His heart had never raced so fast. He analyzed his sensations and realized he had worked endless hours since they left Earth, but he hadn't gotten vigorous exercise... since a week before he left New York. He vowed to run at least three miles a day on the foot-grabber every day until they reached Enceladus. He even set up a checklist on his computer, of all the exercises he planned to do, and what days he planned to do them.

Almost an hour later, before he had actually gone to the gym, Billy's hologram entered his space, smiling kindly. *It's amazing how he calms me down.* Corvis took a deep breath. He wanted to touch the picture Billy's image looked so real.

"I know you're concerned. I would be... terrified in your place, without weapons to defend myself and the children. The ships that are targeting you are so far away that our missiles can't be very accurate. Nevertheless, we *have* started firing. The cluster of ships presents a large target, but within the cluster, the ships are very maneuverable and given so much warning, they will easily avoid being hit. Still, it tells them, in no uncertain terms, that we don't intend to let them take you without a fight."

Corvis felt in his gut that Billy was trying to show him a confident, protective soldier, but he couldn't hide his own anxiety. Moving his head from side to side, Corvis looked at Billy's face. He looked almost apologetic. The worst they'll do is take you as hostages."

That's supposed to be encouraging!?

"They'll be very careful not to damage your life-support systems. Dead hostages are worthless. The other thing is our pilots are very skilled, both at flying and at shooting.

"You're 39 days from Enceladus. Our squadron's range is five and a half days, so you only have to hang in there for

33 days, and our ships will arrive to protect you. Again, your safety is the first priority for all the people of Enceladus.

"I'll let you know more detailed plans as soon as they're solidified. Over."

The image flickered out.

Billy's calm tone helped Corvis breathe again. But the more he thought about the facts of their situation, the more terrified and frustrated he became. *I can't let Svet know until I...we...have a plan.*

He started mentally composing his response to Billy. *We are NOT 39 days out. We're almost 40 days out. That means we are exposed, totally exposed, for the next 34 days. You didn't tell me how fast the bad guys are traveling, so I don't know how much time we've got. Most of all, you don't know how many fighters are in the cluster. Please tell me what the specific plan is.*

Enough! No more planning to go, no more excuses. Go *to the gym,* he told himself.

The sound of the foot grabber got his attention. He was used to the regular "slap, slap, slap" sound of footfalls on the treadmill. His movements on the foot grabber created a rhythmic "Zing, zing, zing" sound. After two miles he had to quit. He was exhausted. *So much for good plans. I'm so out of shape.*

Hide and Seek

Nursery

He was still fretting about how to keep the children from learning of the threat when Svet came onto the bridge.

"Four children were playing Hide 'N Go Seek," she said breathlessly. "Three children are accounted for, but the fourth one is still missing."

His mind was slow to shift. "The child will show up," he said offhand.

"Captain! Franck has been missing for more than 30 minutes. He could be in danger!" she said.

That got his attention. "Oh! You're right. We need to find him. And quickly!" Corvis said, "I'll make an announcement and we'll organize a search."

Over the PA he announced, "A child is hiding somewhere on the ship. His name is Franck. We need everyone to help find him. Please meet me in the gym.

"Franck, please come out of hiding. The game is over. You're not in trouble, but please show yourself right now."

I know I'm an adrenalin junkie, but this is too much, Corvis thought.

Svet said as they rushed to the gym, "Most of the children realize that Franck is missing. And many have already been looking for him."

When we arrived at the place where the children had assembled, Corvis didn't waste time asking if Franck had been found yet. Concerned faces showed that he hadn't. "Each of us must stay in touch with a buddy while we look for Franck so that we don't end up with more missing people.

"If you are six years old or younger, please search your own dormitory, where you sleep every night. If you are seven to nine years old, search the classrooms and then watch the younger children. If you are ten or older, please come with me to the dining room."

When the older children arrived in the dining room Corvis announced, "We need to search any space even half as large as we think Franck could possibly fit into. Keep in mind that he might enter through a space barely big enough for his head. Charity, please take four children and search the kitchen, including refrigerators and ovens, and then, after we've left, search the dining room. Mary, take four children and search Cargo Holds A and B. Charlene and four more children, search Cargo Holds C and D. Gabrielle, take four and look all around the algae tanks and water system areas. Rose, take three walkie talkies, and five children. Start looking in service crawl spaces. Vivian, you and four children look all around the pump houses. Everyone, search inside storage spaces and service ports. Svetlana and I will circulate among you. Go!"

"I'll start by searching the freezer," he told Svet, handing her a walkie-talkie.

As he floated down an aft passageway between classrooms and laboratories, he noticed, as never before, that outside of public areas, wires were neatly bundled and taped out of the way, but not covered. Tools neatly stowed behind work benches were exposed for easy access. Supplies were stored behind netting that a child could easily pull open.

Searching for one small child in this huge space was going to be an hours-long if not days-long nightmare.

"Hello, Svet," he said over the walkie-talkie, "I'm entering the freezer." He didn't want any of the children to accidentally uncover the bodies of the three toddlers who had died of plague or the frozen halves of beef. He looked behind 50-gallon drums of frozen orange juice, huge bags of frozen fruit and vegetables, and 50-kilogram bundles of frozen fish. After 15 minutes he was very cold, and he had convinced himself that Franck was not in the freezer.

Next, he floated up through the main aft portal past B Deck to C Deck, through the gym to the forward service area housing the algae tanks. Perspiration popped from every pore when he entered, so hot and humid was the area. He found Gabrielle and asked, "Have you looked inside the tanks?"

"What?" she shouted over over the noise of the mixers and pumps, "I can't hear you."

"Inside the tanks!" he yelled back, "Have you looked in there?"

"We can't open them!" Gabrielle roared. "The lids are bolted down, and the inlet and outlet valves are screwed in tight!" *That means he couldn't have gotten into them, thank God.*

He floated to the adjacent water and gas storage compartment area. Using handholds for stability, he looked under and behind huge bottles of argon and helium. Then he examined the spaces between gigantic spherical tanks of water and oxygen. He floated above the half-meter water pipes running from the service area to all parts of the ship. There was no sign of the missing child. Corvis was beginning to despair.

As he passed the robot recharging stations, on his way to search the staff area, when the PA system came alive with Svet's voice. "Everyone! Franck has been found. All children, please return to the gym."

Corvis heaved a sigh of relief.

Then she said over the walkie-talkie, "Corvis, please meet us in the Infirmary. Quickly!"

"Who will watch the children?" he asked her.

"Rose and Charlene will keep them busy for a while," came the reply.

Returning to the Gas Storage Compartment, he floated up to Deck B. He was in the Infirmary within 30 seconds.

Seeing Svet's worried face gave him chills.

"In Cargo Hold B, one of the children with Mary saw a foot behind a 50-kilogram bag of flour. She shook it, but it was lifeless. Franck was asleep and he didn't respond when we tried to wake him," she said, "It's very cold in there. I wrapped him in a blanket. He's awake now but very groggy and cranky. He doesn't want anyone around him."

"I'll take over here," Corvis told her, "Please do a roll call, and make sure all doors to areas outside of our common areas are locked."

"I will do that," Svet said, "but some areas, like the gym, don't have doors."

"OK. We'll figure out what to do about those areas later," he said.

Corvis took Franck's rectal temp, got a warming blanket, and wrapped him in it. Franck's core temperature was 29° C or 84.2° F. He started shivering, and Corvis knew that was a good sign.

"Wh...What ha... happened?" Franck asked.

"You got very cold," Corvis said.

"Wh...Where am I?" he asked.

"You're in the infirmary," Corvis replied.

"I haf...hafta get out of here," Franck said, throwing off the blanket.

"You can leave soon," Corvis said, "but why don't you get warmed up first? Would you like a cup of hot chocolate?"

"Yes, please," he said, settling back into his hammock, but not wrapping himself in the blanket.

"What do you remember?" Corvis asked as Franck's shivering subsided.

"We were playing hide n' seek." Then, after a pause, "I went to the place where they store things... I don't remember after that... until I woke up here."

He waited until Franck finished his hot chocolate and then asked, "A storage room is not a safe place for children to play in, is it?"

"No. Can I go now?"

"Yes." Corvis floated with Franck to the gym. Then he found Svet. She looked disgusted and took Corvis away from where the children could hear them talk.

"What?" he asked, "Did you take roll call?"

"I did, and now Erwan is missing!" she said without alarm.

"Why am I not surprised?"

"I recommend we go about our business as usual. If he doesn't show up in a couple of hours, we can do another search. I don't think a search will be necessary. When he does appear, I'm going to be casual, like, 'Hi, Erwan,' how are you?"

"That sounds like the best approach," Corvis replied. "He just has to be the center of attention, doesn't he?"

He had been away from the bridge for almost an hour, and his safety checks were overdue. The second monitor to the left of center showed several blocks of data. Framed in red were data from the Hydrogen Fusion Engines. Engine A: Reactor status: Firing. Containment Structure Competence: micro-stress within tolerance. Thrust: 100%. Engine B: Reactor Status: Charging. Containment Structure Competence: building. Thrust 0%. A blue frame showed data from Magma Plasma Thrusters A and B. Engine A: Helicon coupler: Ion production 100%; Temperature high, within tolerance. Nozzle Magnet: charge: full; Trust: 100%. Data from Magma Plasma Engine B was identical.

A green-bordered graph showed oxygen production and consumption within living spaces "in equilibrium." Within a white frame, the levels of all other gases, including argon, nitrogen, and CO_2 all within normal limits. Internal gas pressure all spaces ranges from 0.34 to 0.75 atmospheres, normal; Leaks: zero. To the right of center, a monitor showed the status of Potable Water Tanks: all full; Wastewater: Flowing, no blockage detected; Water purification: functioning below capacity. Electricity Production: less than capacity; Electricity Consumption: Less than maximum. Burned fuses: zero; Shorts: zero. Screen after screen showed the *Nursery's* systems and subsystems functioning perfectly normally. The fact that all systems checked out 'safe' while Erwan was missing gave him pause. *Automation is a good thing, but we always need to question whether we might be missing something important.*

28
Numbers Revised

JiAnn • Enceladus

"Can you come to the office," JiAnn asked, "I need your help."

"Sure," Billy replied, "I'll be there in 10 minutes."

The office was in what was still called City Hall. The name had been changed officially and in signage, to *Enceladus Federal Building*. Only three stories tall, it contained all the space necessary for the function of government for the Enceladus community. In formal lettering the door to her (now Malcolm's) office read "Office of the Dragomark." The room inside that door was large enough for four people to sit comfortably. Two more could stand. A large monitor was built into the wall opposite the door. Today there were a small fake-wood table and just two chairs in the office.

After Billy arrived and pleasantries were dispensed with, JiAnn stated what she needed help with. "Both Convener Cly and General Dioikis are asking what the satendrites see within the cluster of objects that keep blinking in and out of view. The confusing, incomplete data Malcolm feeds me from the Bubble aren't very satisfying." JiAnn said. "I understand why they want more, but we can't see what we can't see. Do you have any suggestions?"

"Perhaps with the help of the computer, we can see more. Let's run a simulation," Billy suggested, while typing on the office computer. "First, I'll make a 3-D grid of a sphere representing the cluster of objects."

Billy created a globe shape with horizontal, vertical, and cross-sectional lines marked. *"X, Y, and Z axes*, all of which meet at the center of the sphere. We'll start with a black globe to represent that we can't see anything to start with."

"Now, I'll ask Malcolm to place a dot in every location he sees any part of a ship and then erase the dot as soon as the ship disappears. The computer will make a hologram movie of dots coming into and going out of view. Then I'll have the computer draw grey shapes representing spaces where there must be objects blocking our view of ships."

"When will the program be ready?" JiAnn asked.

"It's ready now. It's imperfect. We know the cluster isn't exactly spherical, but the computer will adjust even the shape of the cluster as more and more data come in," Billy replied.

"Let's send it to Malcolm now," JiAnn said.

With the tap of a button, Billy announced, "Done."

Two hours later the computer had enough data to simulate the cluster. As more data were entered, the graphical movie grew sharper.

An hour later still, JiAnn reported to General Dioikis. "A computer simulation run over the past several hours calculates that there are over one hundred fighters in the group of objects. The satendrites have not seen a mother ship, but with that many fighters, there must be a command-and-control ship, and a source of power and provisions, amid the group. They're on a direct path toward the armada and will overtake that group within a week."

"This is very helpful. Will you send me the hologram and continuous updates?"

"Yes, sir," JiAnn replied.

29
Svetlana Informed

CORVIS WAS COMPLETELY PREOCCUPIED, hopelessly trying to figure out ways to defend the *Nursery*. In addition, he dreaded informing Svet about the threat. *I can't put it off any longer*, he thought. He called her to the bridge.

While he waited for her to arrive, he started his reply to Enceladus. "Hi, Billy. I have some questions about the last information you sent. Can you tell me the speed of the approaching enemy?"

At that moment, Svet arrived. "Is this important? The children are having lunch, and I need to get back to help supervise."

"I'm sorry, but yes, it's critically important," he said.

She stood rigid, looking impatient.

Good, this needs your full attention.

"You know about the armada that was moving toward Enceladus. It's now targeting the *Nursery*."

Her face went from angry to scared.

"It's worse. There are over a dozen fighters also headed directly for us," Corvis added

It took a moment for the news to sink in. She looked increasingly frightened. Silent for several minutes, she reached for a co-pilot's chair and floated into it. "What can we do?" she whispered; her face white.

"I've been trying to think of ways to defend the *Nursery*. I don't know that there's much we *can* do. We don't have any weapons. We can train the children to take their seats and buckle up on short notice... That's all I have thought of, so far."

"That's a great plan," she said sarcastically.

"Honestly, if you can think of anything, anything at all, please let me know. We're in a desperate situation. I'm sorry to have to break this news to you."

"It's hopeless. We're just waiting for them to catch up with us, and then...they'll kill us." She was silent for a minute, head in hands. When she looked up, he saw her hands trembling. "I can't face the children right this minute. Can I hang out here while I compose myself?" she asked.

"Actually, I was just going to ask for co-pilots to watch the bridge so that I can go to the gym. Could you monitor the panels for a few minutes for me?"

"I'd be glad to," she said in a softer tone.

On his way to the gym he thought about Svet. *She's not used to this level of stress. I hope a little time alone on the Bridge will calm her nerves. A good workout should help my nerves and my muscles, as well. The days ahead will be rough.*

His first day in the gym would be brutal. He knew it, and he wasn't wrong. He was glad to be alone there. As a warm-up, he intended to run three miles on the foot grabber. In zero gravity whether you run on the floor or the ceiling, there is no resistance and little traction. When he stepped onto the foot grabber machine, bands instantly came out and secured his feet to a treadmill. When he didn't resist, the machine made him move *backward*. He had no choice but to run.

The machine provided little resistance to start, and he was weightless, so he exerted little effort. With a remote device, he gradually increased resistance as he warmed up. After two and a half miles, he told the foot-grabber to release him. It felt like another mile might kill him. Then he did arm curls. With his feet planted on the wall, he pulled against the resistance cables attached to the wall between his feet. Cable exercises approximated weightlifting, but they train slightly different muscles. Another half hour of different exercises followed.

After his workout, he still didn't have any new ideas about how to protect the ship, but he felt considerably more confident. And very sweaty.

He dashed through the bridge and ducked into the bathroom to splash water in his face. Erwan was sitting on the toilet fully clothed.

Corvis jumped and almost shouted but forced himself to speak in an even tone. "Hello, Erwan," he said.

"You didn't even *look* for me!" a glum Erwan replied.

"I didn't know you were lost," Corvis said, "but apparently you are because this is not where you belong. Please come with me."

The shock on Svet's face lasted only a millisecond. "Hi, Erwan," she said, "Did you take a wrong turn?"

"Humpf!" he said as Corvis floated him off the bridge, and into a classroom.

Svet Reports

When he returned to the bridge, he noticed that he had forgotten to close the transmission to Enceladus before he went to the gym. He flipped the switch to stop transmitting.

Agitated Svet said, "I have news from Enceladus!"

"I need to take a shower," he protested.

"Shower, schmower!" she said. "You need to hear this, *now*!"

"Well, all right. Tell me," he said. Then added, "Did you say anything while I was gone? You were transmitting to Enceladus." He floated over to the captain's seat.

"I didn't say anything," she said irritably. "We have more trouble..." But an instant later, she turned bright red, "Oh, my God. He heard me say that?"

"Say what?"

"I said he was handsome!"

"I agree," Corvis said, "his wavy blond hair, his blue eyes..."

"No!"

"No, what?"

"He's black!"

"Billy Birchfield is black?

"No, Tyler Washington... Isn't that a strong name? Tyler... Washington! Lieutenant! Tyler! Washington!"

"He'll get over it. What did you learn?"

"But will *I*?"

"Will you what?" he asked.

"Ever get over my embarrassment."

"Anyway," he asked, "what news did he have for us?"

Her face went from red to white. "That there are a *hundred* fighters from Montenegro chasing us."

Corvis groaned out loud. "Could our situation possibly get worse?" he asked, then instantly made the sign of the cross because one should never tempt the universe with that kind of statement. It's almost as bad as suggesting it will be a *quiet* night on the hospital ward.

30
Armada Disappears

JiAnn • Enceladus

JiAnn wore a dowdy, thread-bare, faded, bluish housedress. She was reporting from her kitchen where she was dicing onions. She stopped when her call was accepted. "General Dioikis, I have unbelievable news. The satendrites tell us that the Northern Armada has now vanished."

She paused for effect.

General Dioikis's large frame filled JiAnn's screen. "Vanished?" Dioikis repeated. As he turned, JiAnn saw that he was at a large table surrounded by what appeared to be his wife and two daughters. The girls were about four and six years old. He stood and moved to a bedroom.

"Sorry to interrupt your dinner, JiAnn said contritely, "but this is important. The armada disappeared into that cluster of objects from Montenegro that had been approaching for several days now. The satendrites say they have been observing the group for a couple of hours, and there is no trace of the armada now. As the cluster swallowed the armada, the satendrites observed closely, but the same objects that hid fighters also blocked their visualization of the ships when they entered the cloud. The hologram is becoming more detailed, but we still don't know exactly what we're looking at."

"And there is still no sign of a mother ship in the group?"

"None. In fact, by now, we're thinking there must be at least *two* motherships in there. Both, no doubt, loaded to the gills with firepower."

"It's disconcerting that we know ships are in that cloud and yet we can't see them. Our problems are not improving. But good work on your part. Keep me informed, especially if the satendrites see any change." Dioikis cut the connection.

31
Message for Svetlana

CORVIS • NURSERY

"MESSAGE WAITING," CORVIS'S MONITOR flashed urgently. He tapped *Accept*. In the hologram a black man looked magnificent in his space uniform, his broad shoulders and biceps bulging, and his smile revealing brilliantly white teeth. He paused the message to examine his image from all sides. Tight black curls glistened. His very dark complexion looked healthy from every angle.

The message began, "Beautiful woman..." so, he knew the message wasn't for him, and he kept it on pause. *Svet was right,* he thought. *He certainly is handsome. And direct! Something good could come of this.*

"Svet," he called over the PA, "please come to the Bridge. You have a message."

When she arrived in the control room, Corvis moved to the navigator's niche, far to the right of the captain's seat, and pretended to busy himself with checking algae-tank levels but listening intently.

"Beautiful woman, news from the satendrites is that the Northern armada has disappeared into the strange group of objects now heading your way. That will make it harder to fight them.

"As for you, lovely lady, I only wish I had seen you first!" the dark-complected one said. "You take my breath away. I'd like to touch your hair and your face, *and* you seem to be the type of person I would like to spend some time with. Please, when this... crisis...is over, let me buy you a drink. For now, tell me your name...unless you want me to keep calling you 'beautiful woman.' Over."

"Samforites!" Corvis blurted, "what in Hell are samforites?"

"You'll have to ask Tyler," Svet said dreamily. She clicked over to *Transmit*.

"Hello, Tyler," Svet began, "you're kind to overlook my... immodesty. I didn't realize I was transmitting, but now I'm glad I was." She smoothed her hair. "My full name is Svetlana Turgenev. Different people have had different nicknames for me. Maybe you'll make up one of your own. Your name feels good on my tongue, Lieutenant Tyler Washington. We should certainly have a drink *if* we manage to survive. I feel like I'm inside a big lazy cow, who's munching grass, mindless that she is being stalked by professional hunters with high-powered laser guns. Even if the cow could run, it would just lumber along. There's no question about the outcome. It feels like we're just waiting for it all to be over. Sorry to be so hopeless, but you might want to reconsider trying to help us. What I'm trying to say is I want you to stay safe, *whatever* happens. Please take care of yourself. Over."

She might appreciate it if I give her some privacy, Corvis thought.

"The computer says that I need to check the temperature in the freezer," Corvis said. "Sorry to leave you."

"Sounds urgent. You'd better go do that. I can stay on the bridge for a few more minutes," Svet replied.

Svet's Birthday

A terrible crisis was brewing that was beyond their control, but their survival also depended upon keeping up their morale on the ship. At 0700 hours, Corvis knew that the children would be finishing breakfast, and Svet would have been up for at least an hour. He floated to the dining room. "A little birdie told me that someone special has a birthday today," he announced to the children. "Today is *Svet's* birthday. Let's all sing happy birthday to Svetlana!" He started singing and most of the children joined in.

He had guessed the odds favored at least half a dozen children had January birthdays. "Today, we're celebrating at least four more birthdays in the month of January." He waited a second. The children were silent, looking at him with open mouths. "Everyone with a January birthday gets an algae jelly!" He waited another second. The children's faces showed their disappointment, just as he wanted. Then he said, "You know what, *everybody* gets a jelly to celebrate January birthdays!"

At that moment eight robots emerged from the kitchen, as he had programmed them to do. The children cheered. Bearing bright yellow jellies for each of the children, they approached the tables.

The children gobbled their jellies down quickly.

"Breakfast is over," Svet said after the children had finished. "Everyone needs to go to follow their leader to class now." Four little robots, each carrying a different colored flag, yellow, red, green and blue led the children, each of whom knew which robot to follow, out of the dining room.

Svet crooked her finger for Corvis to follow her. They floated through the gym to the aft portal, down to Deck C, and through a short corridor. On one side a door read *Staff Lounge*. The other simply read *Chief Operating Officer*.

Svet's cabin was even larger than Corvis's. Perhaps the engineers expected that the COO would do a lot of entertaining. For her digital wallpaper she had chosen flowers of puce and rose, with green leaves and a sand-colored background. It had a very calming effect. A white sheet floated over her hammock, and she had made a pink sham for her pillow from what might once have been a blouse. A scarlet ribbon twined between the cords that secured the head of her bed to the wall. A faint hint of lavender scented the air.

Corvis floated slowly through the center of her large room impressed with how comfortable she had made it.

"That was sweet," she said, perching at the edge of her hammock, "Birthdays were no big deal to my parents, but a few of my friends had birthday parties when I was growing up. As soon as we blasted off, I knew I would never see my family again, so now I just want to close that chapter of my life. I want to stop missing them. I want to just forget all about them."

She looked like she was about to cry.

"You couldn't forget them if you tried. And it would be sad to forget people you loved. Tell me about the family you left behind," he said.

"My parents were already ancient when I was born. My mother was born in 2010. Can you believe that?! They both worked hard just to provide for our little family. We lived in Kostroma, the town where the Volga River meets the

Kostroma River. Kostroma never changes. It's small, but it's only a few hours from Moscow. Daddy wrote icons for a large export company in the capital. He was paid only after he finished a picture, and he was a perfectionist. He earned very little. So, Mama also had to work. She taught kindergarten."

"That must have been difficult," he said.

"It was, but I was their only child until I was 15, when my baby sister, Oksana, was born. Mama was 50. I don't know whether she and Daddy had planned to have another child or not."

Svet floated to her bar and drew two tubes of protein drink. She offered him one, which he accepted. She returned to her berth.

"I love Oksana so much. She's like a little daughter to me. As a baby, she never cried. She only cooed. Daddy left us as soon as he learned that Oksana had Down Syndrome."

Svet floated out off her bunk, apparently lost in thought.

"Mama had to work during the day, so I finished high school remotely while caring for Oksana at home. For three years Oksana and I were never separated for more than a few minutes at a time."

"Wow," he said, "no wonder you were close."

"While I was in college, I called her every day. For the last eight years, Oksana has attended Sheltered Occupation during the day while Mama was at work. I miss Oksana so much... and Mama..." She took a deep breath and angrily wiped away a tear.

Svet's voice had trailed off to a whisper as she floated to the door. She turned to face me. "Thanks for listening," she said, finally, "and thanks for singing to me."

32
Sockey

JIANN HAD BEEN A fan of soccer on Earth. After she attended her first game on Enceladus, she commented to a friend, "It's a very different game here."

Her friend had said, "Yes, it's played on a field covered with 10 centimeters of fluff snow on top of solid ice, a meter thick."

"Sounds like a recipe for serious injuries."

"You got it," her friend had said. "Because of the violence, some people call it 'sockey'. Get it? Half soccer and half-ice hockey."

Today was the first game of the quarter-finals. Billy was playing and JiAnn, of course, wanted his team to win. But mostly, JiAnn just wanted to get her mind off the threat posed by the invaders from Earth.

The match was held in Saturn Stadium, which had more than 6,000 butt-activated, electrically warmed seats, less than a tenth of which were filled for this game. Dressed in long underwear, a wool sweater, long slacks, a long coat, and a knit cap, JiAnn was ready for the freezing temperature of the unheated stadium. She had arrived early to get a good spot.

Half an hour before the match, dozens of other high-occupancy transports were already landing in a well-ordered dance, touching down just long enough to discharge passengers, and immediately ascending out of the way of other arriving transports.

Her favorite place was halfway up and close to the center line. That way she could see all the action, goal to goal. On her way to her seat, she stopped at the concession stand and bought herself an "otter flipper," bread freshly leavened, hand patted into a long oblong shape, quickly fried, and dusted with confectioner's sugar, spiced with cinnamon, and a cup of hot coffee, black.

The ground of the pitch was covered with newly produced, soft white snow. JiAnn watched as drones painted black lines: boundary rectangle, bisected by a center line with a dot in the middle, and a large circle centered on that dot. At each end, goal lines were also painted in black, a large rectangle with an arc protruding in front, a small rectangle inside the large rectangle, a dot centered on the arc halfway between the larger and smaller rectangle, and a very small rectangle outside the boundary line centered on the dot in the goal space.

The lines melted through the snow almost as soon as they were painted, leaving pigment frozen onto the ice below. Then the goals got set.

Before biting into the warm flipper, she smelled it, savoring the scents of pastry and cinnamon. Then she chewed, savored, swallowed and took a sip of hot coffee to wash it down. *Heavenly,* she thought, as her eyes took in the field surrounded by spectators waiting for the game to begin. *What a wonderful community I live in. My friends are blissfully unaware of the coming invasion. As for me, I'm just going to get lost in the game and forget everything else for an hour or so.*

The Blizzards in blue and the Raptors in black took to the field. JiAnn knew she would have had trouble staying upright on the slippery field, but the players, wearing shoes with soft, rubbery treads where Earthling metal cleats would be, made running on the ice look easy.

As the game was about to begin, everyone in the stadium stood for a lusty singing of the new Enceladus national anthem. Her throat tightened with pride. Each player huddled around the center of the field. The Raptors won the coin toss.

At the kick-off, the ball flew almost all the way to the Blizzard's goal. Two defenders glided in, stopping the ball and kicking it to a midfielder. A Raptor collided with a Blizzard, both players falling and sliding several meters in opposite directions. The first blood of the game appeared as a thin red streak in the white snow.

Billy, playing for the Blizzards, scored the first point of the game, heading the ball into the Raptors' goal. *Until recently, I would have noticed him as just another good player. Now I realize just how gifted he is. How could anyone even consider sending the Apprentice Dragomark into harm's way?* She was so consumed with this thought that she didn't notice who had won.

33
Cluster Research

CORVIS · NURSERY

DESPERATE FOR IDEAS ABOUT how to protect the *Nursery*, Corvis remembered Svet's suggestion that he find out more about the cluster of objects chasing them. He replayed Billy's briefing. "A group of fighters, launched from Ghastli spaceport in Montenegro in November…" The briefing was from January 8, so he searched "Montenegro" and "Ghastli Spaceport," and every synonym for these terms he could think of, and dates from October 2099 to January 8, 2100. He only got general articles about Montenegro in return. He tried "Montenegro Spaceport." Still nothing. Just before giving up, he tried just "Ghastli," by itself. He received a long article from the <u>Financial Flash</u> dated May 1, 2099.

Kind of old. But it might be worth scanning. He made a few notes. Title: "Is Brobdingnagian Ghastlich Insane?" Background: On June 23, 2058, Ghastli, aged about 5 or 6 years, was rescued from a troop of baboons among which he had been living. More than a dozen baboons were killed to get the boy away from them. He could not speak but made baboon sounds and walked like a baboon. Resisting all training in personal hygiene and basic socialization, he was placed in a mental hospital in Cape Town, South Africa. On January 22, 2079, he escaped the hospital. Details were spotty after that. He was a capo in the Ahmed crime family for some time. He then murdered Ali Ahmed and formed Family Ghastli. "Appearing naked, covered only in dried blood, Ghastli has a reputation for personally executing heads of crime families who refuse to pay tribute."

He was currently the wealthiest man on Earth...or was until the bombs dropped.

He shared this with Billy, who replied, "Good effort! I'll tell give the information to JiAnn, and maybe she can find out more."

Don't Want to Know

Nursery

When he went to the gym, he found Gabrielle Gondjout and Charity Segy already working out there. Gabrielle wore a yellow jumpsuit, and Charity a pink one. Gabrielle was using a rowing machine while Charity was doing heavy leg presses against strong resistance cables.

"Hello," he greeted them.

"Hello, Cap'n Crow," they chimed together.

He stepped onto the Foot-Grabber for his warmup. "How are you young women doing?"

"You know..." Gabrielle said sadly.

"Life goes on," Charity added without hope.

"Do you know what's happening on Earth?"

"We can tune in the news, but I, for one, don't want to see it," Gabrielle said. "It must be awful."

"We have enough to worry about, ourselves, right here on the *Nursery*," Charity said almost defiantly.

"So, you know that we're being chased?"

"We do! They aren't going to kill us, are they?" Gabrielle hoped.

"It reminds me of when the soldiers were coming to the village," Charity said, her face filled with fear. "I hope we will survive."

"I'm *positive* we will make it," he lied.

"Why do you say that?" Gabrielle asked.

"The Enceladus Space Force is coming to protect us from the bad guys," he said, more confidently than he felt. *Good,* he thought, *now they'll spread positive, hopeful vibes.* "How are the little ones taking it?"

"They don't know what's coming," Charity replied. "I hope you know how to fly the *Nursery* through what's ahead."

"We got our hands full," Gabrielle said, "just keeping them doing their homework."

"It's good you're helping them. Little minds need to learn."

"That's true, Cap'n Crow," Charity commented cheerily. "They're learning every day."

He finished his warmup and attached cables to his ankles and wrists to do stomach crunches.

"How long until we get to Enceladus?" Gabrielle asked.

"We should land in about 16 days, 23 hours, 14 minutes and three seconds, but who's counting?" he stated.

Gabrielle laughed.

34
Lunch with Billy

JiAnn • Enceladus

AFTER OBSESSING FOR DAYS, JiAnn resolved that Billy should not go out to rescue the *Nursery*. She had decided that the *Nursery certainly must* be saved and that the invaders must be defeated, but Billy was absolutely not the person to do it. The only question was how to prevent that from happening. Talking to Dioikis would be worse than useless. In the general's mind, Billy was an ace pilot, chosen by his peers to lead the squadron. *Billy's role as Dragomark Apprentice is a distantly secondary issue to Dioikis.*

It was military strategy, so President Cly had no significant input. She had to appeal directly to Billy.

She called him from her tiny parlor. "Are you free for lunch?" JiAnn asked.

"Sure," Billy replied, "But I'm on call, so I might have to leave quickly."

"I understand. How about the Dizzy Crab?" JiAnn asked.

"Yes! That's a fun place."

JiAnn got a table by the window so they could look out at the cherry grove, where the trees were in full bloom. *I know they are forced into bloom, but they are lovely. In early October,* JiAnn thought, *fresh fruit will be harvested here. That will be a happy time.*

While waiting for Billy, JiAnn watched a crew of three workers in orange coveralls, and seemingly unnecessary white hardhats in the grove, about 10 meters from the sidewalk, hovering around a manhole surrounded by an orange temporary fence. *They're probably working on the electrical system. Not enough equipment for waterworks.*

A couple, both wearing hooded jackets that obscured their gender, walked hand-in-hand on the sidewalk. Two noisy mini-rockets, commonly called cigars or simply gars, whizzed by, about three meters above ground, followed by a personal transport at a more comfortable six-meter altitude. *Life goes on while enemies approach at half a million kilometers per hour*. Her pulse quickened.

When Billy arrived, JiAnn was already sipping her beer. Their table was spread with a red and white checked cloth. Reproductions of ancient rock bands adorned the walls. Old-fashioned soft rock music played in the background. Every table was full of talkative customers, some of them having drunk several shots, spoke rather loudly.

"We were in the trainers today, fighting mock battles with simulated fighters from Earth," Billy said, looking excited as he slipped into his chair.

"That will be serious combat when it comes," JiAnn said, handing Billy a digital menu.

The waiter arrived a moment later. "I'll have a Crab Louis," JiAnn told him.

"I'll have the red snapper with parsnip fries," Billy said, handing the waiter his device, "and a beer like hers."

"I went to a lecture at the observatory last night," JiAnn said as the waiter moved away.

"Was it interesting?" Billy asked.

"Yes, it was. We looked at Earth, 'then and now.' How do *you* feel about Earth?"

"I always thought I would like to visit there some day. Mom and Dad talked about how beautiful it was, what wonderful memories they had and on, and on. Honestly, I got sick of hearing their nostalgia about Earth. I know the names of famous people and places there, but I don't know anyone, personally, who lives on Earth. And yet, I still wanted to see for myself the Grand Canyon, Mount Fuji, the Pyramids, and so on. I know that there were more people there than I can imagine. Now...this war! It sounds awful."

Lunch arrived.

"I'm an Earthling," JiAnn said, "or at least I was born there." She dug into her salad. "I can't help feeling nostalgic... like your parents, I guess. But seeing Earth now through the telescope, it breaks my heart. It's not a little blue marble any longer. From here, Earth looks like a tiny ball of mud. It's brown, glowing faintly orange."

She fell silent as she recalled leaving Earth quickly, with only the clothes on her back, her purse, and her wedding ring. Abandoning her husband, Mike tore at her heart, even though she wasn't sure he would even miss her. *He's probably dead by now.* Missing all her colleagues and students at the university, and her twin sister, JiUdi, leaving without being able even to say goodbye, in order to fly to this secret colony...and now they were dead or dying. Her sadness and guilt weighed on her spirit like a boulder.

"Sorry to be so down, she signed. "How's the snapper?" she asked, not quite ready to broach the subject, the reason for inviting him to lunch.

"I lost you for a while there... the fish is the best," he said. Then, reflectively, "A few months ago, before the war actually started, I wasn't that interested. Earth History Class was boring, just more of the same, one war after another. Earthlings are still stuck in a rut. Far away countries trying to conquer the world, others trying to protect the world, differing opinions depending on what country wrote the history. It didn't seem like it would affect us much. But now that so many people I know are losing people they love, I realize that human beings there, billions of them are dying. It's horrible!" He shuddered.

"Speaking of dying," JiAnn said, awkwardly approaching her topic, "do you think it's wise for the... for *you* to lead the charge against the Northern Confederacy?"

Billy blinked and shook his head in confusion. "Who else...? I was chosen by my teammates to lead the elite squadron."

"That's not my point," JiAnn struggled to continue "You, you have so much to offer...in other areas. You're *needed* ... to interpret for the satendrites...what they see..."

JiAnn froze, hearing Billy's phone buzz. *Oh God, we've just started to talk.*

"I've got to run. Sorry, we have a mandatory formation in 15 minutes," Billy said taking a large last bite of his unfinished lunch and carrying a handful of fries. "Don't worry about me." He paused and followed up. "I've been well trained." Billy was smiling, but JiAnn read tension under the bravado.

I wish your training had included a dash of common sense. "Be well!" she encouraged against all her foreboding.

Again, I didn't say goodbye. And this time, I could have.

35
Mass Gain

CORVIS • NURSERY

HE'D BEEN THINKING THAT he needed to get in shape for the coming conflict. His reactions would need to be lightning quick soon.

Corvis's job as captain of the Nursery was far less physically demanding than that of an ICU nurse. Looking in the mirror while shaving, he noticed that his face looked puffy. *Water? Microgravity effects? More likely fat.* He'd been snacking constantly to relieve his fear.

After arguing with himself over other priorities that needed my attention, he finally convinced himself to go to the gym and check his mass. His weight was zero, of course. In the gym, he climbed into the scale, a contraption with a box about a cubic meter in volume aligned with *Nursery's* direction of travel. He put his hand on top of his head, knowing the ride would be bumpy. The scale accelerated his body against the line of *Nursery's* travel and then with it, over and over. It was like being inside a drink shaker. After half a dozen quick oscillations, the scale stopped moving, and the numbers on the readout stopped spinning.

He got out but had to steady himself because he felt so dizzy. He read his mass and couldn't believe what he saw. His normal weight/mass was 68 kilograms. Now my mass was 72 kilograms.

I'm going to have to eat regular meals, cut out snacks, and get a lot more exercise. Danger was coming. Being overweight wouldn't help.

Since he was already in the gym, he did three and a half miles on the foot grabber.

Squadron Deployed

Enceladus

Back on the bridge, he was patched into the meeting of the squadron. A hologram of General Dioikis, dressed formally in his uniform with all hisribbons and medals, addressed the group. He was the picture of confidence. The pilots were already in their blue jumpsuits and seated at little tables. "You are the hope of all the citizens of Enceladus and of more than 300 children, as well," the general reminded them.

Then he demanded rhetorically, "Were we born to become slaves?"

The pilots thundered "No, Sir! We're Dans!"

"Ladies and gentlemen, you are outgunned more than 20 to 1, but you are faster and brighter than the enemy by far. Your teamwork exceeds my highest expectations."

Twenty to one! How can you say that and just move on to the next topic? Their mission is hopeless, and the Nursery *is lost!*

"You will deploy 15 minutes from now. Do you have any questions?"

The pilots talked among themselves.

A woman raised her hand.

"Pistis," Dioikis said.

"What tactical support will we have?"

"Fifteen unmanned stealth laser cannons deployed three days ago. They'll park near *Nursery* and wait for you there."

A long minute passed silently.

"You've trained diligently. You're ready for your mission. If there are no other questions, take to the stars! May God bless each one of you!"

The faces of all five ace pilots looked determined, not worried, as they filed out of the briefing room.

Corvis's own heart was pounding. Five young pilots blasting off at 1 AM to fight a horde of determined, well-armed Earthlings... His heart sank. *They must be terrified.*

On his screen, the briefing room remained visible though empty of people. "Three, two, one... blastoff Birchfield," echoed in the empty room.

Five seconds later, "Blastoff Washington."

Five seconds later, "Blastoff Pistis."

"Soliva, blastoff."

"Blastoff Reitmann."

A few seconds later, Corvis's monitor went blank.

Suddenly, he was aware of how fast his heart was pounding. *They're really coming to help us,* he thought, *come what may, we're no longer alone in this.*

JiAnn to Squadron

Enceladus

Light flickered as the 3D image of the upper half of a gray-haired woman took form in front of my monitor. She wore a formal black top and looked calm, and self-assured, although she fiddled with her hair. Corvis listened as she addressed the squadron.

"Brobding Ghastli is a brutal crime boss who personally delights in torturing not only his enemies but also his own employees, often killing them afterward. It doesn't appear that he has any experience as a fighter pilot, so he may be directing the operation from Earth. He's very dangerous. You definitely don't want him, or his army, to kidnap the children on *Nursery*. I guess I don't need to tell you to be very careful that you, yourselves, do not fall into his hands.

"All of Enceladus is wishing you well."

Relief at Hand

Nursery

Corvis was more than ready to hear from Billy again. His shape appeared much smaller and less well-defined in the new scratchy new hologram. His surroundings were also different than he'd seen before. He was inside the tiny cockpit of a fighter, dim blue light illuminating his face. Seeing him again, even in this form, sent Corvis's pulse up by at least ten beats per minute. His voice was also different, less clear, with thrumming background noise. His eyes shifted from looking directly into the camera to a downward focus, probably on dials in front of him.

"This message is double encrypted but even so, it must be brief. Squadron A of the Enceladus Defense Force has just deployed to your location. Our ETA is 23 February. However, we will push our machines to the limit, and I know you will press yours, too, so that we rendezvous sooner. Over."

Corvis was only partially relieved. *He knows that my main concern is when the enemy fighters will overtake us*. He tried to keep the irritation out of his voice. "Roger that. When is the enemy expected to catch up with us?"

Should I say more? No. Ask a simple question that demands a straight answer. He hit the "send" button.

He debated whether to call Svet in the middle of her sleep cycle but decided to wait until he had the answer to his question.

Too Little, Too Late

Nursery

Billy's rough hologram took shape less than half an hour later. "Unfortunately, the enemy could arrive as soon as 22 February, and they have over a hundred fighters to our five. But remember, they don't want to kill you. They just want to take you hostage. That's something you don't want, and I certainly don't want, but you *will* survive.

"One way you can increase your speed, incrementally... but then, every little bit does help... is to override the autopilot and aim *Nursery* directly at the center of Saturn. That will maximize Saturn's gravitational pull on your ship. It will take you slightly off-course, but you can let the autopilot do a course correction a couple of days before you land. Over."

Corvis was getting ready to respond when another message came in on a different channel.

"It's a terrifying position to be in, no two ways about it, but I know you'll do all you can to reach us, and we to reach you.

I've already set my engines to full power. I'll burn through fuel at an awful rate, but we'll *all* survive. Over."

Corvis wanted to say that he was afraid for the children, but Billy knew that, and truth to tell, Corvis was afraid for himself. *If the children start screaming, and floating around the cabin, it'll only make matters worse. In the past, Svet has been no help at all in disciplining the children during a crisis. Maybe, if she hears advice from Lt. Birchfield,* I thought, *she'll take it to heart.*

"I need your help on another problem." Corvis transmitted, "Children tend to misbehave when *Nursery* is under attack. If they scream and vomit and move about the cabin they could get hurt. How do I control them, so they stay in their seats? Over."

As soon as he sent the transmission, he called Svet. She floated onto the bridge and grabbed a handhold very close to Corvis, her face registered anxiety.

He filled her in. "Elite Squadron has blasted off. They're coming to us at full speed. Meanwhile, we're using Saturn's gravity to the maximum to help us close the gap more quickly."

"Tell me the truth. When will the Enceladans get here?" she whispered.

"They call themselves 'Dans', and they'll intercept us on February 23 at the latest."

"And the bad guys?"

"Maybe as early as February 22."

Svet pushed her fingers against her eyes as if, by doing so she could counteract the emotional terror with physical pain. "We're dead," she said quietly. "There's obviously no way we can survive."

"No," Corvis said, "Even if they take us, we'll still survive. They can't kill us, or they won't have hostages. They'll actually protect us, at least until they step foot on Enceladus."

"What's the difference?"

"Hope," he said. "Believing that we can escape, either before or after they capture us. That's the difference."

She looked at me directly for a long time but said nothing. She was obviously thinking about what I had said.

"If we're taken as hostages, isn't that even worse than death?"

"No. We could still escape... But let's focus on living today and tomorrow."

"That's all we can do," she agreed, looking defeated.

Code Broken

Nursery

An hour earlier, Corvis had asked Billy how to control the children once the fighting began. Billy's face took shape in front of my monitor again. He looked almost happy.

"Put yourself in the position of a child," Corvis heard him say over the distracting noise, "You can't control kids when they're terrified. Just be with them. Comfort them as best you can. Over."

What Billy said was not at all what Corvis expected from a military man, but it made perfect sense.

"Roger that," he responded, "you're going to be a great dad! By the way, which of us is going to be 'Dad' to *our* kids, and which will be 'Daddy?' I think you'll be 'Daddy.' If that's not a proposal, what is? Over."

A hologram of Billy's face reappeared five minutes later, not long enough to be a response to what Corvis had just said. A red frame with white letters surrounded the image, "Highly Sensitive" and "Top Secret" printed on all four sides surrounded his face.

"We have broken the cluster's code. Will share transmissions, but you *must not* refer to any content or react or respond in any way to what you learn about their strategy. Specifically, you must not change course. Continue toward the center of Saturn. Over."

Oh my God this gives us a huge secret weapon, Corvis wanted to shout.

"Roger that," Corvis said quietly. "On a different topic," he transmitted, "I overheard something about samforites. What are samforites? Over."

A half hour later: "[Double encrypted: As we talk, I will send coded chatter.] As for your 'proposal,' Whoa! I think we should get to know each other, in the biblical sense, first. Make sure we're compatible.

"The organisms: they're called satendrites," Billy responded. "They're single-celled organisms that form a single, vast colony of billions of cells. They float about 20 to 100 meters above the surface of Enceladus. They're attracted, electromagnetically, to the electrical impulses in human brains, specifically in the visual cortex."

"But Enceladus has no atmosphere," Corvis transmitted. "How can they float?"

His answer came while he was eating a large bowl of delicious algae spaghetti. "[We have learned that a General Copenhavlad commands the Northern Armada.] They trail long, almost straight filaments of molecular DNA, about a meter between each nucleus, creating webs that look would look like spider webs, only microscopic, far to small to see with the naked eye. Each nucleus is attached to ten to twenty other nuclei."

"You still haven't told me how they float."

It took another half hour to get an answer. [Copenhavlad to Brobding: We need to accelerate faster. Brobding: We are accelerating at maximum consistent with fuel reserved for possible battle. Be patient. We have the upper hand.]

They're having an internal conflict. That's to our advantage. A general isn't going to like being told to be patient.

"They ride on the steam geysers," Billy was saying, "Their webs resist the steam rising in the geysers and that resistance lifts them above the surface, like kites."

"How do they survive without atmosphere?"

"[Copenhavlad: Five defenders launched from Enceladus. We need to reach *Nursery* before they reach us. Brobding: Small defense. Few defenders. Easy to destroy.]

Unfortunately, he's right. The thought left me hopeless.

Billy said, "The steam provides them with moisture, hydrogen and oxygen. They create a micro-atmosphere around each nucleus, all surrounded by a cosmic-ray-resistant cell wall. They photosynthesize glucose with light both from the Sun and from Saturn. They get trace elements from the geysers. The organisms are fairly well understood, biologically, but people's reactions to them are a complete mystery, at least to me."

"What do you mean?"

"[Copenhavlad: We can move faster outside the swarm. Brobding: If you leave Swarm, you break contract. Swarm collects and goes back to inner solar system.] I mean, some people refuse to believe in them."

"Why don't you just grab a sample and show them?"

"[Copenhavlad: Then increase the speed, damn it!] That's harder than it sounds. First, they're microscopic, even the nuclei, and they're floating over geysers, which means they are constantly moving. And then, the colony is at most three layers thick and the layers are separated by at least a meter. Against the background of Saturn, they are totally invisible. We only see them because they are very faintly bioluminescent, and even then, only against the black background of the void."

"I take it you did, eventually, get a sample."

While waiting for Billy's response I received a scratchy, audio-only transmission from Earth.

"Corvis, this is Jake."

Jake? Who...

"I recruited you to take the kids to Enceladus."

Knowing it would take close to an hour to get a reply, Corvis transmitted several questions.

"It's good to hear from you. How are you? Are you still in Congo? What are you doing?"

It turned out Jake's first transmission wasn't finished.

"You're the only... person I know... who is still alive."

Jake was obviously having trouble breathing.

"Every city of any size has been bombed. It's hot and dark here. Hard to breathe. Fled to Namibia. No reason to bomb the desert. No city near here. Traded my Xamba for a solar-diesel-hand-crank generator and transponder.

"Much cannibalism now. Someone has been circling me for days. Probably will eat me. Wanted you to know some secrets before I pass."

Corvis waited, breathing quietly to hear what would come next.

Billy's reply came.

"[Brobding: When engagement begins, Swarm fighters form first wave.] Yes, after five years of trying, a specimen was collected. By the time it was mounted, it was completely dry, so we could fully see all the structures, but not exactly how they functioned."

Corvis was worried about Jake, but he needed to keep transmissions to a minimum. Billy couldn't help, so he continued their game.

"You said some people still don't believe they exist. The specimen should have convinced them."

"[McMathis (a pilot): Six hours in open. Where's my shield? Not fair! Brobding: You're covered now. No whining.]

Morale problems. That's also to our advantage.

"Some doubters were convinced of their existence," Billy said, "but die-hards persisted in saying that it could be a bacterium introduced to the surface by humans and contaminating the instruments. Other specimens have been collected, but it is hard to know how to convince doubters."

At 2300 hours Svet came onto the bridge. "Tell me what you know. I'm so scared. I've kept the children occupied, so they're not worrying about what's coming. But I can't think about anything else. I'm scared sick. I need news, even if it's bad news."

"Let's go to an officer's quarters. We're not transmitting, but call it paranoia, I still feel exposed on the bridge."

The room was small, but neat and clean. White walls waited for digital wallpaper instructions. The gray netting, that would have contained personal possessions, was empty. Corvis floated into the small habitation and hovered near a ledge. Svet floated to the hammock.

"I just got a troubling transmission from Jake."

She looked puzzled and then said, "Jake! When I think about Jake telling us about this mission, it seems like years ago!"

"He's alive in Namibia."

"I hope he will survive."

"Unfortunately, he doesn't expect to live much longer."

Corvis didn't tell her how Jake thought he would die. "He said he had secrets for us, but he got cut off before he told me what they were."

Corvis floated to the refrigerator and took out an algae juice drink for each of them. "It sounds like a horrible existence on Earth now. I'll keep monitoring. Anyway, whatever the secret is, he seems intent on sharing it with me, so I'm sure I'll hear back."

"Now, about our enemies. First, Enceladus has broken their communications code, and we're monitoring everything they say to each other! What we've been calling the cluster, they call themselves a "swarm." The general leading the Northern Armada, Copenhavlad, and the leader of the Swarm, Brobding, are far from unified. And they have motivation problems. On the other hand..."

"I know the other hand. We're screwed. We're utterly, totally screwed. But we're alive. And we can listen to them talking. So, for as long as we're alive we must do what we can to bring these children to Enceladus."

Corvis was tired, but Svet's little speech brought him back to life. "Yes," he said, "on to Enceladus with our last breath."

Svet offered a high five, and he slapped it hard.

"I've got to get back to the children."

I haven't given Svet enough credit for her will to survive and to fight for the children. She's tough, and she's really dedicated to our mission. More importantly, she's right: we can't give up. We can't let fear cloud our thinking. We have to persevere.

He floated back to the bridge where he immediately heard:

"[Copenhavlad: You can catch up with us. Brobding: Watch me leave]." Billy said, "Each nucleus collects light, and they communicate with each other by electromagnetic signaling over their web-like filaments. Together they have tremendous visual capacity."

"They have, what?"

"[Copenhavlad: I show intersect with *Nursery* 21 February 2200 hours. That's not soon enough. Brobding: Be patient.] They *see*," Billy said, "They communicate. With each other. And with humans by means of electromagnetic cell signaling."

So, the enemy's prediction for the time they will arrive is about the same as Enceladus's estimate. Terrifying.Can you die of anxiety? Corvis didn't bother to take his pulse or blood pressure. He knew they were sky-high. Instead, he tried some self-talk: *This is the only moment you have, and this moment isn't that bad. You're worried about what's going to happen in the future...* He forced himself to take a long slow deep breath. That didn't help much, but contact with Billy did, so he kept up the dialogue.

"I understand why there are doubters," he transmitted, pushing off from one end of the bridge to the other while waiting for information.

"[Brobding: Petersen's group, take port flank of ship. Doan's group takes starboard.]

Oh my God, he thought, *we're going to be swallowed up.*

"We haven't isolated it yet," Billy said, "but they must have some kind of lens that takes in light and focuses it. It seems they record images in their DNA."

"When a cell dies, its body floats down to the surface of Enceladus, I suppose," he transmitted.

"[Copenhavlad: Nursery is definitely accelerating more than expected. Brobding: Won't make a difference once we arrive.] No, when a cell dies, it's caught in the web. Neighbor cells disassemble the constituents. One neighboring cell divides and the constituents of the deceased cell are fed to the two new sister cells.

"Satendrites are very sensitive to electro-magnetic impulses."

"How do you know that?" he asked.

"[Pilot Isolongi: Mayday! Mayday! My main engine failed. Brobding: Use secondary. Mechanic on the way.]

Thank God, they have a problem. They'll be delayed getting to us.

"The colony can act like a single lens, visualizing objects at vast distances in great detail. To do that, they need to communicate with each other somehow."

"But how could you possibly prove that they can see?" Corvis asked.

"[Copenhavlad: We are NOT slowing down for mechanical problems in one of your rockets! What's going on? Brobding: Fighter being repaired. Be patient.] We have to prove two things at once: that they can see and that they communicate with humans."

"That seems almost impossible," he transmitted.

"[Copenhavlad: I will not allow the Nursery to slip through our fingers. Brobding: We have 100 fighters. Nursery will not slip through.]

Corvis grabbed a handhold and listened intently.

"Doubters still doubt, but I think I can convince *you*, at least. We saw your ship and the armadas, in detail, soon after you left Earth. But the cluster was a little fuzzy," Billy said.

Trying to sound bored, even though his heart was pounding outside his chest, he transmitted, "Even though I'm convinced, I'll play the devil's advocate. It's easy for you to say that after the fact."

"[Isolongi: Engine repaired. Full speed ahead.]

That didn't last long. They'll be bearing down on us faster than ever now.

"The fact is that Enceladus planned and executed a response with the best equipment and personnel we could muster long before our telescopes could visualize the problem."

"Point well taken," he transmitted.

"[Copenhavlad: We need to make up for lost time!] Despite numerous events when satendrites have warned us of distant dangers that we were able to mitigate or even avoid, doubters continue to claim that the Dragomark, the one who speaks for the satendrites, is a charlatan," Billy said.

To Tyler

Nursery

At 0400 hours Svet came onto the bridge looking tired and full of stress, but she smelled like fresh lavender.

"I couldn't sleep," she said, "What have you learned?"

"We've talked all night, using code" he replied, "but I haven't learned all that much.

"One of their fighters had mechanical problems, but they fixed it quickly, and now they are speeding toward us fast."

Svet said "I need to send a brief message. It's overdue." She sat erect with a pleasant smile and started.

"To Tyler: This will be short. I want you and I need you. Please stay safe. P.S. I love you. We'll hold each other soon. Over."

She said to Corvis, "This waiting is hard."

She seemed to be looking to him for strength, but Corvis was really scared himself. "Yes," he agreed, "My nerves are all on edge... The elite squadron will be here soon. Meanwhile, try to get some rest."

Earth

"Before you leave," he said, "I want to play for you a briefing on the situation on Earth."

Svet looked apprehensive.

"Over three billion people have died so far. Bombing continues, the strikes too numerous and widespread to count.

"It's impossible to find transports to the Moon or Mars. No more vessels are leaving Earth because all that could lift off have left and none are returning," a female voice reported. "Multiple layers of radioactive dust clouds are absorbing and trapping heat from the sun, but little light is reaching us. More after this..."

"By the way, have you heard anything more from Jake?" Svet asked.

"No. It's been more than ten hours... I'll keep listening."

"I guess he didn't make it," she said sadly.

Radio Chatter [double encrypted]

There had been no sound from the radio for several hours. Corvis rested in one of the bunks on the bridge. Maybe he dozed. He woke up when he heard chatter.

["Repeat. Negative," a blonde woman in a black turtleneck said. Behind her was a large open space with several figures, some walking, some watching monitors on a distant wall. She was obviously on a mothership of some type. "As long as you are under the protection of the Family you will remain in close configuration."]

Corvis watched intently hoping to pick up some useful information.

["But we must have visualization of the squadron from Enceladus. We need to plan a strategy. Can you give us a rationale for refusing our request?"] a woman with brown hair in a gray uniform asked. She looked frustrated as she spoke from a tiny cockpit.

["Negative. Family rule. No rationale will be offered,"] black turtleneck replied.

Corvis's radar calculated their distance to be just over 14,000 kilometers.

Alignment

Billy appeared on Corvis's screen. "The Group, the *Nursery*, and Elite Squadron are all in perfect alignment. *Nursery* is very large, so Group can't see the squadron, and, supposedly, squadron can't see the Group. Over."

"So, *Nursery* is your shield? Over."

Corvis jumped because Billy's response came almost immediately. "Roger. However, the quickest way to your location is a straight line, both for us and for the enemy. I consider you, in particular, precious cargo. I will die before I let you fall into their hands. Over."

"Please take care," Corvis said, "I don't like to hear you talk about your own death. Over."

"Heads up. We're closing in upon each other at a very rapid rate. The cluster is accelerating faster than we had imagined possible. Fighting will begin within one or two days. Over."

Emotions were tearing Corvis apart. Billy's willingness to die for him made me love him even more, while the fact that Brobding and his fighters were approaching so fast had a hold on Corvis's lungs.

After lights-out, sleep did not come, not for Corvis, and probably not for Svet, nor, possibly, for many of the older children, either. In the night hours, Corvis listened to the sounds of the ship every five minutes the clap of distant thunder and the long high swoosh of the release of deadly explosive pressure within the containment walls of one pair of engines, the constant whir of the other engines, the never-ending flow of water to and from toilets, algae vats, dehumidifiers and humidifiers, fans moving air through scrubbers and back into circulation. What Corvis never heard in this small interplanetary town hurtling through space were the sounds of footsteps. At night, even on his monitors, he didn't hear the voices of children. After lights out, the *Nursery* was like a breathing, sleeping, digesting giant organism. The children on the *Nursery* may have slept, but many of the caregivers could not. *This is the calm before the storm,* Corvis thought.

Consultation

"Svet, can you come to the bridge?" Corvis Letred her.

She arrived wearing a yellow jumpsuit.

"We need to prepare the children for the coming battle," Corvis told her quietly.

"How can we prepare them for another battle?" Svet asked. "They have been through so much violence already."

"We'll have to reassure them, even if we're not confident, ourselves."

Svet looked serious. "You and I need to discuss safety. You'll put up the shields before fighting begins?" she asked.

"Definitely! And the children will have to remain buckled in their seats as much as possible." Corvis wanted to say that even a little time out of their seats could be dangerous, but he decided not to argue.

"It's not realistic to expect them to stay seated for long periods of inactivity," she replied. "The older girls and I will supervise and keep them in the cabin. As soon as we have any turbulence, we will get them buckled in quickly."

"It sounds like you've thought about this. Thanks for being prepared. If I can do anything, let me know," Corvis said.

As captain of the ship, he didn't like the sound of the last sentence, but it seemed in keeping with Billy's advice.

Explosion

Knowing that they would soon be in the middle of a fight, Corvis was just about to deploy the shields when something hit the rear of the ship and exploded, sending shudders through *Nursery*. *What was that!?* Near panic, Corvis instantly hit the Shields button and they went up.

According to his monitor, several children were screaming and clinging to Svet and the older girls. They struggled to buckle the children into their seats. Older children sat rigidly in their own seats, looking terrified.

We were hit to stern, Corvis thought. *That means Billy is safe. But that also means the battle has started.*

Corvis immediately tried to replay the recording from the aft camera to see how close the enemy was. But he got a message on his monitor reading, "Error: Aft camera not installed."

The enemy had hit the camera and destroyed it. Corvis immediately transmitted, double-encrypted, to Billy, "We've been hit. Aft camera was destroyed. No other damage noted." Then he turned a midship camera to stern to give him a view of the space behind the *Nursery*. They also had radar coverage.

In front of his monitor, the hologram of a thin man in a teal-blue uniform, gray close-cropped hair, and a neat goatee, suddenly took shape. "*Nursery*. This is General Copenhavlad of the Northern Confederacy, from here we will be escorting you to Enceladus..."

Like hell you will, Corvis wanted to shout in response, but he decided on a more considered answer. He was trying to compose the precise words of his reply when Billy appeared in hologram.

"Negative," Billy countered. "*Nursery* is currently under the protection of the Autonomous Enceladus Defense Force."

Ignoring Billy's transmission, Copenhavlad continued, "Our next shot will take out one of your engines if you do not immediately surrender."

Oh my God, they don't care if they kill us, after all! Corvis took a deep breath and forced himself to remain calm. He remembered that dead hostages are useless. Collecting himself, he resolved to use a businesslike voice.

"Without all four engines, *Nursery* won't be able to steer a direct course to Enceladus," he transmitted with encryption turned off. Corvis waited several minutes for a reply, but none came. The threat hung in the air.

Chatter

A midship camera recorded a bright explosion to stern.

"A globe has been destroyed. We must retaliate," an African man in the teal Northern Confederacy uniform said.

While Corvis was glad a globe had been destroyed, he worried about how the enemy would take revenge.

"We have complete tactical superiority," a shirtless man with matted beard replied. "We will take the initiative when we are closer to the target."

"I'm not comfortable with that," Copenhavlad replied.

"Be comfortable that you are under the protection of the Family!"

Four almost simultaneous explosions lit the void.

Chatter: "You must respond with fire."

They still aren't fighting back. Either they don't have sufficient ammunition, which is extremely unlikely, or they can afford to bide their time, Corvis thought.

"We were contracted to deliver you to Enceladus. We will deliver you. I need no more advice from you."

"[Double encrypted to Billy: Are they aware that *Nursery's* hull, actually five skins are very thin? If our hull is even grazed by a laser beam, we will develop a fatal leak.]"

"[Double encrypted to Corvis: Do you have an escape module?]"

That's right! We could escape in our life raft. But a minute later Corvis despaired.

"[Double encrypted to Billy: Our escape vessel is designed for low Earth orbit. It has almost no propulsion and uses only parachutes to slow its descent. Enceladus has no atmosphere, and so far from help, it's a deathtrap.]"

Corvis's heart felt heavy.

"[But you could inflate it inside *Nursery*.]"

"[Negative. There's no space large enough. But there's a portal out to the Escape Module; it wasn't designed to be brought inside the ship.]" *He's right, though. Remaining attached to the ship, it could provide some temporary shelter if* Nursery *loses its integrity.*

Corvis saw five explosions to port and no apparent response from the group.

Then another four explosions behind the *Nursery.*

Billy's smiling face appeared. Unencrypted he said, "Take heart, my friend, fourteen of their globes have been destroyed. Their fighters are gradually being exposed. They're still almost 12,000 kilometers behind you."

In space, and at this speed, 12,000 kilometers is nothing! Corvis thought. *But Billy is trying to give encouragement.* I heard chatter from the cluster.

"This is unacceptable! We must let them know that they can't get away with this!"

"Watch for a vessel leaving the *Nursery,*" Brobding said.

Over several minutes, Corvis saw two more explosions in the midst of the cluster.

Tyler's face appeared on my monitor, his message unencrypted "Two more of your hiding places up in smoke," he taunted.

Three globes lit up on the outer edge of the Swarm.

Soon I lost count of the explosions: two here, three there, over and over.

Billy's jubilant face appeared again: "Approximately half of their globes have been popped! The satendrites now visualize the full number of fighters."

"How many fighters do they have?" Corvis asked.

Billy's smile disappeared. "You don't want to know."

"Yes. I do."

"101 in the group and five in the armada, plus two heavily armed motherships."

Nursery Sees Group

Corvis had been pushing the *Nursery* for several days at maximum thrust, but now his heart sank. Through the mid-ship camera's zoom lens, he saw rank on rank of fighters in close formation less than 500 kilometers from the *Nursery*. "I see the Group now. They appear as tiny dots. The explosions made them seem much closer. When will they reach *Nursery*?" Corvis asked barely able to speak.

"In less than two hours."

"And when will you arrive?"

"I wondered when you would ask."

A dazzling white fighter with blue wings, red engines, and purple laser guns whizzed past the windshield so close that Corvis jumped. It tipped slightly as if to wave at the *Nursery*. It was followed by four more that flew a bit farther away.

Corvis laughed and cried at the same time. *Billy's here!*

He immediately opened the cabin monitor so Billy and the other pilots could see the children while he made the public announcement. "The Autonomous Enceladus Space Force is here. They're going to take us safely to our new home!"

The children waved their arms and cheered.

Corvis wanted to leave it at that, but he decided to tell the truth.

"Our ride will get rocky before we arrive at our new home. Our ship will get tossed back and forth. When that happens, the safest place will be in your seat with your seat belt fastened."

"I knew you would get here in time!" Corvis transmitted to Billy and the others.

"This is my first time to actually see the children. Even on my little monitor, I can see that they have been traumatized on Earth. I think I speak for the entire squadron: Nothing, and no one will stop us from getting these wounded little kids to Enceladus!"

"You got here much faster than I expected," Corvis transmitted.

"You came to us almost as fast as we came to you! The next few days'll be a little crazy, so buckle up!"

"You know we will!" Corvis replied.

Over the next hour, he watched the cluster get larger on the monitor. Soon he could see details on individual fighters. The smaller fighters were dark brown and black, with dull bronze engines and red laser pods. They were about two-thirds as large as the Enceladan fighters but had just as many cannons. He saw only one larger fighter, and even then Corvis had only a brief glimpse as a round shape blocked it from view. It was mostly yellow. As his pulse quickened, he was glad that with the shields deployed, the children couldn't see the horde of warships closing in on the *Nursery* so quickly.

Another half hour passed in silence.

Suddenly, two more globes exploded much closer to the *Nursery*. Chatter followed immediately.

Copenhavlad: "I command you to return fire."

Bearded one: "Not yet. But we're almost close enough."

"I hired you. I can fire you."

"No one fires Brobding," Beardo said.

So, the one with the beard is Brobding. He's the baddest of the bad guys.

Corvis watched the monitor as three more globes exploded behind the *Nursery*. Then tracer beams flashed into the void in front of them. *When they start firing back, they're really going to unload on us.* Corvis thought. *This is how it ends. It'll soon be over for all of us.* It alarmed Corvis to feel more interested than afraid.

Behind the *Nursery,* white fighters dodged a huge yellow one with a double cockpit, firing repeatedly. The yellow fighter, more than twice as large as those from Enceladus, had beige wings and dark brown engines, with four laser emplacements in front. Corvis counted at least twenty cannons on its surface.

The yellow fighter suddenly erupted in a fireball.

Billy's determined face appeared as he gloated. "One down and only 105 to go!"

Thank God! Corvis watched yellow fighters and white fighters fire on each other for several minutes. A white fighter flew toward the cluster. Two yellow fighters pursued it; a white fighter swooped in and fired on both yellow fighters.

A large blue ray indicated a laser beam, but Corvis couldn't determine the source. Suddenly, a brown fighter in the middle of the Group caught fire.

"This is Lieutenant Pistis," a woman in an Enceladus uniform taunted, "I just killed one of your fighters. Come and get me if you're not too scared."

I don't know if it's a good idea to anger them. Corvis thought. *We're at a huge disadvantage. You're the expert, but* Nursery *is in the middle. You do remember that don't you? Our ship with*

311 children on board? We could die in this conflict. When will the other fighters get here? Hope. I've got to hold on for a little while longer.

"Your fighters will return to the Group," Brobding commanded.

Copenhavlad responded, "We can use the p..."

"P? P? Were you going to say that you could use the paralyzing probe? Like the one you are now experiencing? Did you think I would be stupid enough to accept this contract without carrying the probe myself?

"You have destroyed one of my ships and killed two of my best soldiers!" Copenhavlad shouted.

"I've disabled the probe long enough for your fighters to return to the Swarm."

Four yellow fighters returned to the cluster. Five minutes passed in total silence.

According to Corvis's instruments the closest fighter in the "Swarm" was just 10 kilometers behind the *Nursery*. The most distant fighter was only 15 kilometers behind. *They're here! And they're thirsty for blood.*

Close Combat

"Engage!" Brobding commanded. "Company A to port, Company B to starboard."

Corvis's heart accelerated as a monitor showed dozens of brown fighters redistributing themselves efficiently into two hemispheres. The *Nursery* was about to be surrounded.

Billy's fighters were nowhere to be seen. "Where are you?" Corvis whispered to the air in the bridge.

From behind the *Nursery*, three brown fighters peeled off to port and three to starboard. The void lit up as blue and green laser beams crisscrossed. White fighters appeared out of nowhere. Sparks flew at different, unpredictable angles. The *Nursery* heaved heavily to port, sending Corvis's coffee tube crashing into the wall.

More sparks flew as brown fighters were hit but limped away. Another glowing brown ship spiraled off wildly.

A young woman in an Enceladan uniform, her blonde hair in a tight bun, broadcast. "My name is Lieutenant Reitmann, Harriet Reitmann. I just killed one of your ships!"

I get it, Corvis thought *the Enceladans are goading the bad guys so that they'll make mistakes.*

Four Dan pilots hooted their praise unencrypted.

Two white fighters flew directly toward the cluster. As soon as brown fighters followed, the white ships broke off and two more white ships flew in. Three ships exploded within the cluster as white ships flew off at right angles.

Another blue beam dazzled close to Corvis's windshield. Suddenly, *Nursery* rocked first to port and then quickly to starboard as another brown ship exploded nearby. Corvis's stomach wanted to surrender its contents. His monitor of the cabin showed Svet and the girls comforting the little ones. Many of the children were crying. Corvis wished he could do something to help them.

"It won't be much longer," he announced over the PA.

A thin but healthy man's face smiled. "This is Soliva, Dalisay Soliva, and you can thank my unmanned laser cannons for killing three of your ships."

Four voices shouted without encryption, "Yay, Soliva!"

We're outnumbered, Corvis thought, *and yet our morale is so much better than theirs.*

A brown fighter flew so close to Corvis's windshield that he could count the rivets in along its bronze engine. As soon as he stopped shaking, he decided to leave the bridge and help out with the children.

Just as he entered the cabin, the ship tilted suddenly. An older girl caught a toddler by his ankle as he recoiled from a wall in the cabin. "Good catch, Martha," Corvis said.

"Sorry, Cap'n Crow," a little boy said.

"Sorry for what?" Corvis asked.

"I wet my pants," he said.

Corvis whispered in his ear, "I almost did, too."

The little boy laughed and slapped his thighs.

Svet and the older children helped little ones change their clothes and sip fluids from the tubes robots delivered from the kitchen. One girl steadied another as she floated out of the restroom.

Corvis crouched on the opposite side of the robot Svet was working with and encouraged a little girl to drink some fluid. Suddenly the ship lurched again. As soon as the ship was on an even keel, Corvis urged the girl to take another sip.

Later, he floated to the kitchen and found some small snacks for himself to keep his strength up.

When he returned to the bridge, his eyes went instantly to a monitor. Billy looked exultant on the screen. "That's six down! And most of the globes have been destroyed! Where are you going to hide now, you cowards?"

Corvis was just beginning to breathe easy when about twenty fighters roared forward from behind us, beams firing continuously. Dozens of sparks flared. A fireball indicated a kill. Tyler came on, "Great coordination, guys. That's one more down!"

Two more brown fighters whizzed by inches in front of Corvis's window. A bright flash directly across the bow made Corvis's eyes close involuntarily. A second blaze blinded him again. *Nursery* tumbled 180° one way, then the same amount the other direction.

"Guess you forgot about our unmanned cannons," Pistis gloated.

Four more ships were picked off, in rapid succession, within the formation.

"Easy, peezy!" Tyler crowed.

Before he finished speaking, very near the *Nursery* to port, a bright spark indicated another hit. Corvis couldn't see the color of the fighter that fell away in a glowing ball.

"Mayday!" was all the female pilot could say before the ship exploded.

After about three minutes of continuous laser fight, four more fireballs burned. Corvis held my breath, waiting for the radio silence to end. After two more fireballs erupted, two brown fighters returned to the Swarm.

He had lost count of the number of fighters destroyed, and I didn't know how many, if any, of them were from Enceladus. Corvis hadn't heard Billy's voice for several minutes. *Please let Billy be OK*, he prayed.

Svet entered the bridge just as Billy's face appeared. He looked sad but resolute. "We've lost a hero. A great patriot. An ace pilot. Our sister Harriet Reitmann will be remembered forever. Our four surviving ships will honor her memory by defeating the enemy's 83 remaining fighters. Dans will never be slaves!"

"She died. For us," Corvis said.

"Oh my, God," Svet said, "I must send a message to Tyler."

"Of course," Corvis said.

[Double encrypted: "Tyler, my love. Please don't take any unnecessary chances. I want to see you whole when we reach Enceladus."]

His response was immediate. ["You, too. We all have to be strong and, above all, smart! Stay safe."]

Immediately *Nursery's* monitors showed six explosions.

"That's for Harriet, you SOBs," Billy pronounced.

[Copenhavlad: "You've made a mess of this operation. You're down to 64 fighters, and we're approaching their base. It will soon be impossible to capture the hostages!"]

36
Engine Failure

A FRENZY OF LASER beams crisscrossed in front of Corvis, followed by a rapid succession of explosions to port and starboard.

He caught sight of a streak of brown just before the rear end of *Nursery* was hit and hit hard. The ship went careening off course, and everything not tied down floated to port. Corvis struggled to hold on as he hovered in front of the displays. Fighting continued outside, but Corvis's focus was on the damage the *Nursery* had sustained.

He checked the air pressure, and there was no leak, but a red frame flashed. Inside the warning read "Plasma Engine A failure! Explosion imminent. Jettison Magma-Plasma Engine A."

In fear, he radioed Billy, "A warning says to jettison a plasma engine, but we won't get to Enceladus without it."

Billy replied, "The engine will explode and destroy your ship. Jettison it *now*!"

I can't, but I must! I must! Corvis thought.

The warning now read, "Engine will explode in Ten, nine, eight..."

Corvis forced himself to press the "Jettison" button.

The entire universe instantly went crazy. Everything familiar was spinning past him so fast that he saw everything at once, yet nothing in particular. *I* am *going to* die, he thought.

He instinctively reached out his left hand to grab something, anything, and it was struck by a hard object that twisted his arm in a way it had never twisted before. The searing pain forced me to pull his hand to his chest.

"Billy!" he screamed, "I can't do anything! Everything is spinning!"

"Steady!" Billy said and then repeated, "Steady. Next time something solid hits you, try to grab hold."

Corvis heard Copenhavlad's voice: "Hold your fire!"

He felt a hard whack on his shoulder. Nothing to grab. A slam to his right foot. The spinning was accelerating. He grabbed, but his hands caught only air. The spinning intensified. The next time his feet touched something, he pushed off. After a second, his body crashed into a wall. A handhold touched his hand but was gone in a millisecond. *This has to end soon,* he thought. *A human body can't withstand this kind of punishment. I'll be dead, but at least this hell will end.*

"I can't see anything, and I can't do anything! I'm tumbling out of control, in chaos!" he cried.

"Patience," Billy said, "*Nursery* is spinning very fast. You won't be able to see anything clearly, so *close your eyes* and use your sense of touch. Bend your knees. Next time you touch a wall, curl into a full crouch. Do not push off, but rather, use both hands to find something to hang on to."

Corvis followed Billy's directions. The darkness was not as frightening as the chaos. He felt a portal whiz past and, instantly, the control panel. A handhold escaped his grasp, then another. He grabbed the next one with his left hand.

It nearly yanked his arm off, but he hung on despite the excruciating pain and grabbed the same handhold with his right hand.

Opening his eyes, he was able to focus on an area directly in front of him. Objects he had forgotten about shot past at incredible speed. A pen and an empty drink tube went past, deadly projectiles, both.

"I'm on the wall," he reported, "but I'm several meters from the control panel." Instinctively, he kept his whole body plastered against the wall. One foot found a handhold and the other joined it.

"Try to reach the handhold next closer to the control panel with one hand," Billy instructed.

The instant he released his right hand, it flailed wildly toward the center of the room, taking most of his upper body with it. Pain in his wounded left shoulder seemed to scream. With the focus of survival, he used all his strength to pull his right arm back to the wall. Resisting the strong temptation to grasp the handhold, he finger-walked his right hand toward the next handhold. Grasping that one he folded his wounded left arm under his chest, never allowing it to leave the wall.

The cover of the fuse box flew past. "Billy, I shouted, things that were screwed down are coming loose!"

"Don't panic," Billy replied. "Are you getting closer to the control panel?"

"Yes, but it's a slow process."

"It will get harder," Billy said, "*Nursery's* spin is speeding up. It could break apart soon, so you need to get to the control panel."

This ship is going to break into pieces, Corvis thought, *but until that happens, I'm going to do my best to resume control.*

Corvis's painful left arm was too weak to reach for a handhold, so he reached with his right hand, held, and let his left hand creep up to join it. Then he reached again with his right arm. His legs helped by finding handholds pushing his body forward.

After what seemed like hours of concentrated effort, he reached the control deck. It had built-in handles underneath and on the sides that he had never noticed before. "I'm at the control panel!" I shouted.

"Good!" Billy replied, "Now look for a button that says 'Autopilot' or just 'Auto,' and push it."

"I see it, a huge yellow button, but I can't lift either hand to push it," he said.

"*Nursery* is about to break up. Find a way to push it!" Billy commanded.

Corvis moved his head over the panel and tried to push the button with his chin. he missed. He tried again and touched it with his nose.

"Success!"

Nursery jerked and shuddered violently. The spinning continued but more slowly. After what seemed like an hour, there was another jerk and another shudder. The spinning was noticeably slower now. After several more jerks, he reported to Billy. "The spinning has stopped. I can move around the bridge now. I'm going to check on the children." Corvis imagined lifeless little bodies floating in midair.

At that instant, before he left the bridge, several laser beams flashed across his windshield, reminding him that even with *Nursery* on autopilot, our problems were far from over.

"No firing!" Brobding commanded over the com.

"We're close to their defense system," Copenhavlad argued.

"I have a plan," Brobding replied.

As he floated into the cabin, the jerking propulsion threw him into portal molding. To his surprise, Svet and the older girls were attending to the bruised and bleeding, the jerky movement of the ship making their work harder. He floated close to Svet and whispered in her ear, "How many did we lose?"

"None yet," she whispered, "but some may not make it."

"I have to return to the bridge for a minute, but then I'll start taking the injured to the infirmary," he said.

Just after the *Nursery* jerked, an explosion to port sent passengers reeling to starboard. With the shields deployed, they couldn't see anything outside.

"Are they still fighting?" Svet asked.

"They're still fighting, but I think they're waiting to see whether our ship will disintegrate before they fire on us again."

With that, Corvis returned to the bridge.

37
Plan C

BROBDINGS'S TRANSMISSION WAS SHORT: ["Plan C."]

What the hell is Plan C? Corvis wondered.

Certain that the *Nursery* was doomed, he believed the lifeboat was their only hope of survival. *We should have had a lifeboat drill the first day*, Corvis thought.

The radio silence that followed was almost as hard to bear as the explosions, knowing that the battle was not over. *We're in the eye of the hurricane,* Corvis thought. Over the PA he rapidly announced, "I realize that many of you are wounded, but we're going to do a lifeboat drill. This is just a drill. Repeat, this is just a drill. We will not be entering the lifeboat at this time, but we need to practice how we would get there if needed. Go to the rear of the ship by Dormitory groups. If you sleep in Dorm A, you will go first. Dorm B, follow them.

"Proceed through the gym to its aft portal, then turn to starboard and float through the laboratories to the portal marked 'Escape Module.'

"When you have all arrived at the lifeboat, Svet will take roll."

On his monitor, he saw most of the children float toward the gym. The ship's sudden lurch sent some of them crashing into walls.

Svet blocked the portal. "Please sit down," she said. A few children sat down. But when the others did not sit, those who had been seated floated toward the portal again.

"Captain," she said into the walkie-talkie, the children are frightened and confused, and English is their second language. Could you give the directions just one step at a time?"

"Let's start over," Corvis announced. "Everyone please sit down. Everyone sit down, now." He watched the seconds click by at an alarming rate.

Nursery hauled sideways, but Svet continued to block the portal to the gym.

"If you sleep in Dorm A, *only* Dorm A, please follow Charlene to the Escape Module assembly point."

He watched as Svet floated away from the portal to allow the first group to leave the cabin. When that group had left the cabin, he said, "Now, if you sleep in Dorm B, please follow Rose to the lifeboat assembly area."

The process was painfully slow, and the jerky movement of the ship made it more difficult, but Corvis knew it could save lives.

"If you sleep in Dorm C..."

Seconds turned into minutes. The *Nursery* could be attacked at any time.

Half an hour later, Svet reported, "All present and accounted for, Captain."

"Well done, everyone," Corvis said, "The drill was successful. Please return to the cabin."

Leak

Corvis noticed a flashing red notice: "Warning! Air leak! Pressure dropping!"

His heart stopped. *What more can go wrong?* He wondered.

He pressed "Details" and read "Slow leak: Deck 0, Cargo Hold D. Object piercing all five layers of hull." *That means the object is still in the wall, but the pressure inside versus the vacuum outside could cause the whole shell to fail. I have to act fast,* he realized.

He floated down Forward Portal past Decks B and C to Deck 0 then pushed off and floated past Cargo Hold B to Cargo Hold D. Using a hand-held floodlight, he searched the visible walls. Then he looked behind large objects stored there. Certain that he had examined every square centimeter of the wall, he had almost decided to send a robot to find the object, when up in the corner, where the wall met the ceiling, less than two centimeters from the top of the wall, a small object caught his eye. It appeared to be the handle of a screwdriver, not more than four centimeters long. It must have been left on a workbench, and during the fierce spinning of the ship, it must have been thrown, point first, into the wall. He reached out to retrieve it but caught himself just in time.

Removing the tool would have opened a hole in the only barrier between their temporary home and the vacuum of outer space. It would have resulted in such a tremendous pressure difference that the fabric would have torn, and *Nursery* would have lost all its air and collapsed in on itself. He decided on a safer solution.

Returning to the deck, he quickly programmed a robot to take a tube of sealant, a tube of glue, and several strips of patching fabric to Cargo Hold D. He instructed the robot to apply a large quantity of sealant around the base of the handle of the screwdriver, followed immediately by a layer of glue, to which overlapping strips of patch material were to be applied.

That should hold until we reach Enceladus, he thought, *and that's all I care about.*

Closer Combat

"[Double encrypted from JiAnn: Satendrites report that a single fighter docked with a large mother ship and has remained there for almost twenty minutes."]

Corvis trained *Nursery*'s cameras on the huge, black spherical ship covered with hundreds of laser cannons, and radar dishes. A dozen huge engines jutted from the rear of the ship. It had to have had portals and windshields, but they must have been flush with the skin of the ship, and frosted not to reflect light because none were visible.

["It's been a full hour since our last skirmish. We must not let our guard down," Billy transmitted. "We're almost within range of Enceladus's guided missiles. In three hours, we will be close enough for the regular fighters to join us.]"

Three hours! It might as well be a lifetime, Corvis thought.

An hour later, his midship monitor blinked red, and a circle appeared around a small brown fighter approaching slowly.

He signaled Billy: ["I have company."]

"[Satendrites are tracking," Billy responded. "The fighter's headed toward your ventral belly. I'll come in dorsal.]"

Corvis watched Billy's white ship, first visually, and then on the monitor. On another monitor he saw the brown ship approach from directly behind. The enemy ship grappled the *Nursery* and attached itself sending quaking waves across the entire surface of the ship. In the bridge, Corvis could hear screams from the cabin.

His midship camera showed the enemy craft on *Nursery's* surface. Frantic, but holding his voice in control, he reported to Billy. "Someone in a spacesuit is getting out of the fighter."

Nursery jerked, and then another set of waves crossed its skin. Children again screamed in the cabin. Billy's fighter was now attached to the *Nursery*.

"I'm getting out, too," Billy said.

"Don't, Billy," Corvis pleaded, "it's too dangerous."

"I must. It's the only way I can stop him."

The enemy spacesuit moved slowly, handhold by handhold, along the belly of *Nursery* to its port side.

Corvis watched Billy's space suit crawl equally slowly across the roof.

"You're about three meters in front of him, and ten meters above him," Corvis advised.

"Thanks!" Billy said, "You're my eyes."

No longer able to speak calmly, Corvis shouted, "He's crouching over the external door! He attached something!"

Billy's laser shot missed him by mere centimeters. The enemy returned fire, narrowly missing Billy. Then evil Spacesuit laid flat on the hull for several minutes.

"What's he doing?" Corvis asked.

"His decoder's running algorithms. He's waiting for the sally port to open. I'll try to get him before it succeeds in opening your door."

"Be careful," Corvis said.

Several laser beams passed less than a centimeter over the prone body. The enemy fired even more beams at Billy, some barely missing him.

Everyone on board heard the gears grind as the port slowly opened.

"Svet! Lock the Cabin door!" Corvis said over the PA, "Prepare to evacuate."

Spacesuit disappeared into the sally port, after shooting several times in Billy's general direction. *Nursery* shuddered as the sally port sealed.

Svet darted through the cabin door, then quickly locked it again. "What's happening?"

Corvis was already on his way to the sally port. "Enemy onboard!" he replied.

Nursery jerked again with uneven propulsion.

Rose's voice came over the intercom. "Erwan has Christian with a knife to his neck!"

This can't be happening.

Billy spoke in my earbud. "Is there another port?"

"Emergency port is fifteen meters to stern."

"Open it for me."

Corvis fumbled with shaking hands to unlock the cabin door. Svet came through, and Corvis locked the door again. They quickly floated to the rear of the ship, trailing Rose.

Children's faces registered confusion and panic, but they remained silent.

Corvis pushed off forcefully from the gym's doorway, entered the aft passage, floated through freezers to the emergency port.

He punched in the code to open the external door of the emergency sally port. Precious seconds ticked up.

Svet said to Rose, "Try to get the knife from Erwan and take him to the infirmary."

Rose pushed off.

Billy reported, "I'm in the emergency sally port, and pressurizing. You don't need to wait for me. The port will open automatically."

Corvis knew he had only 15 minutes for the main sally port with Brobding in it, to pressurize.

Both Svet and Corvis rushed back to the front of the ship.

In the cabin a child whispered, "What's happening?"

"It'll be OK," Svet whispered. "We have to take care of a problem up in front."

Again, Corvis had to unlock the cabin door, and then lock it again after they passed. Precious time was slipping past. Corvis tried to program the port not to open, but the computer would not accept the override. Arriving at the main sally port, both Svet and Corvis leaned against the door as it started to open, but the motor was too strong for them.

The enemy was coming through the port. Corvis lunged at Spacesuit as he emerged. He flung Corvis aside like a leaf and then removed his helmet. The hall was instantly filled with the stench of his blood-and-feces-matted hair.

Furious, Corvis threw himself at the monster, again. Again, he tossed him aside.

Brobding removed his spacesuit and laughed as they gaped at his completely naked body, coated entirely in dried blood. Then, turning away from us as if we were of no concern, he headed for the bridge. The ship jerked, throwing him against the doorframe, but he proceeded undeterred.

As Corvis followed him, he heard knocking at the cabin door. Svet opened it to allow Billy in. She quickly locked it again.

Relieved to see that Billy had a weapon, Corvis asked, "Is that a laser pistol in your holster?"

"Using lasers inside this ship would kill us all," Billy warned loudly as he floated toward the bridge. Billy rushed Brobding but was thrown against a console as a sudden 10% surge of gravity accompanied Brobding's change in *Nursery*'s course.

Brobding had captured the *Nursery*.

It's over. We now belong to Brobding, Corvis thought.

"On three!" Billy commanded, not needing to explain what Corvis was to do. "One, Two..."

Nursery jerked, throwing them even more strongly into the monster than they had expected.

He rolled over, laughing. Brobding threw Corvis into the control panel, raising a plume of sparks. Billy he sent reeling to the door. Brobding's focus returned to the dials. Billy spied the large fire extinguisher firmly attached to the wall and grabbed the release lever. He used all his strength to hit Brobding over the head with the massive tank.

Brobding floated, unconscious.

"Get out!" Corvis shouted, "Hurry!"

Billy looked at Corvis for a tenth a second, and then pushed off. The two got out of the bridge just as Brobding came to his senses.

"We can't let him take us." Corvis said.

Brobding was tapping in commands on the console. He seemed completely unconcerned with the rest of the world now that he had control of the ship.

"He won't take us," Svet said confidently. "I'm going to extinguish him."

"How?" Billy and Corvis both asked.

"The same way we extinguished the fire in the dormitory. Keep the door closed for me."

Corvis locked the door to the bridge.

Responding to the click, Brobding tossed a confident sneer toward the window in the bridge door.

Svet pulled the fire alarm handle.

"Evacuate the bridge!" a mechanical voice said.

The fire door closed and sealed the bridge as air whistled out, indicating that a vacuum was being created. Simultaneously, fire alarms sounded throughout the ship.

Corvis rushed to the cabin, found Charity and shouted over the shrill siren, "There is no fire! Try to keep the children calm! It will end soon."

As Corvis returned, Brobding looked at the door, confused, mouth gaping for air, and stunned. Furious, he rushed the door. It didn't open. He pounded on it, but the fire door was built to sustain even an explosion. His fists bleeding, fresh blood trickling from his ears, the vacuum continued to intensify. He soon floated unconscious just inside the door.

Nursery lurched, again.

Corvis managed to turn off the noisy fire alarm. Eager to get *Nursery* back on course, Corvis reached for the door handle.

"No," Billy shouted, "wait!"

A full minute later, Brobding pulled himself to the control panel and, pushing off from there, thrust himself against the door hard. All three of them pushed away from the area. Then he floated, lifeless.

Nursery continued its uneven progress farther and farther off course.

"Just five more minutes," Billy advised.

Two minutes later the three all flinched as Brobding's hands twitched twice. They all jumped in terror. *When is he going to die?*

Hesitantly, when the time had passed, Corvis released the seal of the fire door. Air rushed past us as the bridge repressurized. Cautiously, Corvis touched Brobding's finger. It was ice cold and lifeless.

"His body goes to the freezer, but no one outside the *Nursery* must know that he is dead," Billy ordered.

"How do we get the body to the freezer without the children seeing it?" Svet asked.

"I can take it through the Lobby down to C Deck, past the algae vats, then back up to A Deck and from there to the freezers," Corvis said. "But why are we keeping it secret?"

"We're buying time. We know they've broken our code, so whatever we transmit they read. As long as they think Brobding is aboard and alive, they will hold back. As soon as they know that Brobding is dead, they will attack. They have nothing to lose."

"How do you know they've broken our code?" Corvis asked.

"Brobding told his fighters to watch for a vessel leaving the *Nursery* immediately after we talked about your lifeboat."

"But Tyler and the others will be worried about you," Svet said.

"They know that if I don't send a mayday, I'm fine, but I have to return to my ship in case the enemy attacks again. Copenhavlad's mission is to take control of Enceladus. He needs the children as hostages to force us to allow him to land. He is certainly not ready to concede the battle until the last possible moment."

Billy's body brushed against Corvis's as he passed on his way aft. Corvis nearly fainted as arousal coursed through him. Corvis gave him a friendly nudge in reply.

Billy chuckled.

"I need to get *Nursery* back on course," Corvis said. He felt good floating in front of the control deck once more.

The ship lurched, again.

Svet asked, "Can I send a message to Tyler?"

"It's better that we keep the enemy guessing by maintaining strict radio silence," Billy said on his way to the rear of the ship.

"I understand," she said softly, "I need to take care of the children, anyway."

38
Course Correction

CORVIS QUICKLY CHECKED *NURSERY'S* speed and heading. Brobding had altered our course, but within an hour the autopilot would get them almost back to where they needed to be. Afterward, he floated Brobding's limp, weightless body to the freezer; then he went up to Dorm C and got a sheet, wrapping the dead terrorist in it so that anyone walking into the freezer wouldn't be horrified to see such a ghastly corpse.

Suddenly, he remembered Erwan and wondered whether he still held poor Christian at knifepoint.

Corvis went the short distance directly to the infirmary. Three teenage girls took turns holding the door closed as Erwan pounded against it, screaming.

"Thank you for helping. You can go back to what you were doing," Corvis told them.

As soon as they let go, the door swung open, and Erwan burst out. He was sweating and crying in rage. Aware that he could use his crutch as a weapon, Corvis grabbed Erwan's free arm with his good hand, and floated him down the portal to Deck C, around the gym, and into one of the unused officers' cabins, where he set him free. Corvis half expected him to escape immediately, but Erwan seemed content to stay, pushing off, back and forth, from wall to wall burning off pent-up energy.

"What happened?" Corvis asked calmly, "How did this all start?"

Nursery jerked and Erwan bounced off a wall. "Christian called me a looney!" Erwan cried out.

"That's not a nice word."

Erwan scrambled into a hammock. "So, I hit him."

"Oh," Corvis said evenly, "That's not a good way to solve a problem. Is it?"

"I couldn't just let him call me names."

"What happened then?"

"Christian hit me. *Twice!*"

"That's not good. It must have hurt."

"I had to defend myself! He could have *killed* me!"

"Did you use your words to tell him to stop?"

"No! But it wasn't my fault. Christian started it!"

"What did you do then?"

"I warned him with a knife."

"*How* did you warn him with a knife?"

"I held it to his neck, but I wouldn't have used it."

"Knives are useful tools, but a knife should never be used as a weapon."

"He made me do it."

"That was one choice. What other choices did you have?"

"None. He could have killed me. I had to show him that I could kill him first."

"Let's think about other choices. How could you use your words?"

"I couldn't. He was trying to kill me."

"How about saying 'I'm not going to let you hurt me,' or 'Stop! I'm going to tell an adult!'"

"He wouldn't have listened."

"Maybe. Maybe not. But next time try taking a deep breath, counting to ten, and think of words that you could say instead. OK?"

"I'll try," Erwan said sheepishly.

"Before you go," Corvis said, "tell me, did you get hurt when the ship was spinning?"

"Ooooh!" he moaned, "I nearly died!"

"It was very scary, wasn't it?" Corvis said.

"I think all my ribs are cracked."

"Let me see your chest."

He opened his jumpsuit, and Corvis saw bruises where the seat belts had prevented him from flying around the cabin.

"Are you bleeding anywhere?" I asked.

"Oh, yes," he said, "my leg hurts bad!"

He had a large abrasion where the seat belt had scraped the skin off his stump.

"I would like to listen to your heart," Corvis said, "will you go with me back to the infirmary?"

Since Erwan had been speaking normally and seemed to have no trouble breathing, Corvis didn't think he had broken any ribs, but he used this excuse to get him to breathe deeply. They floated to the infirmary, where Corvis placed a stethoscope on various places on his chest. "Take a deep breath" he said while listening, "breathe out."

"You're healthy, Erwan. But I want to take an Xray, and put a bandage on your stump," Corvis said, putting his stethoscope away.

Just then, the ship lurched throwing both into a wall.

"I don't like the word 'stump,'" Erwan said, "Call it my 'leg.'"

"OK," Corvis said selecting the largest ready-made bandage in the infirmary. "Here's a bandage for your leg." It didn't completely cover the scrape, but it looked impressive on his small body.

After taking a chest Xray, Corvis said, "Let's go back to the cabin."

"I want to go to the dining room," Erwan whined.

"That's not a good idea. There could be more rough rides for a while," Corvis explained, "so it's safer for you to be with the other children."

They floated to the cabin. But as Corvis was returning to the bridge, Mary Ndong stopped them. "Let me try to talk to Erwan," she said.

What can it hurt? My efforts have certainly been ineffective with him, Corvis thought.

"Erwan," Corvis said, "let's go to the dining room."

"What for?" he asked.

"Mary would like to talk to you," Corvis said.

"I don't want to talk to Mary," he said defiantly, "she's ugly."

"That's not a nice thing to say, especially since she's right here."

"I'm not going to talk to Mary," he said.

"I'll give you a jelly."

"OK."

When they got to the dining room, Mary wasted no time.

"Listen, you little piece of garbage," Mary said, before Corvis could intervene, "if you do something stupid like that again, I will personally rip your head off your shoulders!"

"Get away from me you witch!" Erwan replied.

"Whoa, whoa, Mary," Corvis said, "I think you should join the others in the gym."

"And Erwan, you used words this time. That's good, but were they nice words?" Corvis asked.

"No," Erwan mumbled, "but I'm scared of her."

"That's no reason to call her names. You can go back to the cabin, now," he said. "A robot will bring you a jelly."

Corvis quickly made his way to the bridge.

When Svet came into the cockpit, he told her about his conversation with Erwan and about Mary's attempt to "help" Erwan. "I think Erwan's going to be an ongoing problem."

"I do, too."

"And I think Mary speaks her mind."

"She won't back down to anyone," Svet agreed.

"She has lots of potential, doesn't she!"

"She certainly does," Svet said.

Attending the Injured

"I need to attend to the children who were injured while our ship was spinning," Corvis said. "Some of them may need emergency treatment."

"Nearly all of them were hurt," Svet replied sadly.

"That's why we need to triage all of them," Corvis said. "Those with the most serious injuries get treated first. Let's get the older girls to help unless they're too badly injured themselves."

"That sounds like a good idea."

Once the girls were assembled in the front lobby, Corvis explained the procedure. "As we pass through the cabin, I'll look at each child and say either 'red,' 'yellow,' or 'green.' Every 'red' child must be taken to the infirmary immediately; every 'yellow' child may wait quietly in their own hammock for their turn; and 'green' children are good to go. They won't need any treatment."

He had to work quickly, as he had 312 potential patients to check. He started with Svet, who, amazingly, only appeared to have several bruises. "Ice those when you have a chance," he suggested.

Mary Ndong had a headache, and she had no memory of the ship spinning. He sent her directly to the infirmary where he could watch for other signs of concussion. Rose, how are you?" he asked.

"Oh, Cap'n Crow, it was terrifying. I was so scared for the children. I didn't think most of them would survive..."

Corvis broke in, "You. How are *you*?"

"I'm fine. Just a few bruises."

"Would you go with Mary? I'm sure she can find her way on her own, but help her get settled, please, and then come back to help us in the cabin."

The other four teenage girls all had welts from their seatbelts but were fine otherwise, and able to help with triage.

As he looked each child over and asked a few questions, he found sixteen with differing amounts of blood on their garments. These all were sent immediately to the infirmary. Twelve more had swollen arms or legs, indicating either fractures or strains. One had a stiff neck, and the child cried when Corvis touched his head. All the rest had painful bruises but were eager to get up and play.

After looking at each child, and before going to the infirmary, he again assembled the older girls. "Is one of you willing to help me treat the injured children?" he asked. The girls looked at each other, but none volunteered. After a few seconds, he said "That's fine," and turned to leave.

Rose called after him, "I'll come."

In the infirmary, all the exam rooms were full, as were all the waiting hammocks.

"Rose," he said, "would you check on the children? If one of them needs something, would you get it for them? Most importantly, if there is an emergency, please let me know right away."

"OK, Cap'n Crow," she replied.

Dominic, the boy with the stiff neck, concerned Corvis. First, he fitted the boy with a cervical collar. Then, he quietly asked, "Do you know where you are?"

"I'm in a spaceship," Dominic replied.

"Do you know how your neck got hurt?"

"The ship was rolling and rolling, and my head bounced around and around."

"Can you feel this?" Corvis asked, pinching the small toe of his right foot.

"Yes," he said.

"And this?" he asked, pinching his left thumb.

"Yes."

"Can you raise your arms?" he asked.

"Yes," Dominic said, but didn't move.

"Show me," Corvis said.

He raised his arms, just as the ship jerked. He immediately moaned and held his head.

"Push your foot into my hand," he told him.

His leg press was strong.

"I think you'll be fine," he said. "Please wear that collar for a couple of days, and no rough housing. OK?"

"OK, Cap'n Crow."

"Take it easy today, Dominic," Corvis said. "You can go back to the cabin now."

"Thanks, Cap'n Crow," he said, as he pushed off.

"Rose," Corvis said, "the next child can come to this exam room now."

He moved to the next station. Five-year-old Miriam was crying, the left leg of her jumpsuit was bloody. "Rose," he said, "can you help me in here?" He washed his hands and put gloves on.

When Rose arrived, he told her, "I need to look at Miriam's leg."

Miriam screamed when they moved her leg.

"Miriam," he explained, "I need to cut off part of your jumpsuit."

Mary held her hand for comfort. With scissors, he cut the leg of the jumpsuit off. As soon as he saw her leg, I understood her pain. Slightly less than a centimeter of white bone protruded through the skin of her thigh. Around it the skin was dark, and blood was oozing at the site.

"I'm not qualified to set this bone," he told Rose. "But I will have to check how much bleeding there is." No other part of her jumpsuit had blood on it, so he only had to check the leg. He used gauze to dab around wound. It was bleeding, but not profusely, and the blood was deep red: venous blood.

"Miriam," he said, as he pinched her left toes, "can you feel this?"

Before he finished the sentence, Miriam replied "Ouch!"

While touching her toes, he assessed them for circulation. They were warm and pink, and her capillary refill was less than three seconds, so he knew she had circulation to her foot, at least for now."

"Will you move those toes?"

"No!"

He wanted to treat her pain, *and* he wanted her to remain calm, so he drew up a combination painkiller and sedative in a syringe. "This medicine will help take away the pain, and it will help you rest," he explained. "Look at Rose while I give you the shot, OK?"

"I'll give that about 15 minutes to kick in," he told Rose after the injection. "Can you stay here with her for a while?"

"Certainly."

The next three patients had bleeding wounds, but luckily, none of them had broken bones or other problems. He was able to quickly clean the wounds, apply bandages, and send them on their way. Three more children from the waiting room had bunks in exam rooms.

It was time now to apply traction to Miriam's leg. As he floated in, the ship listed and he tumbled sideways. Fortunately, the exam room was equipped with a traction harness. "We'll help you put this little vest on," he told her. "And then we'll put a band around your ankle. Traction in the weightlessness of outer space is different from what we do on Earth."

Out of the large assortment of traction cables, Corvis decided to try three kilograms of resistance. The clamp of the first cable attached to the top of the vest, and from there to a ring fastened to the wall. The second resistance cable clamped into a ring in the padded anklet.

"Rose," he murmured, "would you talk to Miriam? I'm going to pull the ends of the bone apart and try to get the exposed piece of bone back under the skin." Holding the upper part of her thigh, he gently pulled the lower part away.

Miriam screamed, but the exposed end of the bone slipped back under the skin. He immediately attached the lower resistance cable to the opposite wall.

"Good girl!" he said heartily, "Your bone is inside the skin now, where it belongs! I'm going to stitch the skin together, so it doesn't pop out again."

Again, he leaned close to Rose. "When I tell you, can you keep Miriam's mind occupied? Maybe ask her to count backward from 10 to 1." He cleaned the area around the wound carefully and got the tiny syringe and the sutures ready.

"OK, Rose" he said, "keep her thinking."

"What are the names of all your brothers and sisters?" Rose asked Miriam.

Corvis injected a small amount of local anesthetic above and below the wound, while Miriam named her siblings. After a minute, he made a single stitch and tied it off, and then another. Meanwhile, Miriam seemed determined to name *all* her relatives. She paused when she saw Corvis look up.

"We're all finished," he told them. "Except to put the bandage on. Now we just need to keep your leg clean until we reach Enceladus, okay? Meanwhile, I'll keep you as comfortable as I can. Why don't you stay in this hammock for a while? Is there a video game you like to play?" I asked. "We have hologram games. Or you can sleep if you want to. We'll leave the traction on for a little while, OK?"

They'd been working for two hours by then, and he thought Rose might be tired. "Would you like to quit now?" he asked her gently.

"Yes, Cap'n Crow," she said, "I would like to take a break."

"Thanks so much for your help."

"You're welcome."

Nursery shifted again.

He wanted to check on Mary Ndong, to be sure she didn't have a concussion, so he went to the exam room where she was resting. The entertainment center wasn't on, and she seemed to be asleep. He couldn't be sure, of course, since she was blind. "Mary," he said softly.

"Yes, Cap'n Crow?" she said immediately.

"You're awake, then," he said.

"I was just thinking about all the things that have happened to me," she said in a small voice.

"You've lived through so much. You're a strong woman," he said. "Do you want to talk about it?"

"Yes," she said firmly. "When the ship was spinning, I thought my blindness might have been a blessing. I could feel things hit my skin, and the spinning made me sick to my stomach, but I also heard the children screaming. I was thinking, 'This is how I finally die.' I wasn't as terrified as the children were. Whatever they were seeing made them scared."

"I think you might be right. To be honest, to save the ship, I had to close my eyes. Maybe blindness can be a blessing once in a while."

"As the spinning slowed down, I thought, 'Maybe this isn't my time to die. I wonder if there is a reason for me to live.'"

"I'm sure there is," he told her. "You're here for a reason. For now, you do need some rest, but I'll check on you occasionally. I may have to wake you up, but then you can go right back to sleep."

He next checked on three children with swollen appendages: two arms and a leg, and two children who had been bleeding. None of the children with swollen limbs seemed to have fractures, but he X-rayed them just to be sure. There weren't any fractures in the group. He iced each of their injuries, setting a timer for twenty minutes in each exam room. In between these, he checked on two children with blood on their uniforms. In both cases the wounds were simple abrasions. He cleaned them and put bright cartoon bandages on their "owies" and sent them back to the cabin.

As he was removing the ice from the last of the three children with swollen extremities, the ship rocked, throwing him, sore shoulder first, into a wall. He had to stifle a couple of words the children didn't need to hear from the captain.

When he went to the waiting room to call two more children into exam rooms, Rose was entertaining them.

"Oh, I thought you were finished," he said.

"No. I just needed a little break."

"Great! I really appreciate your help."

In the next exam room, he met four-year-old Loic who was accompanied by Charity. His left forearm was swollen. "What happened to your arm?" he asked.

"It bended," Loic said.

"Let's take a picture to see the bone inside," Corvis said.

He X-rayed Loic's arm and immediately saw that he had a green-stick fracture of the ulna. "Uh-oh, the bone in your arm is broken," he explained, "I'm going to put a cast on your arm so that it will heal straight and strong."

The 3-D printer quickly applied the cast, which was made of strong polymer.

"We need to leave the cast on your arm for six weeks," he said. "That way if you fall the bone inside won't break all the way. Do you understand?"

"Um-hmm," Loic replied stoically.

The ship suddenly lurched, and Corvis steadied himself. "You can go back to the cabin now," he told Loic.

Next, Rose entered with three-year-old Jennice. The little one had blood on her jumpsuit from the collar bone to the armpit, due to an abrasion caused by the seatbelt rubbing away the skin.

"Do you have an owie, my cousin?" he asked.

She nodded solemnly.

He cleaned the wound and applied a large yellow bandage.

"You can take Jennice back to the cabin now," he told Rose.

He then checked on Mary and she seemed fine.

After three more hours, he had treated all the remaining children who had been hurt while the *Nursery* was spinning. Exhausted, he returned to the bridge.

Testing

A day had passed in complete radio silence. Knowing that Billy's fighter was attached to the *Nursery* was comforting. It meant he was close, and ready to fight if necessary. Charity reported to me that they had asked Erwan to promise not to cause any more disruption. *Hmm! That'll last about an hour.*

"Thank you," Corvis said.

He could now see both motherships. Brobding's, he had studied earlier. Now he looked at Copenhavlad's brown-and-purple craft. It had three disc-shaped decks stacked on top of each other with hundreds of laser canons mounted on the periphery. Beneath the ship, three gigantic engines propelled the ship through space. A large windshield wrapped around the front of the top deck, and a smaller one looked out the rear.

Watching the monitors, he saw a fighter emerge from the Swarm. Billy's squadron immediately fired on it, and the fighter instantly returned to its place.

It seemed strange to Corvis that the enemy would try to strike, knowing that Billy was in the cockpit, his ship ready any instant to fly into action. But, of course, the enemy didn't know where Billy was. Brobding's ship also was docked to the *Nursery*. Outside of the *Nursery*, no one had any way of knowing the condition of either Brobding or Billy. On the other hand, *Nursery* was back on course for Enceladus, so anyone could easily conclude that Brobding was not in charge.

Finally, Copenhavlad broke 33 hours of complete radio silence. Standing proud in his formal uniform, he announced to the Swarm, "Expeditionary Group. In the absence of your leader, I am taking command of the swarm. You will..."

A hologram of a small Asian woman's head and neck appeared suddenly. Her voice broke in: "No! Brobding is still in control, and I am his woman, his second-in-command! I give commands in his absence!"

"We are approaching the range of Enceladus's full defenses. We must strike now, or our mission will be lost," Copenhavlad said in an authoritative voice.

"You will wait for my directive!" Brobding's Woman countered.

A minute later, four large yellow space fighters engulfed the *Nursery*, two to port and two to starboard. Four Enceladan fighters met them head-on, and a barrage of laser beams soon sent them back to the safety of the formation.

Half an hour later, Corvis watched two sleek missiles streak into the cluster. Two brown fighters exploded silently in the vacuum of space.

Billy's hologram form appeared near Corvis's screen, his message was not encrypted. "To all ships, friend, and enemy, those missiles came directly from Enceladus. We are now within the range of more than a thousand of our land-based missiles. Pilots would be more stupid than I think they are to leave the Swarm from now on. But we will stay nearby to protect the *Nursery*. Over."

Corvis's reaction was strange. He felt weak and lightheaded. *I guess the good news allowed my body to stop producing massive quantities of adrenaline.*

Immediately, the Asian woman's head appeared above my control panel. "Release my husband to me and I will set you free," she ordered harshly.

"Unfortunately," Corvis transmitted, "your husband is our safe passage to Enceladus. He and his ship will have to stay with the *Nursery* for the time being."

A dozen brown fighters exploded from the cluster toward *Nursery*. Within seconds, a barrage of large laser beams tore apart two targets among the deviating fighters, and the surviving fighters quickly returned to the group.

Brobding's 46 remaining fighters then retreated toward the center of the solar system taking different routes, leaving the two motherships with only four fighters to defend them. "I order you to return to formation!" Woman shrieked.

Two minutes later, the woman pleaded with the departing ships in a different voice. "Don't abandon me. Have pity upon an old widow. What's going to happen to me now?"

Moments later, the spherical mother ship raced back toward the sun at full speed.

39
Congratulations

A HOLOGRAM SHOWED A jubilant Billy. "Congratulations, team, you've defeated the enemy!"

"Svet, can you come to the Bridge?" he said over the PA.

"Yee haaaw!" Dalisay shouted.

"Magnificent!" Tyler crowed.

"Sweeet!" Ophelia said.

Nursery hauled to port as Svet came through the door.

He played her the tape.

She gasped. "It's over? The battle's really over?", she asked.

"It is! Shall we thank the pilots for helping us?"

"Can I go first?" Svet asked.

"Sure."

"This is Svetlana Turgenev, the Chief Operating Officer of the *Nursery*. First, I want to thank Harriet Reitman, if she can hear me. You died to save the lives of 311 children, and my life. I'll never forget your sacrifice. To the rest of you, pilots, my heart is full of gratitude and joy that you have conquered the enemy. And a special note to Tyler: I love you."

She looked at Corvis and nodded.

"For my part," he began, as the ship heaved and he recovered, "I want to congratulate Ms. Turgenev, who killed Brobding. Billy and I would still be fighting him if she had not literally *extinguished* him. There are six girls in other parts of this ship who deserve my life-long admiration. I call them girls because they're not yet legally adults, but they are heroes by any definition of the term. Their maturity and mental toughness have repeatedly amazed me.

"And you pilots demonstrated skill, nerve, and valor beyond what anyone could imagine. Thank you for saving all our lives!"

A large, clear colorful hologram of JiAnn wearing a tropical print top, standing next to General Dioikis, wearing his dress uniform, in sharp contrast to the scratchy holograms of the pilots, took shape in front of his monitor.

"Every screen, large and small, on Enceladus," JiAnn said, "displayed telescopic images of *Nursery* tumbling, out of control through space. Not one person spoke out loud as the ship spun faster and faster. I for one, could not breathe as it appeared that the ship was about to break apart under the pressure of that force. That anyone could save the *Nursery* from certain destruction was nothing short of miraculous!"

Remembering the ship spinning out of control made Corvis feel like vomiting. *There* are *some things that are worse than death.*

"Corvis, I don't know how you did it, but you're an amazing pilot and an even more amazing leader!"

General Dioikis spoke. "I couldn't be prouder of the pilots of the Elite Squadron. All soldiers of the Autonomous Enceladus Defense Force are gratified by your success in fighting off the enemy. President Cly, with the Joint Generals, concurring has created the new E-Ring Medal of Valor to honor your exceptional bravery in service to Enceladus. Upon your return to this community, Harriet Reitmann will be the first to receive this award posthumously; and immediately, the rest of you be awarded the E-Ring Medal of Valor.

"All of Enceladus is eager to welcome you home!"

Nursery jerked, and Corvis's mind returned to the first moment he saw the ship. He remembered when it was new, still in the hanger. He remembered President Gbonkta, who took such risks to secure this ship for them, and General Kasavubu, who planned the military strategy to get them safely blasted off, and how Ms. Kongo got the children ready for an adventure none of them could have imagined. Jake, who wheeled-and-dealed to get all the stuff in order and wheedled Corvis into taking on this impossible mission. *Thank you,* he thought, *wherever you are,* however, *you are, thank you.*

Plea

Corvis monitored an exchange between General Copenhalvad and General Dioikis.

"Enceladus, this is the commander of the Northern Confederacy Task Force," General Copenhalvad said. "We surrender unconditionally. Over."

"You and your fighters will not be taken prisoner. Over," General Dioikis replied.

"Then permit us to land in peace."

Dioikis said, "That will not be possible."

"We do not have enough fuel to return to the inner solar system. I and my crew will perish," Copenhavlad insisted.

"I doubt that you would have come this far without sufficient fuel to return to the inner solar system."

"The Revised Geneva Space Accords require you to save our lives."

"The Revised Geneva Accords specifically prohibit use of paralyzing probes. You have them. And you have, very recently, used them. Moreover, you were warned while you were still in the inner solar system that you would not be allowed to approach, much less land on Enceladus. You did not come in peace. You killed one of the pilots protecting the Nursery. You *will not* land on Enceladus."

Several minutes passed without further chatter.

Corvis watched the four yellow fighters and the brown and purple disc, which had once been such a threat, retreat, without further protest. Mesmerized, he observed until the formation of five ships became just a dot, and then disappeared completely.

The *Nursery* continued its herky-jerky progress toward Enceladus.

40
Honor Guard

ENCELADUS

CORVIS RAISED THE SHIELDS that had protected the *Nursery*, and announced over the PA, "The bad guys are gone. And we will be in our new home tomorrow... whoa!" as *Nursery* listed.

His chest swelled involuntarily as he saw twenty Enceladan fighters flying in close formation together to meet them. Ten took up positions to port, and the other ten to starboard. Billy's four remaining ships flew in front of them for an hour, and then sped away.

Corvis watched the interior monitors as children floated to the alcoves and waved at the fighters.

He didn't think they intended it, but he could hear conversation between pilots in Elite Squadron while they returned to Enceladus.

"What about you, Pistis?" Billy asked, "What are you going to do when we get home?"

"The monthly yak race is Saturday."

"Oh, yeah!" Billy said enthusiastically, "Who do you think'll win?"

"Norbu's favored," Ophelia said, "but I bet a cube on Kiba. They're paying 10 to 1 if he wins. He's still young, but he's getting better. He could surprise everyone."

"I heard all our yaks come from one mother. Is that true?"

"Yes and no," Pistis said. "Only one live cow was brought as a young calf to Enceladus, but frozen sperm from 50 bulls came with her. She and each of her six daughters were fathered by different bulls, and then *they* were inseminated with sperm from different bulls, so there's a fair amount of genetic variability in our herds. The exact genealogy of each yak, male or female is carefully recorded. That way we maximize variety in the gene pool.

"What about you, Billy? What'll you be up to?"

"I've got a soccer match day after tomorrow night," Billy said, "but I don't know if coach will let me play, since I missed practice all this week. If they're smart, they'll let me play, though. I'll still be really hyped from our battle."

Both pilots laughed.

It's going to be great, just passing a ball back and forth with Billy, Corvis thought, remembering his soccer cleats in his little duffel bag.

41

Preparations

JiAnn

JiAnn HAD BEEN IN the Bubble when the satendrites revealed that the Swarm had broken up and departed. Her heart felt lighter knowing that the Apprentice was on his way home. From General Dioikis, she learned that the elite fighters would land at 2600 hours and that they would complete their debriefing an hour later. She planned to welcome them home and thank them, more personally.

She also knew that the Chamber of Commerce had formed a Decorations Committee and a Food Committee to prepare a Welcome Home dinner honoring all the pilots and welcoming the new Earthling children to Enceladus. Social Services had already organized a system by which foster parents would be introduced to children to determine whether there would be good chemistry between them. The children would sleep in the college dormitory for at least the first two nights. During that time, the children of the *Nursery* would get to know their new families during the day.

JiAnn tried to occupy her mind to quiet her still raw nerves. She planned to wear a conservative black suit to meet the pilots. She typed up what she would say, but reading what she had written, she realized that it didn't really matter exactly what she said. All that mattered was that JiAnn wouldn't be able to really believe that Billy was safely home until she saw and touched him.

42
Visualizing Enceladus

CORVIS

ON THE OVERSIZED SCREENS in the auditorium and cafeteria, Corvis periodically posted real-time photos of Enceladus as seen through the ship's telescope. Sometimes it appeared as a speck in the void, other times, its shadow appeared as a black spot on Saturn's enormous yellow disc. By twelve hours out, Saturn half-filled his view from the pilot's seat. Its brightness was blinding. *Saturn radiates more heat than it receives from the sun*, he remembered. Enceladus, itself, was almost pure white.

Watching activities in the classrooms, he noticed that more and more time was devoted to instructing the children about life on Enceladus. With them, he watched an instructional film on Enceladan architecture. A woman's voice said, "Ice is the main construction material on Enceladus. Our 'outdoor' structures are very large. They are maintained at 0° C., or 32° F., so that the walls don't melt. Indoor spaces are small, because it takes lots of energy to cool the air close to the walls, while keeping the rest of the house warm. Ceilings are high because our children grow tall in the very low gravity of this moon."

The next film was called *Farming on Enceladus*. It sounded interesting, so he watched most of that one, as well.

"Farming on Enceladus started *before* the first humans arrived. Robots built the first dome in 2072, and they tended the first garden. The first settlers, Maud, and David, arrived on November 19, 2073. Within the first residence, meant for two people, six more settlers squeezed in while their residence was being finished."

He marveled as Dome Alpha, the first little dome, was scanned and the camera focused on a sign above the door of a small house. The sign read "Kline Museum."

"Robots prepared the soil, made from tank-grown algae, and they planted the first crop on this moon. Robots made a hundred mounds of the soil. They planted one seed of squash next to one seed of corn next to one bean seed. A hive of bees had come with the robots, and they pollinated the crops. The numbers of both bees and vegetable seeds increased dramatically over time.

"That first dome was only 20 meters in diameter. The habitable area on the surface of Enceladus was just over 314 square meters, or 3,380 square feet, considerably less than a tenth of an acre. The dome was only ten meters high at its highest point. Humble beginnings, indeed.

"The second dome was 200 meters in diameter, and 100 meters tall. It enclosed more than three-quarters of an acre. After that, all domes have been half a kilometer in diameter. We currently have over 2125 acres, or 864 hectares under domes."

Corvis saw larger and larger domes, and a variety of crops and farming techniques came into view.

"But this doesn't begin to tell the story of our agricultural output. Terracing and intensive farming help us to produce far more food on Enceladus per acre than is typically produced per acre on Earth. In addition, from the beginning our algae tanks have produced more than enough food to sustain our entire population in an emergency. Thousands of tons of dried algae are stored in ice warehouses outside the domes where the vacuum of space keep all biological processes to a minimum.

"The ocean under the icy surface of Enceladus provides us with an almost unlimited supply of fresh fish. But we take only as much fish as we can eat. And we return live shrimp, raised in tanks, kilogram-for-kilogram for the fish we catch. We also have an unlimited supply of hydrocarbons, brought to Enceladus in large tankers from another moon of Saturn, Titan. A wide variety of plastics, some harder than steel, and others almost as hard as diamonds are manufactured here.

"Enceladus Colony was conceived as a safe harbor for humans in case of a nuclear war on Earth. Far-sighted scientists designed aspects of the settlement to protect many other animals, both to feed us and for us to enjoy.

"We have chickens, of course, as well as pigs, and yaks.

"So, what can you expect to eat on Enceladus? We produce most of the vegetables and fruit that are commonly eaten on Earth, such as wheat, corn, and tomatoes. And we serve fish, pork, chicken, and beef (yak, that is)..."

Slowing Down

Nursery

As soon as the threat of being taken hostage passed, Sal the computer revised our course to land on Enceladus. On this day, Corvis started firing the retrorockets. While

Enceladus has little gravity, the center of Saturn was still pulling hard. For the first time in three months, our children were feeling constantly increasing Gs. For the final landing sequence, Corvis typed in the title of the program "Land on Enceladus," and Sal took over.

Svet spoke over the PA system. "This will be your last breakfast on the *Nursery*, children. We get to eat up all the leftovers of our Earth-food! Also, classrooms will be open so that you can draw pictures and write in your journals about how it feels to finish your long, dangerous trip. It's a holiday. No school today!"

In front of his monitor, a hologram took form. Corvis displayed its message on the cabin screens. "*Nursery*," a woman in scrubs said, "this is Lorna Graham of the Enceladus Health Department. I need to orient you to our Immigration Procedures.

"We have very strict infection control protocols that must be followed to the letter. As soon as you land, drug- and disease-sniffing drones will pass through every space in your ship. All doors must be unlocked, including closets, cabinets, and storage rooms. No one will be permitted to leave the ship until drones have examined every space in the *Nursery*.

"When you exit your ship, you will be taken by bus to the entry tunnel. In the tunnel, you will be sprayed with micro-fine antiseptic mist. Most people are not even aware of it, but it can cause a mild allergic reaction in rare cases.

"Nursing aides will meet you at the end of the tunnel to guide you directly to the showers. While you're showering all your clothes and hand-held items, including stuffed toys, will be fumigated. You must not take any food items off of the ship.

"All personal baggage must be clearly marked with the owners' names. These items must be *left on the ship*. Personal items will be processed and delivered to your residences later the evening of your arrival.

"Is anyone on the ship ill?"

Corvis turned off the cabin monitors and replied. "No one is ill," he said. "But nearly all of us were hurt while the ship was spinning out of control. Two need to be taken off on stretchers. In addition, we have the bodies of three small children who died of Mbiximia pestis. We also have a nine-year-old boy with serious behavioral issues that we didn't know about when we left Earth."

"Very well," Nurse Graham said, "we'll have gurneys ready. The coroner will have to examine all three bodies. Hold back the child with behavior problems. He can exit *Nursery* with the crew. Do you have any questions?"

"I know this is not your area but is there someone we can talk to about the burial of the children?" he asked.

"That will be an important event," Nurse Graham said, "so perhaps the Dragomark Emeritus would be the one to talk to.

"Do you have any other questions?"

"Not that I can think of," he said.

"If any health issues arise, or if you have questions later, Health Department personnel are on standby to assist. Welcome to Enceladus."

Those words sent chills through his body. *We're really here!*

Dans See Nursery

Nursery had no landing gear. They had to make a belly landing and hope the structure that had barely survived the stress of rapid spinning would hold together. Sal had to bring the *Nursery* almost to a complete stop before touchdown. Even in Enceladus's tiny gravity, our mass of over 30,000 kilograms was enough to destroy the *Nursery* if it landed at even 5 kilometers per hour straight down. *While thin, the five layers of the hull are almost infinitely elastic. We'll survive... I hope,* Corvis thought.

General Dioikis asked Corvis to put him on the PA system. He wore a formal uniform with lots of ribbons and pins. "Welcome, children of the *Nursery* to your new home, Enceladus.

"Some of us have been watching your journey for more than a month. Now that you're here, all Dans will be watching you land.

"Your ship is the largest mobile structure let alone spacecraft, that many of our people have ever seen.

"Even though we have prepared a runway of very soft snow, your touchdown will be bumpy.

"After such a long time in space, your body, and anything you lift, will feel heavy. So, conserve your strength.

"We all look forward to meeting you in person very soon!"

Corvis had been monitoring the cabin. The younger children hadn't paid attention to the general's speech, and the older children got more and more excited. By the end, most of the children were literally bouncing off the walls.

Svet made an announcement: "There is food in the cafeteria. Feel free to sit at your normal table, and robots will bring snacks to you. Be thinking about what you want to wear for your arrival on Enceladus."

Onboard the *Nursery* a celebration had begun.

Corvis watched as the settlement came into view. Large ice-glass domes stood close to the huge circular runway. These were dwarfed by even more gigantic domes in the distance. Even from 10 kilometers away, the ground at the base of the domes looked lush and green. He wanted to think about anything but what might happen to the *Nursery* and all its inhabitants, in the next few minutes.

With Sal in control, his work was finished. He could just relax. Then, suddenly, he realized that he hadn't packed his own belongings. Plus, he'd been wearing his light-green jump suit for two days. He had to shave, shower, and change.

After his shower, he felt clean and fresh. Since he only had two jump suits it wasn't hard to decide what to wear for arrival: the light blue one. He left the dirty green one in the hammock, along with his small duffel bag. He was both excited and fearful. He imagined the children were even more eager to get out of the ship.

"OK, space-people," he announced, "it's time to buckle up for landing on Enceladus. If you need to go to the bathroom do it now. Then please go to the cabin and be seated."

As he sat in the captain's seat, he felt barely perceptible gel automatically fill around the back of his body and his neck as part of the landing sequence. Seatbelts deployed. For 15 minutes, he feared they all were going to die. He had to trust Sal, the computer. That wasn't easy. Even though he was sitting in the pilot's seat, the computer was in complete control... it seemed like they were coming straight down, and it felt like they were falling far too fast.

Suddenly, they bounced. Hard. The windshield and all monitors suddenly went totally white as a cloud of soft snow rose around the *Nursery*, then very slowly fell back to the moon's surface. According to the altimeter, they ascended fully 20 meters. Traumatized children screamed. Several seconds later they bounced hard, again, but went up only 5 meters this time. Again, the children screamed. The ship bounced several more times as small jets guided the *Nursery* around the circular runway. They scooted along the soft runway on *Nursery*'s ventral surface, around and around the circle. Finally, they came to a stop. The Sal detected no leaks. *Nursery* had survived the landing and, as far as Corvis knew, so had all the passengers.

His seat, which had been in a fully reclined position righted itself, and his seatbelt stowed itself.

"Welcome to Enceladus," he announced over the PA as soon as he found his breath. "Your seatbelts will release now, and you may go the alcoves. You will see a line of float busses coming to the *Nursery*. They'll take you up to one of those domes."

A small vehicle approached. "Please open your main port for the drones and health workers," Ms. Graham announced over the radio.

Fifteen minutes later, the little float had equalized pressure with the *Nursery*. A dozen drones, two robots, and three healthcare workers entered the lobby while Corvis watched on his monitor.

"Several drones and robots will be coming through our ship," he told everyone. "Three Dan helpers are with them. Svet will give you final instructions about leaving the *Nursery*."

He quickly programmed all the robots to follow the orders of the Enceladan authorities.

The children watched in awe as the large silver robots, so different from the small white ones they were used to, rolled through the cabin and on through the rest of the ship. *Nursery* felt so much smaller, now that the tiny gravity of Enceladus dictated an 'up' and a 'down.' Drones buzzed busily around and between their seats, then exited the cabin to examine the other parts of the ship.

The healthcare workers wore disposable scrubs that covered them from neck to ankle, under long white lab coats. Blue face masks and blue head and shoe coverings completed their attire. Some of the children appeared afraid at first, while others vied for attention from the first outsiders they had seen in three months. Workers spoke with each child.

"Hi, I'm Tom," one said.

Before he could ask, a four-year-old responded, "I'm David."

The boy next to him piped up, touching Tom's face. "I'm Jacques, and I'm three!"

After an hour, Ms. Graham again appeared on Corvis's screen. "Thanks to your cooperation, we have gathered all the health data we need for the moment. There will be more questions in the future, of course. You're now free to disembark."

Corvis heard Svet announce over the PA, "When your name is called, please, walk to the Lobby. Please stay in the cabin until your name is called. I know you are excited to get off the ship. It won't be long now.

"Groups of 10 to 12 children will enter the sally port. The air pressure will go down, and your ears may pop, but you will be fine. You will go directly through a tube into a float bus. The bus will take you to the dome, where you will go through another tube, and some adults will meet you inside. All your personal belongings will be given to you this evening, so you don't need to worry about them right now.

"Rose, Gabrielle, and Charity will go with the first group. Your little bundles will follow once everyone has left the ship."

I'm not needed on the Bridge, now or ever again, Corvis thought. He felt a strange sadness. Even before leaving the ship, he had nostalgia for the job of captain. He waited in Reception to encourage the children as they left their rickety spaceship and emerged into their new home. Their tiny, battered, bandaged frames seemed even more vulnerable than they had appeared three months earlier, around the campfire in Gabon. But now Corvis knew them each by name: Mary, with her facial scars, tall David and short John, his faithful copilots, tiny Jaques... Off they went, limping, leaning on each other for support into waiting busses.

Finally, came Dominic in his cervical collar, Loic in his cast, and Miriam on her stretcher. One-legged Erwan briefly held the hand of his new Dan friend. Svet and Corvis, his left arm in a sling, were the last to leave.

General Dioikis had asked Corvis to leave all internal systems running so his engineers could determine the most efficacious way to cannibalize every bit of the ship. It still felt strange to leave the *Nursery* with all systems still running.

Three months ago, their ship was in mint condition, and now the salvage operation had already begun. He smiled at the irony.

43
Setting Foot on Enceladus

THE INTERIOR OF THE bus was white, white seats, white walls, and white frosted windows. The ride took less than five minutes. As it came to a stop the recording repeated, "Please wait for the tube to pressurize. The door will then open, and you may depart the bus. Please be sure you have all your belongings."

The final bus floated up to an opening to a tunnel. A sleeve sealed to the door of the bus, and air whistled as air pressures equalized. Corvis imagined news cameras were rolling as they stepped out of the tunnel onto Enceladus's tundra. The gravity of Enceladus, feeling almost nonexistent, still gave him a clear sense of being on *terra firma*. It felt very strange. He noticed children push off from walls as if testing to see whether they were still weightless. They jumped high but came back down to the ground. They were also shivering. The living areas of the *Nursery* had been heated, the Arrivals Hall much less so.

As they had been warned, they had to go directly to the showers. It felt strange to take off all his clothes as soon as he arrived. The shower room looked and felt like any other athletic facility, but he knew that the "water" was a strong antiseptic mixture. Brief health screenings followed, after which, each of them was given a wristband for "walking quarantine." And they gave each person an ugly, but warm, gray overcoat, since they had all come from African summer to this icy moon.

After the extensive health precautions, they were set free to meet the hundreds of Dans who had come to receive them. Corvis's eyes had trouble focusing on individuals; there were so many different people dressed in a wide variety of styles and colors. He heard bits of conversations in many different languages. Food stands and gift shops lined the walls of the large Arrivals Hall. The scents of fresh popcorn and other snack foods permeated the environment, making him hungry. People he didn't know waved. He looked around and realized they were waving at him. He waved back and smiled.

Finally, he saw Billy and Tyler attired in their sharp dress space force uniforms. Tyler and Svet embraced and kissed a long, lascivious kiss in front of everyone. Billy tackled Corvis and gently wrestled him to the ground, taking care not to hurt Corvis's injured arm. They kissed.

Corvis had never been happier than in that moment. He didn't want to get up.

He could only see the few children who had been with them on the final bus. "Where are the rest of the kids?" he asked, nervously looking around.

"Most are already with their foster families. The rest of the children are safely in the hands of Social Services," Billy reassured him. "Let's relax and enjoy ourselves. I'll walk you to the school, where we'll have lunch." The air outside was freezing. Corvis pulled the arms of his coat closer, and Billy threw an arm over his shoulders. A sidewalk led through the lawn surrounding the white Arrivals Building to a street. Each building on both sides of the street had landscaping with shrubs and flowers close to the building, and lawn out to the sidewalk. "How do they get flowers and grass to grow in this frigid air?" Corvis asked.

"All our plants have been genetically engineered to withstand the cold. We don't have seasons here. What you see is what you get... all the time," Billy said grinning.

The buildings were long and deep, and most were five stories tall. A sign above the front door of a blue building read "Tethys Residence." The one on the next building read "Europa Residence." Between two of the buildings was a terraced "Community Garden," with colorful flowers, large and small, and vegetables of several varieties in neat rows.

"Does everyone live in a large residence," Corvis asked, "or do some people live in separate houses?"

"We all live in residences," Billy replied. "It's more practical. Heating is a real challenge since ice is our main building material; so private houses would be prohibitively expensive to maintain."

A minute later he announced "We're here. This is where we'll have lunch."

A semi-circular driveway fronted the bright-red three-story building. A border of flowers framed a small lawn. A half dozen bike racks lined the walkway to the entrance.

"Since all of these buildings are made of ice," Corvis asked, "how is it that they're different colors?"

Billy smiled. "After the building is erected, it is sprayed with a kind of water-stucco dyed with different colors."

The Decorations Committee had adorned Mimas Elementary

School Gym in blue, green, and yellow stripes, the colors, and design of Gabon's flag. In the center of each table was a bouquet of yellow and blue flowers with lots of greenery. Corvis was relieved to see all our children there, each with a foster parent or two.

"Dans love gatherings like these," Billy explained.

People milled about. Corvis overheard one adult say to another, "This is my new foster son, Henri. What is your daughter's name?"

"This is Serena," the other adult replied.

Precisely at 1625 hours (on Enceladus noon is 1625 hours, the middle of its 32-hour, 50-minute day) lunch was served. After a green salad, they each got a bowl of soup with fufu, a traditional Gabonese dumpling.

Before the main course, Svet, smiling broadly yet flushed, asked for directions to the restroom. Tyler followed. They didn't return to the meal.

An hour after lunch began, it was time for dessert.

Dessert

Billy invited Corvis to his apartment, and they left just as dessert was being served. Billy had something even sweeter planned. They walked to Europa Residence.

"I live on the third floor," he explained.

A silver-headed butl-bot with a shiny black body and white tie met them at the door, wearing a white apron. "Good afternoon, Sir Billy," it said.

"Good afternoon, Bot-bot," Billy replied. "This is Corvis. He will be staying with us."

"I'm pleased to meet you," Bot-bot said. "Do you like coffee in the morning?"

"Yes, Bot-bot, I do."

"We're running low on bread and beer..." Bot-bot started.

"Take care of the supplies, Bot-bot," Billy said.

"We've had several visitors while you were gone..."

"Not now, Bot-bot," Billy cut it off.

His apartment was simple. A light blue spread covered his bed. The kitchen consisted of a sink, a fridge, a 2-burner stovetop, a built-in oven, and a dishwasher. A counter that also served as a bar jutted a little more than a meter into the living space. The living room had a black sofa and matching chair and a coffee table. A door led to the bathroom.

When he started taking off his uniform, Corvis stopped him. "Please, let me," he said quietly.

Corvis undressed him as slowly as he could, which is to say he practically tore his uniform from Billy. Billy undressed Corvis with matching vigor.

After they had both come, Corvis said, "Sex in extremely low gravity is something I could get used to." Billy laughed. A few minutes later, they got dressed.

"Bring your coat," Billy said, "I'll show you around."

They walked for a couple of hours, while Billy showed Corvis the hospital, the federal building, and other points of interest. They stopped for a snack at about 2130 hours at the Moon Beam Deli. Billy had a yak-tongue sandwich, and Corvis had a chard and kale salad with raisins and peanuts dressed with balsamic vinaigrette.

"Which would you like to visit first," Billy asked, "the zoo, or the botanical gardens?"

"Why don't we go to the zoo? That would be fun."

"Great choice. It will give you a chance to ride on a float-bus."

"I already rode on one, from the *Nursery*. Remember?" Corvis said.

"Yes," Billy said, "but you'll actually be able to see out the windows of this one."

After our snack, they walked a short distance to a bus stop. A float-bus descended to let them on.

Billy walked past the driver to a seat.

"Don't we have to pay?" Corvis asked.

"We pay, all right," Billy replied, "in our taxes."

A few seconds, later they arrived at the junction of the current dome with the next one to the south. The sign above a wide archway read, "Busses only."

"This is one of the agricultural domes," Billy said, "the zoo is about a quarter of a kilometer from here." Verdant fields of corn, cabbage, and other vegetables spread out below us, with robots tending the crops. The bus landed in front of a building with a new sign, reading "Enceladus Zoo," in blue letters; but in front of the first word was a caret, pointing to the added word "Autonomous" in red.

Inside the building, a turnstile met us. The sign read "18+, 1 Ecu; 3 – 17, 0.5 Ecu."

"What does that mean?" Corvis asked.

"It means if you're 18 or older you pay one cube. 3 to 17 you pay half a cube."

"Umm... What's a cube?" Corvis asked.

"The cube is our unit of currency," Billy explained. "It's backed by the total number of cubic meters we have under domes. The number of cubes in circulation increases little-by-little as new domes are completed, so we don't have inflation. There is a direct relationship between the area we have for crops and our prosperity."

He paid their entrance fee, and they went inside. Almost all the live animals within the zoo were of the common economic variety: yaks, sheep, dogs, chickens. Most lived outdoors in the cold, while others had heated shelters. Some animals represented didn't seem to have any economic value, such as cats, guinea pigs, and pangolins.

"Why pangolins?"

"Once we had sufficient genetic variability in our farm stock, Earthers sent us a few live specimens of endangered animals. Enceladus is a kind of secret gene repository. You'll see much more of that in the botanical gardens."

Niches in the zoo also had holograms displaying native fauna, while recorded lectures explained each species. They included "snowballs" and "walking cracks" from the surface, and dozens of fish from the ocean deep below Enceladus's ice. One diorama was devoted to satendrites which Billy had taught Corvis about. They walked and sat, talked and passed time in comfortable silence.

"You must be tired," Billy said.

"On the contrary," Corvis said, "it's so nice not piloting a ship while tending to the physical ailments of 312 wounded children that I'm really enjoying myself. I love being with you."

A few minutes later, Billy said, "Sorry to end our time in the zoo, but we need to head home and freshen up for dinner."

"Do we have a reservation somewhere?" Corvis asked.

"Didn't you know?" Billy asked, looking at him oddly. "You have a formal dinner with all the kids and the President. Speeches, and all that."

"Awww... do we have to?" Corvis pretended to whine.

"I don't, but you do," Billy said, grinning. "You're one of the 'guests of honor, buddy.' We must be at the high school by 2800 hours. And we have to get you a pair of pants and a shirt on the way."

"I don't have any cubes," Corvis told him.

"It will be my 'Welcome to Enceladus' present to you'."

"I'm glad I'll see the kids tonight. I worry about them, being away from them for such a long time. Can't help it."

"They're not your responsibility now. Let their parents take care of them."

"Sounds funny, 'their parents.' To me they have always been orphans."

"Now you get to have a life of your own... after tonight, that is."

Dressing for Dinner

A float bus stopped at 2630 hours and took them to a shopping district Corvis hadn't seen before.

"This is where I buy most of my clothes," Billy said, as we entered a men's store. "Do you have any Earther sizes?" Billy asked the clerk. "My friend here needs a pair of slacks and a shirt."

"But of course," the clerk said, looking Corvis up and down. "Inseam about 19 centimeters?" he asked.

"Spot on."

"We don't have cotton that short," he said thoughtfully. "Can you wear wool?"

"That would be great," Corvis said.

He showed him a brown pair of pants, a dark blue pair, and a black-and-grey check pair.

"Let me try the blue pair," he said.

They fit perfectly.

"Now, your shirt size would be about a nine-centimeter collar and 17-centimeter sleeves?"

"You nailed it, again," Corvis said.

"Right this way," the clerk said, a bit smugly. "We don't display all the shirts, just the color and pattern selections. Please make your selection and then I will bring out your shirt."

There were more than 20 options to choose from. One pattern caught his eye: it was a kind of abstract plant in dark blue with big, bright red abstract flowers, on a white background. Corvis held it in front of himself so that Billy could see it against his new slacks. "What do you think?" Corvis asked.

"It's perfect," Billy said, "I like tropical designs."

Corvis hadn't been on Enceladus even one full day yet, but it felt like his new home. He had expected it to feel claustrophobic, being restricted to the protection of the domes, but so far at least, it felt quite roomy. And as for Billy and him, it seemed like they had been with each other forever, even though they had never dated or gotten to know each other except during the crisis of fighting off a powerful enemy.

"I don't have my own place yet," Corvis said. "Can I spend the night with you?"

"Strange question," Billy said. "I just assumed we would spend tonight and all the rest of our nights together."

"You don't know how good that makes me feel!"

When they got back to his place, Billy asked "Do you want to shower first or me?"

"I've already had two showers today," Corvis said. "I hope I don't need a third." He enjoyed getting ready for a night out together, even though it was business-related. Concerned about whether his buttons lined up, he asked Billy, "Am I straight?"

"No," he said with a crooked grin.

Corvis kissed him.

Dinner was in the gym of the only high school on the moon, with the imaginative name "Enceladus Secondary School." Again, a careted 'Autonomous' had been added to the beginning of the name. Corvis figured it would take some time for the moon's signage to catch up to the new governmental reality, and whoever was manufacturing the new signs stood to make millions of cubes.

Located just south of Saturn Stadium, and immediately west of the convention center, the building was unusually high at six stories. Two wings had been added, and these had been extended, over the years as more Birth-Dan children reached the appropriate age. The central building was purple; the building to the left, also six stories, but much larger than the central building. It was dark blue, and the wing to the right was green.

As they approached, Billy said, "The gym is the third largest indoor meeting place in town. It's always booked."

When they got to the door, Corvis blinked and said, "This gym is gigantic."

"Normally, it's sectioned into four separate gyms, actually."

In the periphery around the tables, children ran and played. But for the occasional missing limb, and their dark complexion, Corvis might not have recognized the children from the *Nursery*. They had traded their jumpsuits for normal kids' attire. Classrooms scattered around the gym offered age-appropriate entertainment of various kinds.

"Care for a drink?" Billy asked.

"What're they offering?" I asked.

"Cocktails, beer, wine, non-alcoholic punch..."

"I would love to have a margarita," Corvis said.

Enceladus didn't disappoint on that measure. Billy returned with their drinks just as a woman stepped onto the stage. "Please take your seats," she requested.

Adults and a few teenagers slowly obeyed.

Corvis noticed Svet sitting next to Tyler at a table across the room, surrounded by a black family of older and younger adults. She looked radiantly happy. *Probably Tyler's family,* Corvis thought. He saw Mary, and knowing she couldn't see him, he went over and greeted her. She looked great in a simple black dress with a string of white beads.

"Soup will be served while our first speaker, President Hashkeh Naabah Cly, welcomes our new immigrants. President Cly?"

Corvis recognized him right away, of course, but the president looked small on the stage. "Good evening, ladies, gentlemen, and children. We extend a warm welcome to our new residents who have traveled for three difficult months to reach us from Earth.

"First, I want to thank those who prepared the delicious food for this banquet..."

The pumpkin soup was delicious, with a little zing, but not overly spicy.

The speeches went on and on. Children came to the table, ate a few bites, if they liked the food, and ran off to play again. Most adults spoke quietly until they had had too much to drink. For the main course, we had choices of chicken, beef, or vegetarian. Beverages were red wine, white wine, beer or water for adults, and milk or water for children.

"The children from the *Nursery* seem to already have assimilated with their new peers," Corvis whispered to Billy.

"Are you surprised?" he smirked.

Corvis smiled, feeling very contented.

While waiting for dessert, they made their way over to Tyler and Svet's table. On their way he heard a little voice behind me say, "that's Cap'n Crow!"

A child Corvis didn't recognize looked up at him and said, "Hi, Cap'n Crow."

He crouched down and offered a handshake. "Hi," he said, "what's your name?"

"I'm Thed," the child said.

Three-year-old Elizabeth from their ship, tugged at his hand and excitedly told him, "This is my fosser mom! I got a fosser dad, too!"

Tyler got up even before they arrived and greeted Billy with a strong hug and pat on the back. Svet looked beautiful in a low-cut, strapless red dress. She and Corvis also hugged. "Looks like our kids are doing fine in their new home," he observed.

"It certainly looks that way."

They returned to their seats for dessert. When they tried to leave one person after another wanted to talk either to

Billy or to Corvis. Finally, Billy took Corvis's hand firmly, and while talking, eased them both toward the door. "If we take the bus," Billy said, "we're captive. Let's walk. It isn't that far; less than half a click."

"Even though our days were lengthened during our trip, today feels like a really long one," Corvis said as they exited the high school.

"I hope you saved a little room for dessert," Billy replied.

"I have saved three month's-worth for tonight's dessert! It's just that the length of an Enceladan day in real life is different from what it seems when I'm watching the time on three different places on Earth plus the time on Saturn."

"My parents still find it strange for the date to change every 24 hours, regardless of the time of day. And three new days start on Saturn during just one on Enceladus. But Birth-Dans have never known a system where the date only changes in the middle of the night, so it doesn't feel strange at all to us."

They walked in gathering darkness along a well-lit road, holding hands. It wasn't any colder as night was falling. Corvis brought Billy's hand up to his heart. "I can't believe all of this is true," he said.

"All of what?

"Being here. Being off that herky-jerky ship. The kids being settled. Feeling happy and safe. Being with you. Being loved by you."

"Get used to it. It's real and it's permanent," he said.

"Even at night this place is beautiful."

"Seeing it through an outsider's eyes helps me see my home in a new light," Billy said. "I'm glad you're here."

"It's been a fantastic day," Corvis said as they entered Billy's apartment.

"And long!" he added. "Even for me. I can't believe it was just this morning that I was watching you land!"

The bag Corvis brought from New York, along with his dirty green jumpsuit, had already been delivered. Billy must have told them where to send the things.

"I don't normally wear pajamas," Corvis warned.

"You don't need no PJs for what I'm going to do with you," Billy replied.

44
First full day on Enceladus

CORVIS OPENED THE LITTLE bag he had brought with him from New York: some underwear, a couple of old shirts, a toothbrush, and a razor. He quietly hung his shirts in Billy's closet, then picked up the clothes that they'd flung on the floor the previous night.

A robot brought fresh coffee.

Billy was awake already when his perso rang. He set his perso on speaker. He heard Tyler's voice. "Are you free for breakfast?"

"Sure. Can I bring a guest?" Billy asked.

"Of course."

They both brushed their teeth and dressed quickly.

"Tyler's residence is only a hundred meters from here," Billy told Corvis.

He imagined a short, brisk walk. He had a surprise in store. Dozens of people were standing on the sidewalk, waiting to greet Billy. He'd become an overnight celebrity. He seemed genuinely surprised, as well, and casually chatted with people as they walked.

They arrived at Tyler's building and took the elevator to the fourth floor. Billy knocked.

Tyler opened the door. His flat was the same size as Billy's, but it looked completely different. The walls were red and green with black accents. A lion romped across his bedspread. Corvis smiled when he saw Svet wearing one of Tyler's shirts. And apparently nothing else. The tail reached down past her knees, and the sleeves had been rolled several times, and still her hands barely cleared. Corvis had never seen her looking so happy or sexy.

The bacon smelled divine.

While setting out breakfast, Tyler announced, "We're getting married!"

Billy replied, "So are we!"

Questioning raised eyebrows constituted the only proposal Corvis ever got. His nod was his acceptance. "Let's do a double wedding," Corvis said.

Smiles all around.

"I like it," Svet said with a grin. "Three husbands and one wife."

"If you have no objections," Billy said, "I would like JiAnn to do the service."

"Good choice," Tyler agreed.

"I want to do it as soon as possible," said Svet.

"So, I don't change my mind?" Tyler joked.

Tyler and Svet had prepared a large omelet and lots of toast with butter and jam. We all had coffee.

"I wonder how the children passed their first night on Enceladus," Svet said.

"I'm sure they did fine. They had each other, and plenty of helpers if they needed anything," Corvis said.

While Corvis was eating Billy put his strong hands on Corvis's shoulders. *That feels good, but is this the right place for intimacy?* He pulled, and Corvis noticed that he had been slumping. "Thanks," he said, noticing that both he and Tyler sat very straight.

After breakfast, Billy and Corvis thanked Svet and Tyler, and Billy and Corvis took their leave.

On the sidewalk again, Corvis told Billy, "I need to check on the older girls who lost their babies."

"And I need to meet with JiAnn." Then Billy asked, "Will you have dinner with me?"

"You *ask* if we'll eat together," Corvis laughed, "but inform that we'll be spending the rest of our lives together. Of course, I want to have dinner with you!"

"And meet my parents?"

"Oh, my God! This is *real*!"

"Don't worry. They'll love you."

Settling In

Corvis had some trouble finding the older girls. With the help of several Dans along the way he finally found the university where the younger children were housed in the gym, and the older girls in a visitors' dormitory. He thought the young ones might be disoriented and a little shy. He was surprised to find them all running and jumping, laughing, and playing with Enceladan children. *They're now Dans, too, Earth-Dans.*

He approached the reception desk in the large lobby. "May I speak with Rose, Gabrielle, and Charity?" he asked the receptionist. "They're older girls, newly arrived from Earth."

Five minutes later, they came down the stairs. They settled in a small visiting room. Two settees and two chairs lined the walls, and a small table with five chairs stood in the middle of the room under a tasteful chandelier. The deep burgundy drapes were pulled back, and the lighting was warm.

He leaned in and quietly asked them, "How are you doing?"

"Not so good," Rose admitted.

"They let us see the faces of our babies," Charity said, "but said that the Health Authority required tests... and then, they took our babies away again."

Rose touched the back of Charity's hand. "Even if they're free of disease, they'll have to remain in the morgue until the day of the funeral. Just imagine how this hurts us."

"Their laws require that my baby either be cremated," Gabrielle said, "or buried in the cemetery outside the Bubbles."

Rose held Gabrielle's hand, and said, "We can visit the cemetery as often as we wish, but we must wear spacesuits to go outside the domes. The temperature of the gravesites is -187° C. to -193° C. It's hard for us to put our babies from the jungle into such a cold place. I know they're not suffering there, but I can't stop thinking about them out there in the cold. I cry all the time."

"Your babies are at peace now," Corvis said. "Frozen at such a cold temperature, they will remain unchanged for centuries."

Speaking for all three, Rose said, "We are sad, of course, but we must accept the customs of our new home. We can never go back to Shimbezu."

"Is there anything else?" Corvis asked. "Anything you need?"

"I know Mary will attend the funeral," Gabrielle said. "I think she will need help. She had a miscarriage on our trip. She'll want to be included. Do you think someone could guide her?"

One more thing for my checklist, Corvis thought. "I'll talk to her."

He spent a good part of the rest of the day consulting with social services about the children's placements and the activities they would be engaged in.

"It's been a challenge for us," the social worker admitted. "We've never had so many children enter the system all at once before. Fortunately, we had almost three months to prepare. Hundreds of people volunteered, but even with careful planning there'll still be glitches."

Next, he set off for the hospital to visit Dominic and Miriam. When he arrived at the hospital, he almost walked past it. It was smaller than any hospital he had ever seen before, at only five stories tall. The first two stories were light brown, and the top three stories were white. Once inside, he discovered that the first two floors were doctors' offices and labs, and the hospital itself started on the third floor.

"Hello," he said to the receptionist. "I'm Corvis Santos, and I'd like to visit Dominic Ondo and Miriam Mengue."

"Oh, those are the children from the *Nursery*," the man replied. "Dominic Ondo has been discharged, but Miriam Mengue is still here. Corvis Santos is listed as her guardian. Do you have identification?"

Fortunately, he had put his wallet in his pocket before leaving for the day, unlike the three months on the *Nursery*. "All I have is my New York state driver's license."

The receptionist laughed. "That'll be fine. She's in Room 507." The elevator listed a sixth floor that wasn't visible from the street. Beside "6" it read "Emergency." *Odd to have the Emergency Department on the top floor.*

As he walked to the room, he looked around. It was a very modern hospital, with all the latest equipment. It smelled clean. On the way to Miriam's room, he passed double doors with a sign above reading "Intensive Care." *Maybe I'll be working there soon.* He realized that he was much more mature and capable than he had been just three months earlier. On the other hand, fatigue settled over him as he thought about the long stressful hours he would spend there. *I'll sort that all out soon enough. Right now, I'm a guardian and I'm about to visit my five-year-old.*

When he arrived, a doctor was talking with her. He washed his hands and then introduced himself. "I'm Corvis Santos, Miriam's guardian."

"Hi, Cap'n Crow!" Miriam piped up, brightly. "I get to go home today!"

"I'm happy to hear that," he said, taking her little hand in his.

"I'm Doctor Carter," the woman said. "We did surgery last night under implied consent. She had received good care on the *Nursery*, making it easy to set the leg. She's already been up and walking. Her foster parents were in earlier, and I reviewed discharge orders with them. We want to observe her for a couple more hours, and when her new parents return, we'll make sure everyone understands that Miriam must not put weight on that leg for six weeks while the bone heals."

"Thank you for your help, Doctor Carter," he said.

"No problem, Captain Crow" she replied as she left the room. Then, she ducked back in and whispered, "If you're not busy, I'd love to take you to dinner."

"Sorry," he said, "I have a prior commitment."

"I met my new father-brothers," Miriam cried happily, "They signed my cast. See?"

He exclaimed over their scrawled signatures as she told him about them. He stayed with her for a few minutes, and when she drifted off to sleep, he quietly left.

As he started to leave the hospital, he decided to take advantage of the fact that he was there. Returning to the Reception desk, I asked "Where will I find Human Resources?"

"That office is in Room 215. That's downstairs in the East Wing," the receptionist informed him.

Moments later, he stepped up to the receptionist's desk in HR. "Hello," he said, "My name is Corvis Santos..."

'I recognize you from the news," the woman said, "Welcome to Enceladus."

"Thank you. I'm here to apply for a position as a registered nurse."

"Wonderful!" the woman said. "The initial application takes about ten minutes to fill out. After that, you'll have an interview with the nursing director and two others. You can step into the booth to your left and fill out the application."

The "application" was completely verbal. A generic avatar said, "Please spell your full name."

He spelled his name.

"Please spell your address, using letters and numerals only."

He replied, "I don't yet have a permanent address."

The machine replied, "Using only letters and numerals, please spell out your address."

With the help of the receptionist, he was able to give Billy's address and contact information as his own. In a few minutes, he had finished the application.

He returned to Billy's apartment just in time to get ready for dinner.

45
Dinner with the Birchfields

"I DON'T HAVE ANY nice clothes, except the things you bought me yesterday," Corvis fussed. "Can I wear them again tonight?"

"Yes, of course, that will be fine," Billy assured him.

"I'll have to wear that ugly gray coat," he sputtered, while putting on his new blue slacks.

"Here. Wear this sweater instead," Billy said, tossing it to Corvis.

The cream-colored bulk-knit sweater felt like putting on Billy. It smelled like him. He hugged himself.

"Oh, this is perfect," he said, "I love it!" It was huge on him, of course.

"Head up, proud chest, tilt the pelvis forward," Billy advised.

Oh that feels sexy!

As they left for the Birchfields', Corvis was so nervous you would have thought he was going to dinner with Brobding.

Billy's fan club followed them all the way. Billy loved the attention.

The Birchfield's unit was on the ground floor. Billy knocked softly. A not-very-tall woman, about 5'10", met them at the door. *I thought she would be taller.* She had ordinary brown hair, worn in a pageboy cut. She wore denim pants and a long sleeve print top. Her feet were bare.

Billy doffed his shoes and pointed at Corvis's.

They entered the living room in their socks. It was about the same size as Billy's flat, with the dining room occupying the far end. *Obviously, this apartment is larger than Billy's,* Corvis thought.

"Come in," Mrs. Birchfield said, "Hi, Billy." They kissed each other on the cheek. "I recognize that sweater. We gave it to Billy last Christmas." She winked at me. "What can I offer you to drink?"

Corvis asked, "What do you have?"

Mrs. Birchfield laughed. "Beer, wine, iced tea..."

"I'll have a beer," he said.

"Me, too," Billy said.

Billy followed her into the kitchen, and Corvis followed both of them.

Their kitchen wasn't large, but it was designed for efficiency, with a range-top, and oven, dishwasher, and refrigerator all built into the wall. The sink was larger than Billy's and the countertop was twice the size of his. Looking at Billy, Corvis asked, "Did you grow up in this apartment?"

"He sure did," Mrs. Birchfield replied.

Billy handed me a beer, and we headed into the dining room.

"Every night... well, almost every night... he ate dinner at this very table.

"Right off the bat, I knew he was special. My labor was so easy, but he was such a long baby. Fifty-six centimeters!"

Billy rolled his eyes. Apparently, he'd heard all this before.

"And he was such a good boy," she continued, "he got along so well with other children..."

Even though she didn't stop for a breath, Billy interrupted, "Mom, he doesn't need to hear every moment of my life up to 18 years."

"OK, Billy, she said, looking at me, "but he was and is exceptional. "So, you're getting married!"

"How did you know!?" Billy exclaimed, "I thought *I* was going to tell you!"

"Same way I always knew when you did something bad at school before you got home. Enceladus is a small town, and news travels fast."

"So, what do you think?" he asked.

Corvis couldn't breathe while waiting for her answer.

"What do *I* think?" she replied. "Aren't you glad you waited for the right guy?"

At that moment, Mr. Birchfield came through the front door and took off his shoes. He wore a white shirt and tie, and grey slacks. He was obviously some kind of professional person. "Well," he said, "the happy husbands have come for dinner, I see."

"We're not married yet," Billy protested.

"Soon enough." Mr. Birchfield was about 6 feet tall. He looked short next to Billy. He gave Corvis a big hug.

Dinner was fried chicken. "This is absolutely glorious," I enthused, "especially, after three months of algae pretending to be food."

Billy put his hands on Corvis's shoulders and straightened his posture.

That does feel good, but it adds to my self-consciousness, which I don't need at this moment.

Billy's parents pretended not to notice.

"Fred and I are both Earth dans, like you," Mrs. Birchfield laughed. "We made the long voyage, and as Billy has heard a million times, we ate enough algae on that trip to last us a lifetime!"

Billy rolled his eyes again. "I *have* heard this a million times, so what's one more?"

Mrs. Birchfield looked at her plate.

During dinner, Billy said casually to Corvis, "By the way, JiAnn would like to meet you."

"OK," Corvis said. "When?"

"After supper, about 2700 hours."

"Tonight?"

"Yes. Can you do that?"

"I don't have anything else to do," Corvis said, thinking, *except make love with you, which I've been waiting for all day.* "But what about your soccer match?"

"How did you know about that?" Billy asked.

"I heard you talking to Pistis about it after you left the *Nursery*."

"I didn't realize we were transmitting to the *Nursery*. Coach wouldn't let me play," Billy said, "I missed practice."

"But you're a hero!"

"Eh? But rules are rules."

As Corvis got up and walked toward the kitchen, he caught Mrs. Birchfield's eye and motioned with his chin for her to join him.

"Mrs. Birchfield..." he began.

"Please, call me Betty," she replied.

"Betty, I want to give your son a wedding gift, but I don't know what he would like."

"Give him something symbolic, not expensive," she said, "What is an interest you both share?"

Nothing came to mind, immediately.

When he went back to his seat, Billy said, "Don't sit down, Honey. We need to leave to go to JiAnn's."

Meeting JiAnn

Caverns Residence, where JiAnn lived, was half a kilometer away. The crowd waiting for Billy was even larger than before.

Once they were on the sidewalk, Corvis stretched up, trying to whisper in Billy's ear. "I want to make love with you."

"That'll happen tonight, trust me."

Billy shook hands with nearly everyone he met, and then said repeatedly, "I have a meeting I have to attend, and Corvis and I need to talk." Afterward, the crowd followed at a respectful distance. As they walked, Billy said, "JiAnn's still one of the most influential people on Enceladus. She's now Dragomark Emeritus, but she still sees whatever the satendrites see. She has the ear of President Cly and any of the representatives she wants to consult with. You'll love her, and she'll love you... But don't forget to treat her with respect."

Holding Billy's hand, Corvis said, "And you're just the Apprentice, Ace Pilot, and hero of Enceladus." Pointing over his shoulder with his chin at his followers, "In case you hadn't noticed."

He chuckled.

JiAnn, dressed in a skin-tight, strapless black evening gown, opened the door wide and gave Billy a long hug. Then, after looking Corvis up and down, she hugged him, also. *For starters, I'm obviously significantly underdressed for the occasion.*

Billy tapped Corvis's shoulders, and Corvis straightened them, lifted his chest, and cocked his pelvis.

JiAnn served tea. It tasted like some decaf, herbal concoction, smooth, but uninteresting. "So, the wedding will be March fifth, I understand," JiAnn said.

Surprised, Corvis looked at Billy, who raised one eyebrow. "Svet suggested the date," Billy said. "By the way, go light on the tea."

"Yes," Corvis said, "that's right."

"At Saturn Stadium," JiAnn said.

Before Corvis could express his dismay, Billy said, "I wanted a small affair, but President Cly vetoed that idea."

"As would I," JiAnn said.

After three more sips of JiAnn's tea, Corvis was feeling no pain, so he just grinned. "Anything is possible," he said, happily.

"Now, about you," JiAnn said, holding Corvis's hand. "You're going to be the husband of a very famous man. And he will love you with all his heart."

"So, I'm learning," Corvis said. "I mean the famous part. And he will be a wonderful dad to our children. That, I already knew."

"And you," she said, "you're a good mate for him."

"Speaking of children..." Corvis said, taking another sip of the bland tea.

JiAnn looked quizzical.

"Three small children died during our trip. Would you consider talking to their moms about a memorial service?"

"Of course," she said, "Anything else?"

"Just some information. Where can I get a shoebox and some wrapping paper?" he finished his tea.

What seemed like one second later to Corvis, their conversation was apparently over, because JiAnn stood, as did Billy, who hadn't touched his tea.

Corvis stood... but his knees buckled, and he sat right back down. He vaguely heard JiAnn and Billy laughing.

Corvis didn't remember walking home. But he *did* remember *never* to drink JiAnn's tea again.

46
Planning the Memorial

JiAnn • March 1, 2100

JiAnn wore pink pants and a light green top to meet with the three Gabonese girls, who looked too young to be mothers, in the dormitory visiting room. "Tell me about yourselves," JiAnn invited.

Rose started. "We come from an area of Gabon called Shimbezu. We live... lived, that is, in a beautiful green jungle. It has been a long trip, and we know we can never return. In fact, we know that most people on Earth are now dead."

Charity said, "Soldiers of fighting warlords repeatedly attacked our villages. Each of us was raped. The fathers of the babies we lost were vicious soldiers who murdered our mothers in front of us. But our babies... we loved our babies." Charity fell silent.

Gabrielle picked up the theme. "Now we, along with all the Gabonese children, are here, on this frozen moon that you have turned into a beautiful garden."

"I've never had a child myself," JiAnn said, "I can only imagine your loss.

"How did your babies die?"

Charity answered. "My Anabelle got bone plague. She had a high fever, then she had seizures and died."

"I'm so sorry. You've already lived a lifetime in your short lives," JiAnn said, "Hopefully, your life here will be much happier."

JiAnn opened a screen and laid it on the table where all the mothers could see the images.

"The cemetery was designed years ago," she said, "Eventually it will have the shape of a bouquet of flowers, but for now just the first pedal of the first tulip is taking shape. Two adults and two children are buried on Enceladus now. "These four are buried in the outer edge of the pedal, but your children, being small could fit in the very center of the flower. Would you like that?"

The young mothers nodded.

"When would you like to have the service?" JiAnn asked.

"As soon as possible," Rose said, "this evening?"

JiAnn gulped, then paused. "You and your children are heroes to all Enceladans. Future generations will recognize their names. Could we do the service day after tomorrow? That will give our citizens a little time to prepare."

Their eyes did not meet JiAnn's.

"As you wish," Rose said. They all nodded "yes."

47
Helping Mary

CORVIS

CORVIS HAD CALLED AND arranged to meet with Mary Ndong at the dormitory. She wore a knee-length white dress that contrasted beautifully with her dark skin.

"How have you been doing?" he asked.

"I'm fine," she said, smiling and lively. "I already have a job. I'm playing piano at the high school, both for music classes and also to accompany instrumentalists and vocalists."

"Wow!" he said, genuinely impressed. "That sounds like a great gig!"

"I love it. Most of the kids are just a little younger than me."

"How do you learn what melodies to play, since you can't read sheet music?"

"There is Braille music, but I haven't used it. If I need to, I listen to a recording. But generally, I just have them start playing their piece, and then I join them, improvising. I have a good memory. The next time they arrive I know exactly what I'll play for them. For me, it's easy and fun! Best of all, I get paid for doing it, *and* I will get free lessons once a week."

"Sounds perfect," Corvis said. "On another matter, there are a couple of events coming up. One sad, and one happy. The memorial for the three babies who died on the *Nursery* is coming up..."

"Maybe they would like to have the song Lucy Aubameyang wrote," she said.

"That sounds like a great idea... to me. Why don't you talk to them about it?" Corvis said, "The other is my wedding. I hope you'll attend."

"Oh, Cap'n Crow! I'm so happy! I wouldn't miss it!" she enthused and reached out for a hug.

"Good," he said, after they hugged, "so what I want to know is whether you would like someone to guide you in the procession?"

"I generally walk by myself, thank you. I have good intuitions about my surroundings, and I use tongue clicks to keep me from bumping into things. But in a formal procession it might be nice to have a tapper."

"What's a tapper?"

"Someone who taps me once to turn left, and twice to turn right, and three times to stop. Abasi and I work well together. I will ask him. Thanks for the idea."

"Sounds like you've got it all figured out. Where will you stay when you leave the dorm?"

"Oh, we've moved out of here already. Four of us older girls are living together for now. But I would like to get a place of my own. They don't mean any harm, but they don't realize that when they move a piece of furniture, I bump into it, bruising myself. Or in the kitchen or bathroom, it's hard for me to find things when they have been moved. Living alone would be much easier."

"Let me know if I can help out in any way," Corvis said, shaking her hand.

Now there's a confident, talented young lady. She'll go far.

Loving Billy

March 2, 2100

Being with Billy was heavenly. But whenever they went out in public, crowds followed them. Billy loved chatting, shaking hands, and hugging people. He really soaked up his new fame... but Corvis just wanted to be alone with him.

At lunch, Billy said to Corvis, "You don't like the crowds, do you?"

"You must have been reading my mind!"

"Let's go fishing!" he said. "It's different on Enceladus."

"I would like that. Though I'm not sure I'll be much good at it."

"It doesn't matter whether we catch anything or not. What matters is that we'll get away from the crowds, away from the city, down into the caverns," he said. "We'll have time together, alone, in a really different environment."

"I'd like that."

"It's decided, then. We'll leave tomorrow morning." That night Billy was like a little kid, checking his tackle box, making sure we had long coats, lanterns, gloves, poles, and then rechecking the tackle box. "We'll be gone all day, so, we'll take a picnic basket with food for three meals and snacks, and two six-packs of beer."

This is what it will be like living with a celebrity. Invasive crowds will irritate me, but we'll get away by ourselves once in a while, Corvis thought. *Billy is so hot I can't blame people for wanting to warm themselves at the fire.*

"Let's make sure to pack a blanket."

"I can't stay overnight," Billy said.

"No, but the most fun part for me will be making love with my beautiful fisherman!"

Billy laughed and grabbed Corvis, and they had the best sex ever.

They lay in Billy's bed, hands on each other's bare chest, savoring the moment, feeling so at one. "When we have kids, our lives will change," Billy said. "We might not have long quiet moments like this..."

"True, and they'll be so cute. We'll be busy and loving every minute."

"And you're a nurse," he said, "so when they get hurt or sick, you'll know exactly what to do."

"Then, they'll go off to college..."

They were both naked when JiAnn called to discuss last-minute details about the memorial service with Corvis.

"I'm sorry, Billy, I can't go fishing tomorrow," Corvis told him. "We'll have to make it the day after tomorrow."

Memorial

A throng of people followed the mothers, who clutched their near-weightless little bundles. JiAnn was waiting when the group arrived at the sallyport.

Since most of the crowd would not be suiting up to go outside, JiAnn said a few words, and a small choir of the older children, led by Mary, sang the song "Shimbezu."

Only the mothers, Svet, JiAnn and Corvis suited up. They tested their radios before entering the super-cold vacuum outside the domes. *Nursery* loomed beside us. Brobding's brown fighter was still attached to the roof.

Nursery looked like a gigantic casserole being raided by ants, as a constant stream of workers carted its contents to waiting float-wagons.

They walked half a kilometer on the path. Above the path, a sign in the middle of a white ice arch announced, "Enceladus Cemetery." Two tiny cameras, one facing the path approaching the cemetery, and one facing the tombs, stood guard, recording anyone entering or leaving.

Two hundred meters down the path, Corvis saw a mound with a narrow path spiraling to the left up to a ten-meter summit. As they started up the mound, they passed two large, white crypts and two smaller ones on our right, arranged as a gentle crescent. On top of each crypt, Corvis read a name and the dates of birth and death, and a photo of the deceased. At the top of the mound, they found three small, open crypts, with baskets inside, with the cover for each leaning against the side.

JiAnn read the 23rd Psalm. Mothers laid their bundles in their baskets and tucked their baby blankets around them, and then placed the lids of glass-ice on top.

After a long moment of silence, JiAnn said, "Little children from Earth, you will not be forgotten, forever." These words had been carved into the ice plaque above their tombs.

My heart ached.

48
Fishing Trip

CORVIS HADN'T BEEN VERY excited about going fishing until the morning arrived. Realizing how nice it would be to have a whole uninterrupted day with Billy, he asked, "How much leave do you have?"

"I usually take my leave as soon as I earn it, but since I served 24-hour days for 10 days, and double that for hazard-pay, I have accumulated three days off. I work four on, three off, so I could right now take 6 days off in a row right now."

"Can you ask for at least a couple of days for our honeymoon?"

"Sounds like a plan!"

They dressed, packed up their stuff, and started off. Billy carried the huge "picnic" basket.

"Stand up straight, tight core," Billy reminded Corvis. "This morning we have a long hike, so I'll tell you how the entrance to the caverns was created. It happened accidentally."

They walked on a narrow path between rows and rows of tomatoes.

"Robots had capped a geyser for the first geothermal power plant. It was way out in the boonies at that time. One of the first things David, the first Dragomark, learned about satendrites was that they were suffering stress due to a large hole in their colony. He traced the cause of the hole to the lack of steam in the capped geyser.

"Rather than move the power plant, he programmed a robot to drill a new geyser 100 meters from the original geyser. The satendrites partially recovered, but output dropped from the geothermal plant.

"He drilled 12 small new geysers in a circle around the capped natural geyser, and then put a lid on the artificial geyser. Voila!"

"Voila, what?"

"Power output rose to 100%, and the satendrites recovered completely."

Just as they came to the juncture of the one dome that had become the city dome, with one of the many agricultural domes, three drones buzzed them in rapid succession.

"Teenagers! They love drones, and they love using them to be obnoxious."

As they entered the next dome, Corvis saw rolling hills growing different crops. They stayed on the path between fields of celery and wheat.

"You were going to tell me how the entrance to the caverns was created accidentally."

"That's about it," Billy said. "A settler was out exploring one day and looked down into an artificial geyser. She saw nothing. That is, she couldn't see the bottom, but the ice was striated, with natural places for feet and hands to hold on to. The steam was warm, but not extremely hot. She was curious, so she started climbing down into the geyser. Two meters down, she found herself in a gigantic cavern. That cavern led to a deeper cavern, and so on down to the ocean."

"Wow! What an amazing discovery!"

"Truly. The earliest settlers knew there was a gigantic ocean under all the ice of Enceladus, but it might have been years before fishing, either commercial or sport fishing, would've begun if she hadn't climbed down" he said.

"Look, there's a yak grazing. These hills are beautiful. They look natural, except for being perfectly symmetrical."

"Yaks are great! We race them, kids love to pet them, and they provide wool, meat, leather, and other byproducts. We don't have slaughterhouses on Enceladus; rather, vans visit the fields, stun, and slaughter yearling males, instantly and supposedly without pain, and transport the carcasses to the butcher factory. A similar process produces chicken meat. The hills are part natural and part artificial. We live close to the south pole to take advantage of the geysers. This region is also called the 'tiger stripes' region because of natural fissures in the ice. Outside the domes, in the valleys, we harvest 'star dust' that has accumulated over the millennia. Dust contains lots of iron, but also tiny olivine particles that, when placed under heat and pressure, produce beautiful gems. Robots build perfectly circular domes over the natural topography. Then we terrace the ice to maximize agricultural output. Infrared light from Saturn is as important as heat from the sun for growing our crops. Domes help to keep both air and a bit of warmth inside and protect us from harmful cosmic rays."

They had come to the southernmost point of the southernmost dome.

"It's time to suit up." He deposited two coins. Billy looked Corvis up and down. "Even when you stand up straight, you'll take a small adult."

"I can't get over it. No one on Earth ever called me small!"

"In case you haven't noticed, Birth-Dans grow tall because of the low gravity of this small moon."

He punched 'S,' and a closet door opened. Two more coins, and he punched 'L.'

Even on the *Nursery* Corvis had never worn a spacesuit, and he looked at his, clueless how to begin. Billy, on the other hand, was clearly an old hand.

"To don this type of spacesuit," Billy said, "just step into the lower part and pull it up a little. Now, put your arms over your head and stand up into the upper part. That's right. Good. Now flip the clamps on the left and right to attach the top to the bottom.

"Next the gloves and shoes. They're in this cabinet over here. There are seven sizes of shoes and gloves. You want a tight fit for your gloves. The tricky part, if you're suiting up alone, is clamping down the fitting around the gloves. You got it. Step into your shoes, and seal them to your suit.

"Finally, you just slip the helmet onto your head and clamp it to the suit at the neck. I'll guide your hands the first time. Outside the domes, ultraviolet rays are deadly, so find the knobs on the left and right side of the helmet. Turn either one of these to lower the filter and raise it back up," Billy said, "Try it."

Corvis did. "Oh, it gets really dark! And the helmet doesn't turn with my head."

"No, you have to twist and bend to see outside the range of vision of the helmet."

"That's cumbersome."

"If you think it's difficult putting on a spacesuit out in the open, like this, you should try doing it inside the small cockpit of a fighter."

"That would seem impossible!"

"It's hard, but machines make it easier. The upper part, stowed behind the seat, comes out automatically, and then the seat reclines entirely. The lower part is in the nose of the ship. The boots are already attached, so it's like putting on very long hip boots. You must keep your toes pointed the whole time until you're all the way in."

"So, the correct size suit for the particular pilot must be loaded into that particular fighter ahead of time."

"Actually, the whole fighter is kind of fitted to the individual pilot. The seat is made from a mold made by the pilot sitting in a special apparatus. The spacesuit is made to our exact measurements, not like these six sizes fit all."

"Six sizes? I only saw three."

"There are three child sizes, as well."

Outside the sallyport, this part of Enceladus looked more like Corvis had pictured it: blinding white underfoot, yellow looking at Saturn, and ink-black void pierced by billions of incredibly bright stars.

"Where's Earth?" Corvis asked, over the radio.

Billy studied the universe above for a minute. "Oh, it's already set."

After they had walked another kilometer, they arrived at the entrance to the caverns. It was nothing like what he had expected. A square, white building, four meters tall and ten meters on each side, marked the spot. An even larger building stood just to the south. A rush of steam escaped as Billy opened the sealed door.

"Can we take our suits off now?" Corvis asked hopefully, as they stepped inside.

"No, there's no natural atmosphere down here," he said. "We'll take off our suits inside my hut."

"It's obviously very humid in here, and yet my visor doesn't fog up. Why is that?"

"It's still close to freezing in here, but air circulation keeps the inner surface of your visor much warmer, so water doesn't precipitate on it."

They climbed down a few stairs cut in the ice and came to a pair of plastic rails. "The ladder goes straight down," Billy said, "Go down facing the ladder. Turn on your headlamp and follow me."

Billy strapped the bulky one meter "picnic basket" onto his back. Climbing down the ladder into the utter blackness was awkward in a spacesuit. After more than ten meters Corvis's foot touched ice.

"The next cavern below this is straight down for another two kilometers. The hard way is to continue climbing the ladder. The easy way is right here: the elevator. The elevator takes two minutes. The ladder takes a couple of hours... and *you* get to carry the picnic basket. Which do you want?"

"The elevator!"

"There's a freight elevator about a quarter of a kilometer from here, by a different entrance, under that large building you saw. That's for the commercial fisheries. It's really big, and it smells of fish."

Billy deposited another coin and the elevator door opened immediately.

Two minutes later they exited and walked down what appeared to be a deep subterranean, long, middle class, apartment complex. "These are the fishing huts," said Billy.

"Huts, indeed!"

A few meters later he said, "This one's mine."

He inserted the key, turned the nob, and pulled hard. The door unsealed, and they went in. The door sealed again after them. "Now, we can take off our suits. Your ears will pop because the air pressure is lower in here."

A moment later, taking off his helmet, Corvis scanned Billy's "hut." "This is bigger than my efficiency in New York." Even with artificial light, the unpainted walls reflected the pale blue color of deep ice. The effect was magical.

"Yah, we like 'roughin' it' *easy.*"

They started unloading the basket. Excited to be in this new, alien place, Corvis laid the tablecloth, and then they spread out the sumptuous feast Billy had assembled. Corvis must have been looking horny because Billy laughed,

"Food, first, then blanket."

"Now I see why it doesn't matter whether we catch any fish."

Billy had brought a three-course meal complete with champagne. They were both very hungry. "Eat lots of vegetables," Billy suggested. "You need to stay healthy."

After dinner, Corvis said, "I have a gift for you, that I brought all the way from Earth." He watched Billy's expression. He didn't seem particularly interested in the present.

Billy held the present to his heart. "Thank you!" he said, "I'll unwrap it after I unwrap *you.*"

After they had sex, there was no savoring the experience.

"It'll be dark out." Billy said. "We need to get back. Help me pack up our stuff."

That irritated Corvis. "Yes, sir!"

"Don't get snippy," he said. "You'll need a good night's sleep before the wedding."

"Look, I'm marrying you, not joining the army. I don't take orders from my husband."

"It wasn't an order," he said, "just an observation."

He's right. We do need to get back. When everything was packed, we put our spacesuits on. That's when Corvis started feeling claustrophobic. The closeness and sudden darkness terrified him.

Billy must have noticed Corvis's rapid breathing. "Breathe slow and deep," he said.

That was the last word either of them spoke until they got back to the apartment a couple of hours later. But Corvis's mind was going a mile a minute. *I can't wait to get this horrible spacesuit off.*

Then, as they walked in the dark, *I don't want to go back to his place. I'm tired of him telling me how to stand, what to eat. I need my own space. I need a place where I can go to put myself together when I'm about to have a meltdown. I know, I can go visit Svet and Tyler, but Tyler's Billy's friend. I need to have some friends of my own.*

When they arrived back at Billy's place, Corvis had rehearsed what he would say. "I know I was the one who wanted to get married as soon as possible, but I'm not sure I can go through with this tomorrow."

"That's fine," Billy said. "We can put it off. That's not the end of the world."

"Thank you for being understanding. It's late now. I don't want to wake people up to give them the bad news."

"No," Billy said. "Anyway, sleep on it."

There you go again telling me what to do.

49
Double Wedding

TRY TO SLEEP ON it Corvis did. That morning, in addition to being sleep deprived, he really had the jitters. He now had second thoughts about committing to live the rest of his life with Billy, but this was to be a major public event, and he could see the headlines "Recently arrived war husband leaves hero Billy standing at the altar!" On a personal level, marriage seemed like a deeply personal thing to Corvis, and all of Enceladus was going to be watching. He fretted about his hair, his fingernails that no one would even see, his shoes. Billy, on the other hand, casually put on his dress uniform, as if it was just another routine event. He just smiled, like he was born to thrive in the limelight.

Billy didn't ask Corvis about the pronouncement that he wasn't ready to get married. In fact, he didn't say anything.

Doesn't he care what I'm feeling? Is he afraid that anything he says might send me running off in anger? Corvis didn't say anything, either. As they took a limo to the stadium they looked out their respective windows. *I do still love Billy, but I feel trapped. I'll go through the motions, and if the marriage doesn't work out, we can get a divorce.*

Every non-essential Dan was seated in Saturn Stadium as their procession formed up at the entrance. The band played a triumphal march as Billy and Corvis, Svet and Trevor entered at the head of the cavalcade. Next came the other fighter pilots and their escorts and attendants. After them came JiAnn, as officiant.

The instant the children from Gabon and their new families entered the stadium, the crowd began cheering wildly. The children of *Nursery* wore dresses and shirts made of the fabric they brought from Earth, accented with the bead jewelry they had given each other for Christmas. They all looked so proud and happy. The older girls marched confidently, nodding to left and right. All the children stood tall with chests proud and waved to the people in the stands. Even the toddlers seemed to have grown a few centimeters, as they sensed they were the center of attention. *Nursery* families sat in places of honor.

Svet took Corvis's breath away. She had transformed herself from a schoolmarm into a gorgeous bride. Her hair was beautifully coiffed using extenders. She dazzled in her white gown with its two-meter train. The lace at the very low bodice had seed pearls sewn into the design. She carried a beautiful large bouquet of blue forget-me-nots, red lilies, and delicate green leaves.

Billy and Tyler also looked ultra-sexy in their tailored navy formal uniforms, that emphasized their muscular physiques, adorned with newly awarded E-Ring medals of valor. Corvis wore a black tux with scarlet bowtie and matching cummerbund. Caught up in the excitement, he forgot his doubts.

In the stands, people waved flags of the old colony and the new sovereign nation, as well as flags of Gabon and many other Earth nations.

They all took their places on a dais in the middle of the field. Close-ups of significant people, as well as randomly selected attendees flashed on the three-story screen at the end of the field. The band continued playing until the procession finished.

When a gigantic flag of Enceladus rose on the flagpole, the crowd spontaneously stood and sang the national anthem in unison. The band, taken by surprise, joined the crowd a beat late. Then silence descended. Even the smallest child did not make a peep.

The stadium was cold, barely above freezing, and even though the seats were heated, many people brought blankets.

JiAnn's voice echoed throughout the stadium. "We have gathered today to join two heroic couples in marriage..."

Because of the cold, the ceremony itself was brief in the extreme, the bare minimum to make us legally married. JiAnn first addressed Trevor and Svet. "Do you, Trevor, take Svetlana to be your legal spouse?"

Trevor responded, "I do."

"Svetlana, do you take Trevor to be your legal spouse?"

Svet said, "I do."

"I pronounce you married from this day forward."

JiAnn then turned to Billy and Corvis. "Corvis, do you take Billy to be your legal spouse?"

He said, "I do."

"Billy, do you take Corvis to be your legal spouse?"

When Billy said, "I do," the crowd erupted in cheers. Even the two of us couldn't hear JiAnn pronounce us legally married. Confetti and streamers flew.

President Cly then addressed the assembly with an uncharacteristically brief statement. "Everyone is invited to a powwow in the Assembly Hall immediately."

The crowd cheered wildly, as people began exiting.

Only the die-hards paid any attention to the formal recession. Those on the dais and the families of the Nursery exiting through the Home Team locker room.

The Assembly Hall was a short walk, about 250 meters, from the stadium.

50
Wedding Banquet

THE INTERIOR OF THE Hall was a gigantic, general-purpose meeting area. Hundreds of people were already seated.

Corvis's eyes bugged out as they entered. Row after row of long, narrow tables welcomed guests with beautiful, what appeared to be, china and silver settings, crystal glasses, and centerpieces of beautiful flowers, all of it recyclable. Hundreds of robots were stationed around the gigantic room, ready to serve food and beverages from huge carts with separate sections for hot and cold foods.

Children dressed in their finest clothes chased each other. Adults chatted and sipped beverages, but stopped mid-sentence when Billy walked by.

If there's one thing Corvis had learned about Dans, it is that they love feasting. Head tables were set on the stage. At their table, JiAnn was seated to Corvis's left, Billy to his right, to his right, his mother, and to her right his father. At Tyler and Svet's table, Tyler's parents sat on his left, with Svet on his right. General and Mrs. Dioikis sat to the right of Svet.

After the main course, President Cly started the toasts. "I rise to toast not only these two couples as they begin their life together, but also the brave pilots who brought these wonderful children safely to our moon: Ophelia Pistis, Dalisay Soliva, and Harriet Reitman of blessed memory, and two of the husbands, Tyler Washington, and Billy Birchfield. We bless you and we thank you!"

The hall thundered with a lengthy "Hear! Hear!"

Billy's father offered a toast. "Here's to my new son-in-law. Brave, courageous, and smart enough to choose the best."

Tyler's father toasted Svet.

Then Billy stood. "I rise to toast four people. Mom and Dad, I wouldn't be here without you. You believed in me and encouraged me to excel. To my buddy Tyler: I love you, brother. We survived hell together, we got married together, and we're going to watch each other's kids grow up together. To Corvis, what can I say? I loved you the first time I set eyes on you. The adventure is just beginning."

Finally, Tyler toasted his parents and Svet. "Last, but not least," he said, "I want to toast Billy, who always makes me feel like I'm the only person in the room. You truly listen to me, and occasionally, you even agree with me."

Everyone laughed.

Corvis was getting antsy. He just wanted to take Billy home and live happily ever after.

At the end of the toasts, a huge, four-tiered wedding cake, extravagantly decorated with dozens of different types of flowers, some of which grew on Enceladus, and of many which didn't, rode atop a white satin-covered cart that wheeled itself down the aisle. Above it floated a gift wrapped in white, topped with a large golden bow.

A new chapter in the lives of all Enceladans had just begun.

The End

Cast of Characters

- **Corvis Santos**   23 years old at beginning of saga Born December 23, 2075. Original profession: ICU nurse. Recruited to pilot the *Nursery* a remodeled space cruise ship carrying 314 orphans to a secret colony on Enceladus, a moon of Saturn. Unmarried at the beginning of the epic.

- **JiAnn Prophet**   49 years old at beginning Born January 21, 2050. Second Dragomark, interpreting messages from satendrites to the leaders of Enceladus Colony. Revered for her wisdom. She is both classy and foxy.

- **Billy Birchfield**   25 years old Born August 30, 2074. Handsome. Athletic. Disciplined military. Fearless warrior. Strategist. Captain of Elite Squadron of defensive fighters. Apprentice Dragomark. Corvis's love interest.

- **Brobdingnagian Ghastlich**   Exact age unknown, probably about 47 years old. Born about 2052. Raised, during formative years by baboons. "Kidnapped" at seven years of age by humans. He hates humans. Grew up among criminally insane. Rose to power by barbarian grit. Contracted to deliver General Copenhavlad and his troops to Enceladus.

- **Svetlana Turgenev**   24 years old Born January 18, 2075.

Capable manager of large university dormitory, recruited to be Chief Operating Officer of the *Nursery*. Tough and disciplined yet nurturing of children. Self-assured and yet vulnerable.

- **Jake Erlmuter**   Friend of Corvis. Recruiter for staff to take 314 orphans from Gabon to Enceladus.

- **General Dioikis**   Commander of Joint Chiefs of Enceladus Defense Department.

- **Convener Hashkeh Naabah Cly**   Head of State of the Enceladus Colony. First president of the independent nation of Enceladus.

- **Tyler Washington**   Second in command of the Elite Squadron. Billy's good friend. Svetlana's love interest.

- **Mary Ndong**   One of the teenagers on the Nursery. Tortured and blinded by soldiers in Gabon.

- **Persephata Typhon**   One of Brobding's lovers.

Acknowledgements

- Thanks to Floyd Largent for his professional editing and attention to detail.

- Thanks to Perry Kirkpatrick for her amazing cover art.

- Thanks to cartographer Hamid Ullah for his stunning maps.

- Thank you to my writing group Write Night Washington for offering truly constructive criticisms of the rough draft and rewrites, even though most of them don't even like sci-fi.

- Thanks to my family who encouraged me and listened to me enthuse about characters and plot.

About the Author

R Cody Carver is author of the **Corvis Epic**: Book One: **Black Bird from Blue Planet**, Book Two: **Crow on Ice Moon**, Book Three: **Raven between the Stars**, and the prequel: **Polku Tallus, Time Traveler**. Cody lives in Seattle, WA.

Stay Tuned For

Crow on Ice Moon

Corvis Epic Book Two

Follow on Facebook: **Corvis Santos**

Made in the USA
Monee, IL
13 January 2024

50710393R00201